PRINT EDITION

SOL OF THE COLISEUM © 2015 by Mirror World Publishing and Adam Gaylord
Edited by: Robert Dowsett

Cover Art © 2015 Guerdrum Art

Published by Mirror World Publishing in September, 2015

Mirror World Publishing
Windsor, Ontario
www.mirrorworldpublishing.com
info@mirrorworldpublishing.com

ISBN: 978-1-987976-09-0

For my parents, who gave me stories.

Sol

OF THE COLISEUM

ADAM GAYLORD

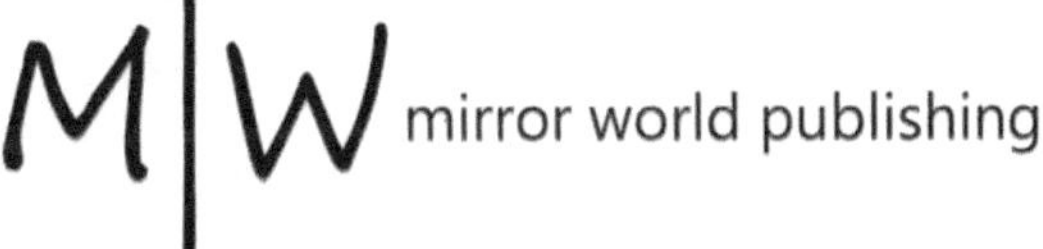

1.

A baby's cry.

Grall was sure that was what he'd heard. In the depths of the Coliseum a person became accustomed to various cries of pain or despair. Prisoners, men broken physically or mentally, called out in the night. Spoils, the women given to victorious fighters to do with whatever they saw fit, cried out often. The beasts, crazed by captivity and seclusion, howled and cackled. Even Grall, though the proud young guard would never admit it, sometimes fought back tears that came in the dark. Over time, one could learn to block out the sound completely.

But the cry of a child, an infant, a sound that had no place in this world, could not be ignored.

Grall made his way slowly down the roughly-carved stone hall, unenthusiastic in his search for the sound's origin. He knew what was expected of him when he found the child. His stomach clenched at the thought.

"I don't need this," he thought aloud, his voice barely a whisper. "I should be in bed." In truth, only minutes before he had lain wide awake, willing dawn to come and give him a reason to abandon his tossing and turning. With the day came his duties; blessed menial tasks he could lose himself in, briefly forgetting his loss.

Grall had come to the Coliseum only a few months before. He had been a guard in the city of Astrolia, capital of the Astrolian Empire, until he refused to participate in a drill using live captives. His protests changed nothing. The captives had died regardless and he had yet again angered his captain, the man that controlled his fate. As punishment he had been transferred to the Coliseum, a post feared by guard and soldier alike. Far more than the danger and brutality, what inspired dread for the post was that for all intents and purposes the Coliseum was a closed system. Be you slave or guard, once you entered it you probably didn't leave. He had begged his captain, promising him utter obedience. But for the Captain, Grall had made it personal. It mattered not at all that Grall's young wife had just given birth to their first son. Neither did it matter that he would probably never see either of them again. Even if he managed to be one of the few to live long enough to see retirement, his son would be grown with children of his own.

He had been all for packing their meager belongings and making a run for it, but his wife's cooler head had prevailed, as always. They lived in the middle of the Astrolian Empire, two week's hard ride in any direction from free lands if they had a mount, which they didn't. She was still weak and sore, not yet recovered from a difficult childbirth. Most importantly, they had a brand new baby. In the best of times the road was no place to raise a child, and they would be in hiding.

"No," she had answered stoically through her tears, "you will go to the Coliseum. You will send us your pay. I will raise our son."

He protested and argued to the point of exhaustion, vainly fighting the logic in her words. Eventually he conceded, packing his bag and leaving his family, barely started, standing at their doorstep.

He still grieved for the son he would never know.

And now there was this.

"I don't need this," he repeated to himself, stopping outside the door to the women's barracks.

They had promised to take care of it.

He knew the mother. She was a slave in the luxury boxes. As sometimes happens, one of her wealthy male patrons had an eye for her and he raped her after she refused his advances. She'd hid the pregnancy well at first but eventually her condition became all too obvious. Grall had been sent to deal with it. The women of the barracks had assured him that though uncommon, such things were not unheard of. The baby would be disposed of in a quiet manner. He had relented.

An infant howling down the halls was not a quiet manner.

Grall took a deep breath and opened the door. His broad frame and barrel-chest filled the doorway while he let his eyes adjust to the dimly-lit barracks. Women were sitting awake in their bunks, eyeing him with considerable disdain. He made his way down the candlelit center aisle toward the source of the disturbance, avoiding the hostile glares and trying to keep his face passive. He didn't want to be here any more than they wanted him here. The object of his quest lay wrapped in a blanket and was held by a rather large cook. He saw the mother lying in a bed off to the side, unmoving. The sheets were soaked with blood but it was her face that drew his gaze. She had obviously been beaten, badly.

"She panicked," the cook said flatly to answer his unasked question. "She confronted the father. He did that and she gave the last of her strength giving birth to this boy. We've named him Sol."

A heavy silence settled over the room; the baby was finally quiet, as if showing respect to his deceased mother. Grall's gaze lingered on the dead slave, her many bruises contrasting with her pale skin and long blonde hair. In life she had been beautiful, a curse for a woman in the Coliseum. In the peace of death she still held her beauty, despite the violence she had encountered.

"And now you're here," the cook broke the silence accusingly.

"I'm sorry. Melina was well liked," he said, attempting civility.

The cook nodded. "She never let this place get to her."

He nodded, recognizing the compliment. There was a long pause.

"You can't keep it," he said plainly, surprised at the feeling he was able to keep out of his voice. Several hisses sounded behind him. The cook neither responded nor moved. She just sat holding the child.

"You know the rules as well as I." He could feel the animosity radiating onto his back from the bunks.

"What life could he hope to have here?" he asked, almost pleading, bristling at the tone of his own voice. He was a guard of the Coliseum; he didn't need to explain himself. Who were these women and this cook who sat unmoving? Had they taken care of things as they promised, he wouldn't have to be down here at all.

He straightened up. "I'll deal with it," he said firmly. Moving the last few paces toward the cook, he felt the women stir behind him. The cook made to strike him and several cries of protest sounded as he reached for the baby. But something unexpected happened, something amazing. As Grall reached for the bundle, his hand was met by the child's. Without fear and with a strong little grip, the baby grabbed one of Grall's fingers and held. He froze, as did the women.

Had it been any other guard, hard and embittered with years of service, nothing would have changed, but for Grall that tiny hand struck with the force of a blow. He shuddered visibly, staring wide-eyed at the child. All was still. Grall knew his duty, what was expected of him. The problem with duty was that it belonged in the Coliseum and he was no longer in the Coliseum. Looking at this tiny baby, feeling it holding his hand, the guard was home.

The little hand holding his finger melted Grall's resolve. The women saw it immediately and smiles passed around the bunks. Grall didn't see them, he only saw the child. He sighed and then without a word he slowly straightened, turned, and walked back the way he had come.

From that moment on, Sol was a child of the Coliseum.

Sol's world smelled of stew. Predictably, the sensation set his stomach rumbling. These days he always seemed to be hungry and the meager rations of a Coliseum slave didn't help much. He was chronically too skinny, despite the fact that an extra portion often found its way onto his plate, a sacrifice by one of the others, usually Oci. Her voice echoed around the giant stew pot he sat inside, scrubbing away as she rambled on about her tasks as head cook. Sometimes he felt bad that the aging woman gave him food off her own plate but whenever he protested she assured him, quite thoroughly, that she was portly enough as it was, a fact he found hard to argue. Her size was the butt of more than one joke around the kitchen, most of them started by her and all of them good natured, but Sol couldn't think of anyone, slave or guard, that held any animosity toward Oci. How could they? With a kind word and her toothy smile, perfectly matching her stark white hair and contrasting so markedly with her mocha brown skin, she made the Coliseum galley feel more like a home kitchen.

For Sol she was the closest thing to a mother he had ever known. Living in the women's barracks, it sometimes seemed that he had a dozen mothers on rotation. He had been brought up in some small way by almost every slave and guard in the Coliseum. "It takes a village," Oci often said, but when he scuffed a knee or needed a scolding, most often it was she who filled the role.

He knew of his real mother; Oci often said he had her green eyes. Further, Melina's fate had not been kept from him. For Sol she was a kind of mythical figure, a woman of beauty and strength who fell stoically to the Coliseum. "A woman who," as Oci often told him, "never let this place get to her."

A hard rap on the side of the huge cauldron quickly brought him from his musings. "I don't hear scrubbing!" Oci chided. He returned to his efforts; Oci didn't stand for slacking. "I haven't forgotten what tomorrow is!" she chimed. He could hear her excitement over the sound of the brushing.

"Chili day?" Sol asked jokingly. They had been playing the game for weeks.

"I swear child, if you're not eating you're thinking about eating. Tomorrow's your ninth birthday, as if you didn't know."

Sol knew and he had been counting the days. Last year, the women had worked together to make him a beautifully-woven and very soft woolen sweater. About three times too big at the time, the sweater would still fit for a little while yet. Oci had stashed ingredients aside for months and made him a birthday cake with real frosting. Best of all had been Grall's present: two more hand-carved miniature gladiators, each complete with a little sword and painted armor. The two figurines took their place next to their worn and battered predecessors in Sol's growing wooden army. Each year Grall added to the collection. This year he hoped for a carved beast to participate in the imaginary tournaments he staged in the back hallways.

Oci shared the boy's excitement, but for her it was different. Sol's anticipation was that of a child's. His blond-haired head was filled with hopes for sweets and treasures. That kind of excitement was contagious and she felt it too. More though, for Oci the anniversary of the boy's birth represented something. It meant that for another year she and the others had beaten the Coliseum. Moreover, in spite of the Coliseum, or perhaps through it, they had made something beautiful. Nothing was kept from Sol; he knew the hardships of his home as well as anyone his age could. Such realities could have easily stolen his innocence and left him hard and bitter before his time. Perhaps it was her efforts and those of the others, or maybe something Melina had passed to the boy. Regardless, somehow Sol remained a child, full of youthful energy and a spark that brought life to a place designed to take it away.

Because the truth was that as much as Sol needed Oci and the others, they needed him just as much. He held a power over those in his life that he could never appreciate. In his boyish smile, always at the ready, he gave them normalcy and he gave them purpose. In a place where it was easy to give up, he gave them a reason not to.

Sol finished scrubbing and hopped out of the pot. "What's next?" he asked.

Oci answered by pointing at yet another huge cauldron in the far corner.

"Aw, not another one?" Sol whined.

"Yes another one and another one after that. And the sooner you get started the sooner you'll be done." Oci instructed, hands on her hips.

"And then another one the next day and another one the next!" he complained.

Oci smiled sadly. "Yes, darlin', and another one the next." Then she added a little more cheerfully, "Until you're too big to fit in any of my pots and they assign you somewhere else."

"Like the cages!" he said excitedly. "Grall took me last week and showed me a welk-dog! It was huge! He said it took five men to get it in the cage and –"

Oci interrupted, "I've told Grall to keep you away from those animals."

"But Oci…"

"No buts! You don't know what kind of diseases those things are carrying. And fleas! You have no business being around those cages."

"I told Grall I want to be a handler. Or even one of the hunters who catch them from the wild!"

Oci paused. "And what did Grall say to that?"

"Oh, you know him. He told me there's no outside and to keep my dreams in the Coliseum, just like always."

If Oci was Sol's foster mother then Grall filled the role of surrogate father. She never tired of seeing the way the duty-driven and often gruff guard softened around the boy. The two played games in the halls for hours when Grall wasn't on duty. On occasion he even let Sol tag along with him on his rounds. Oci wasn't always thrilled by what Grall showed the boy but one thing they did agree on was the need to keep Sol's head out of the clouds and inside the Coliseum. There was no point in getting the boy's hopes up.

Oci nodded. "Good. He's right, there's no use in troubling yourself about the outside." She returned to her work. "And, there's no way you're going to end up a handler. Maybe you can get a job in the boxes carrying drinks or –"

It was her turn to be interrupted, this time with a crash as one of the guards, Yance, opened the door and knocked over a stack of tin plates.

"Damn foolish place to put these." he grumbled, kicking the formerly-clean plates out of his path.

Oci shook her head "I'll keep that in mind," she said without conviction.

"Right," he said, looking around slowly. There was a long pause.

"Did you need something?" Oci prompted.

Yance continued to look around, a confused look on his homely face. "Yes," he answered slowly.

Another long pause. Oci caught Sol's eye with a sideways glance. Yance wasn't known for being the brightest. Sol covered his mouth to suppress a giggle. The slight motion caught the guard's eye and seemed to trigger something. "The boy. He's needed."

"He's not done here," Oci responded a little too quickly.

Sol knew Oci didn't like having him out of her protection any more than necessary. However, her reply had been awfully close to back-talk and Sol could see the guard bristle.

"But if I'm needed, of course," Sol interjected quickly. He didn't want any trouble for the sometimes too-outspoken Oci. It wasn't the first time that he feared their unique situation with Grall had made her forget her place and such forgetfulness could be costly. Besides, he welcomed an excuse to forgo more cauldron scrubbing.

Yance relaxed. "Right," he said. "Let's go."

Sol gave a shrug to Oci who returned it with a frown as Yance lead him out the door.

Sol wasn't sure where they were going, he just hoped it wasn't the Trash River. On the very lowest level of the Coliseum, deep beneath ground level, flowed an underground river. Unearthed in a cave-in a few years before, it had been put to good use. Rather than being hauled up and out, every piece of trash down to the last chamber pot was trekked down and dumped into the flowing black water. For security purposes, a large grate had been installed at the point where the water flowed out of the chamber. It wasn't installed particularly well, though, so whenever a large piece of trash got stuck, the water would push against it and threaten to bring the whole mess down. That always called for a mad scramble to dislodge the errant piece and sometimes meant that Sol, secured by a rope, would be lowered into the river to cut apart the clot.

It always made for an awful experience. The swift running water was cold and smelled terrible. The ceiling at the exit to the chamber nearly met the water and it made a terrible sucking sound. No matter how the guards assured or threatened him, he could never shake the feeling he would be swept away. He was of the opinion that they should just take the rusty old grate down. It didn't reach all the way to the river bottom, anyway. Not that it mattered; no one in their right mind would jump in that water.

Yance's mumbling caught his attention. "All the way back to the surface. Couldn't send someone else…"

The surface? He remembered the last time he had been on the surface. About a month ago, he had been pulled out of the kitchen and herded through these same passages with other slaves pulled randomly from their duties. No explanation had been given but the reason became clear enough upon reaching the surface.

The slaves, their eyes squinting in the bright of the day's twin red suns, had been steered roughly toward a group of guards surrounding a single figure kneeling in the sand at the point of several spears. Sol recognized the young man as a new arrival to the Coliseum, though he didn't know his name. He knelt with his head high, despite the swollen eye and busted lip he had clearly just received.

Brought to a stop in front of the figure, the group was addressed by the Captain of the Guard. "Welcome to class! Today's lesson: What happens to a slave when he's stupid enough to try and escape?"

The group exchanged nervous glances but the young man didn't react. With a nod from the Captain, one of the guards reversed the grip on his spear and brought the wooden shaft down hard across the slave's back, knocking him face down into the sand.

Instead of staying down, which would have been smarter, the young man pushed himself upright again, head held high, his jaw set.

"Again!" The command came and again the blow fell.

Again the slave pushed himself up.

"Well, what are you waiting for?" the Captain demanded angrily. The blows came much faster then, over the youth's back and head, allowing him no chance to right himself. Several of the group closed their eyes to the beating only to have a whip crack over their heads. "You will watch this!" screamed the Captain. It continued for what seemed to Sol like an eternity. Finally the Captain brought the beating to an end with a wave of his hand. There was a long silence.

The Captain smiled smugly and turned to address the slaves. "This has been a good lesson –" he started to lecture but then stopped, noticing that his pupils' attention was not on him but on the ground behind him.

Slowly, ever so slowly, and with obvious difficulty, the slave pushed himself upright one more time. His head lolled to one side, blood running from what remained of one ear.

The guards shifted uncomfortably on their feet and the Captain frowned. He walked slowly up to slave and roughly grabbed the young man's hair, bending the youth's face up to meet his. "Why?" he questioned. "Why even try? What do you hope to gain? You can't change your fate, you must know that. Then why?"

The slave's breath came ragged. He struggled to speak and the group collectively leaned forward to hear his answer. Sol could see him try, could sense the importance of the reply, but the beating had been too severe. His jaw was broken and wouldn't function. All that the effort produced was an unintelligible mumble.

The Captain shook his head and let the boy's head droop back down. He stepped back and motioned to the largest of the guards. "Raise the flag," he commanded.

Sol watched, horrified, as the powerful man brought his spear to bear through the rib cage of the now screaming youth. Raising him off his knees, the guard wedged the butt into the ground such that the spear was pointed straight up into the sky. The slave's screamed reached a fevered pitch as he slid slowly down the length of the spear. The whip cracked constantly as the Captain tried to force the group to witness the grim spectacle. Mercifully, the screaming stopped before the slave reached the bottom. All was quiet save the low sobs of some of the group. Sol's own face was streaked with tears he hadn't known he was shedding.

The Captain cracked the whip a final time. "Tell your bunkmates what you've seen today and his foolishness won't have been in vain." He turned and walked away. "Class dismissed."

Sol felt a tear run down his cheek at the memory and quickly wiped it away lest Yance notice. He needn't have worried since the guard now seemed more interested in a loose thread on his uniform.

"So why am I needed?" Sol ventured to ask.

"Shut up," was the only reply.

Eventually daylight replaced torchlight as they reached a short corridor that opened up to the Coliseum floor. Walking out into the light of the suns, Sol looked over the massive structure he called home.

The original lower half of the great bowl was carved into the stone floor of the valley itself. Shaped in a huge oval, the sand-covered wooden fighting floor was surrounded by walls twenty feet high. Below the floor sat waiting rooms, cages, and an intricate system of pulleys and winches designed to open the gates and trap-doors in the walls and floor. Farther below ran miles of tunnels connecting to underground dungeons, kitchens, and guardhouses. Above the walls ring after ring of stone benches rose up to the ground level interrupted only by a single level of luxury boxes about midway.

Originally the fights, tournaments, and races had been intended only as a means of placating the masses. While entertaining the

Empire's poor was still their main purpose, the games had become unexpectedly popular with the upper business and ruling classes. Soon the single ring of luxury boxes carved into the stone became insufficient and a second level had to be added. Made of the finest materials, the half that rose above the valley floor was the definition of opulence. Crystal chandeliers hung from the ceilings and richly-embroidered tapestries draped the walls. Silver and gold fixtures adorned the washrooms and an army of maids, cooks, and servants responded to the every whim of wealthy patrons as they delighted in the carnage below. It was one of the ironies that gave the Coliseum such appeal that although they sat on hard stone slabs exposed to the elements, the poor masses sat closer to the action and therefore actually had better seats than their wealthier counterparts.

Sol quickly scanned the floor and to his relief saw nothing to warrant suspicion that there might be a repeat of last month's lesson. Slaves were hard at work hauling basket upon basket of sand up from the under-stadium. The wooden fighting floor had to be replaced every few years and it had been a while since the last renovation. As a result, those that worked immediately underneath it were subjected to a steady rain of sand that had to be hauled back to the surface during off-days.

Sol was led toward the largest of the arched entrances that ringed the Coliseum floor. All of the other arches lead to holding cells or down to the under-stadium, but this particular arch marked the opening to a long tunnel that served as the lone passage between the Coliseum floor and the outside world. Sol's pulse quickened as they entered the passageway and worked their way up the long ramp to ground level. In the distance he could see the bright half-circle that marked the outside. This may have been the only tunnel in the Coliseum he had never been in and he glanced excitedly at Yance in the hopes that the guard would reveal their destination. Could it be that he would be taken outside? Yance plodded along taking no heed of the boy. Worse, Sol was sure his pace had slowed. To the boy it seemed they couldn't walk fast enough.

Progressing up the ramp he could see two figures silhouetted to one side of the gate, one of which was obviously a guard. The other had to have been one of the most miserable figures Sol had ever seen. The man was covered in black grease from head to toe. Scrapes and cuts littered his body and one arm hung awkwardly from his shoulder. As they approached, Sol could make out an echoed argument. "I'm sorry, I can't do it. It's too small. I damn near lost my arm up there."

"That's an idea," responded the guard. "Ya might fit if there's less of ya."

Sol couldn't tell if he was joking or not.

The greased man seemed to think he wasn't. "You wouldn't? I'd bleed to death before I got to the top!"

"So?" asked the guard.

"So then he'd clog up the whole mess and we'd never get him out," chimed Yance. "Get him out of here. I got someone better."

Sol and the greased man exchanged looks of sympathy as he was led away.

"Well, get to it," Yance commanded.

"Get to what?" Sol asked.

Yance sighed at the chore of explaining the situation. "Somthin's jammed up in the gears that run the gate. You're gonna go up there and fix it." He pointed to a small opening in the stone and mortar ceiling. Through the opening ran the massive chain that connected to the counterweight that raised and lowered the latticed gate.

Sol eyed the opening. "How am I supposed to get up there?"

"Climb the chain, stupid boy."

"But it's covered in grease!" he balked.

Yance swatted at him. "This isn't up for negotiation. Get up there!"

Sol dodged the swat and moved to the chain. The massive links were as long as his forearm and just as thick. He placed a foot in the bottom link and began to climb. Reaching the opening he glanced once more at Yance and then squeezed his way in. The passage was wide enough for the chain and precious little else. If he kept his arms above him he had just enough room to squeeze between the wall and the chain. Slowly he climbed, feeling rather than seeing his route. A dim light told him there must be an opening up above but he couldn't make out where. The air was stale and fumes from the grease stung his eyes. His knees and elbows were soon scraped and smarting but still he climbed. Finally he reached the large hollow that housed the complex jumble of gears and cogs that comprised the inner workings of the door's counterweight system.

The light was brighter here, a fact he appreciated as he began his search for the jam. He didn't know anything about the actual mechanics of the door so he just looked for something that looked out of place. Gears and axles crowded the space making movement difficult. So intent was he in solving the puzzle that for a time he didn't even consider the source of the light by which he worked. It wasn't until after struggling over the top of a large cog that he saw the opening. It was above him but well within reach when he stood on the cog, which was no easy feat in itself.

It was a window; square with thick bars set in its sill, it had seen better days. The stone on the bottom had been nearly weathered away to the point that one of the bars had fallen out completely. Sol took a deep breath and tried the opening left by the gap. With considerable effort he was just able to squeeze his head through. He was rewarded with his first ever look at the outside world.

He gawked, transfixed by the scene that splayed out below him. Merchants with their carts lined the near side of the street, hawking their wares to the passersby. The smell of roasting meat wafted up to Sol, as did the chorus of the venders. Across from the Coliseum sat a row of shops. Sol watched a woman haggling with a salesman in the front of the closest one. Above the shops apartments looked out over the street. He gasped and nearly slipped off the cog when he realized he was being watched through an open window across the way. A large grey cat sitting on the sill held his eye. It sat like a statue, almost completely still. Only the flick of its tail betrayed its sentience.

Sol tore his eyes away from the feline as a ruckus sounded below. He watched as a merchant chased a boy through the crowd, yelling and waving his fist. The boy, no older than Sol, carried a small bundle he had obviously just stolen from the vendor. The boy was much faster and looked certain to get away, but as he chanced one last look back over his shoulder he smacked right into a particularly rotund pedestrian, sending him toppling backwards. The merchant was on him in a flash. Grabbing the thief by the arm, he dragged the boy kicking and biting back to his cart directly below the window. Sol watched as the merchant opened up the bundle revealing two roast hams.

Sol mourned for the boy. He understood hunger well but he also understood that getting caught stealing meant a certain death sentence. Crouched behind the merchant's cart, the boy had calmed considerably though the merchant kept a tight grip on his arm with one hand. With the other he grabbed the boy's chin, forcing them face to frowning face. Sol strained to hear was said but to no avail. The merchant released the boy's chin then produced a long dagger from his belt. Sol's stomach dropped and he prepared to look away when the blow came.

Much to his surprise, it never did. Instead, with a quick confident movement, the merchant sliced one of the hams in half and handed it to the boy, who was obviously just as surprised as Sol. Standing, he took the other ham and a half and placed them back on his cart. Then he turned back to the dumbstruck boy. The two regarded each other for a moment before the boy slowly extended his hand. The merchant smiled and extended his own. After a brief handshake they parted ways leaving Sol to reflect upon what he had just witnessed.

He wasn't able to ponder long before Yance's yell echoed up the crawl space. "What the hell is taking so long?" Sol sighed. Given the chance he felt he could stay and watch from his window forever. Unfortunately that wasn't an option, so with a final glance at the cat across the way he went back to his search. Or at least he tried to. His head, which had just squeezed through the space in the bars, did not seem nearly as inclined to squeeze back through the other direction. He yanked and pulled until he thought his ears would tear off but still he remained stuck.

"You'd better not be screwing around!"

Sol began to panic and he fought back a scream that would only add to his predicament. Who knew what would happen if the street goers below suddenly looked up to see a head poking out twenty feet up the Coliseum's outer wall. He twisted and strained, the skin scraping off the sides of his head. He tried banging at the bars that held him, first the left: *tink, tink,* then the right: *tonk, tonk.* He stopped his thrashing and tried the two bars again. The left repeated its solid *tink* and the right its less-than-solid *tonk.* He grabbed the right bar with both hands and twisted with all his might. His heart skipped a beat at the sound of the bar scraping in its setting. Back and forth he twisted and shook the bar and slowly it loosened. He could hear bits of stone tumble off the sill as he worked, giving him hope. Finally the bar popped out, sending Sol staggering back precariously on the large cog.

"Don't make me come up there!"

Sol barely heard the idle threat. Holding the newly removed bar in his hands, he stared at the doubly-large opening he had just created. He didn't need to climb up to see he could easily fit his whole body through now. The possibilities swirled in his mind and he sat down on the cog as a wave of dizziness swept over him. He could escape. He could drop himself out the window and run. The gate was stuck, that's why he was up there in the first place. By the time they realized he'd jumped and they made it out, he'd be long gone. The kindly meat merchant below might even help him. He could find a family and get a cat.

He could be free.

The thought was completely foreign to him. For the boy the outside was an anomalous concept. Like the Empire, the outside world surrounded his own, permeated it, but remained always invisible. He knew he should be ecstatic. He had before him what every Coliseum slave dreamed of: a way out. He stood back up on the cog and looked down from the window again. The crowd below went on about their business, unaware of his presence. He looked at the multitude of faces he didn't know. He looked at the carts and the shops. He looked at the alien world. He looked at the cat.

Faces passed before his mind's eye: Oci's, Grall's, the youth's as he slid down the spear. He closed his eyes and listened to the mumble of the crowd. In the distance a bell chimed slowly, marking something Sol knew nothing about. The smell of the street below mixed oddly with the fumes from the grease that covered his body. He opened his eyes and looked down at the bar in his hand. He knew the answer to the puzzle of the jammed gate. He also knew this might be a once in a lifetime chance.

He stood looking at the bar for what could have been forever then slowly, as if raising a great weight, he restored it to its setting.

Now sure of what he was looking for, Sol returned to his search. It wasn't long before he spotted it, the first bar to fall from the window, wedged between the wall and a cog. He braced himself on a stationary bracket and kicked at the bar. It shot out immediately, sending the cogs spinning and turning. The long chain worked along its path, whizzing by Sol as he clung close to the wall. With a loud thwack the mechanics stopped and Sol knew the gate had hit home.

"It's about damn time!" Yance's yell confirmed Sol's success.

Sol took one more long look at the window and then started his climb down with a sigh.

Over the years he would tell himself a myriad of different excuses for why he had stayed. In his youth he would reason that it was because his birthday had been the next day and that he had wanted cake and presents, a rationale that sounded hollow even to a boy. As he grew older he would try to approach it more logically. He would reason that the drop from the window had been too far, that he had feared being turned in, that he didn't want to end up sliding down the shaft of a spear. He would also reason that any other slave wouldn't blink at these kinds of possible consequences.

In his heart of hearts he knew why he stayed. He wasn't any other slave; he was different. Outside of the Coliseum he had no people, no home, and no family to go to. Inside he was Sol, pot scrubber. Outside he was nobody. His bed was here. His people were here. The Coliseum was his home.

Sol paced the small dimly-lit holding cell, pausing briefly at the roar of the crowd from the Coliseum above, the sound echoing through the stone tunnels. Soon the cheers would be for him, either in victory or defeat. This was to be his inaugural bout, a test of the months of training Grall had put him through. The guard had been wise in seeing the likely path of a young man in the Coliseum, figuring it was only a matter of time before he would be thrown out on the fighting floor.

Grall had taken it upon himself to train the boy in secret. Teaching a slave to fight wasn't a condoned activity to say the least. In the same dark halls where they had played together short years before, Grall trained Sol in knife play, boxing, grappling, and swordsmanship. He had been uncertain as to how such training would take. Sol had always had such a peaceful demeanor. There were times when Grall worried the boy was growing up too soft for his surroundings, but Sol proved himself a good student and it wasn't long before the pupil was able to match the teacher in every discipline. As Sol's abilities grew, so did his confidence. In an ironic twist, the other guards started to take special notice of the muscular young man with a swagger a slave should never have. It was agreed that some time on the fighting floor would take him down a peg.

Now, on the eve of his sixteenth birthday, that time had come. As he continued to pace yet again he worked over the situation as Grall had explained it. "You'll wait in the holding cell until a guard comes for you. Once you reach the gate to the floor, you'll be given a weapon. Wait for the gate to open then run out. Survey the floor. Don't look up at the stands. Too many first timers put themselves at a disadvantage because they waste time gawking at the crowd. Figure out how many fighters are on the floor, what the props are, if they can be used for cover. Try to get your back to something so that you can concentrate on protecting your front. When it's over, give the crowd a wave then drop your weapon and head back to the tunnel you came from. I'll try and meet you before you make it to the Pit."

The Pit, as it was affectionately known, marked another first for Sol. New fighters were housed in a large communal barracks accepted by most as the worst room in the Coliseum. Reputedly crawling with parasites and disease, it was a place of violence. A new fighter sometimes stood a better chance of surviving his first bout than his first night in the Pit. Thankfully for Sol, the combined mortality rate kept turnover in the barracks high. If he could survive his first few bouts he would likely be moved to a shared room, an option Oci had been pushing Grall for ever since learning his fate as a fighter.

The aging cook was distraught at the news. She alternated between blaming Grall for forcing him into the bouts and begging the guard to take him out. As with Sol's move to the Pit, Grall simply didn't have the power to do either. Sol tried to console and assure her on several occasions but to no avail.

He jumped at a sharp rap on the door, surprised when the guard to enter was Grall himself. He smiled nervously. "You're leading me out?"

Grall shook his head. "No, just checking in. You ready?"

Sol shrugged. "I guess so."

"Really?"

Sol sat down on the small wooden bench. "No. I know what I'm supposed to do but I don't have any idea how I'm going to do it."

Grall sat down beside him. "I'm glad to hear you say that."

"What? Why?"

The large guard smiled. "The last thing you need is to go into this thing thinking you know just what to do. It's better to approach it with a clean slate and pick up the pieces as you go."

"But what if I don't pick up the pieces?" Sol pleaded. "What if I get cut into pieces?"

Grall frowned. "Do you think I would get cut into pieces?"

"No, of course not. But–"

Grall interrupted. "Then since you best me more often than not, you won't either."

Sol hung his head, his shaggy dirty-blond hair draping his face. "But if I don't get cut, then I'll have to do the cutting. I'm not sure I can."

"Oh." Grall nodded in understanding.

The two sat in silence for a time before Grall spoke again. "Do you remember The Cave-In?"

The stone tunnels under the Coliseum were constantly being expanded or repaired. Small cave-ins were not uncommon but one such incident was huge. An entire system of tunnels running east away from the Coliseum had collapsed to some degree or another. A couple dozen slaves had lost their lives and for a time there was concern the whole tunnel network may have been compromised. For anyone living in the Coliseum at the time the incident was known simply as "The Cave-In".

Sol shrugged. "A little."

"You couldn't have been more than five or six at the time. A small body was needed to work around the boulders and check on the support structures so you were it. Oci was worried sick but you scampered through nooks and holes a cave rat wouldn't go through. Didn't even blink. Then they took you to the south tunnels where the cave-in was the worst. I was up in the pens dealing with a sick rink cat when word came up there was a problem. I hustled down expecting to see you under a rock. Instead you were standing in front of a pile of boulders, arms crossed in front of you, refusing to go into that damned hole. The guard, Rakett I think his name was, was fit to be tied."

"That guy was always a jerk," Sol interjected.

"Well that *jerk* was about to jam you down that hole with the pommel of his sword. You wouldn't do it. I'm not sure I ever knew why. Do you remember?"

Sol had a faraway expression. "There was a hand," he said quietly.

"A hand?"

"It was sticking out from the rubble, all pale and stiff. It looked like it was reaching for me." He smiled sheepishly, "I still have nightmares about that damned hand."

"Down in the hole?"

Sol nodded.

"Huh, so that's what it was. Well anyway, Rakett was in a fury and I couldn't do anything about it. He outranked me. I didn't know what I was going to do. So I asked you, kinda desperately, 'Sol, please go down the hole.' Rakett started to chew me up and down for butting in but then, without a word, you climbed into the hole."

"You asked me to. I guess I just figured you wouldn't unless it was safe."

"That's what I figured. You did what you needed to do and you did it for me, because I asked."

Sol nodded again.

Grall put a firm hand on Sol's shoulder. "Remember that today. You're going to go out there and do what you have to do, not because you're fighting for you but because you're fighting for me and for Oci and for everyone else in here. This is your home. You're fighting for your home. Hold on."

Grall stood and walked to the cell door. Opening it, he grabbed something from just outside and then returned to sit by Sol. The dim torchlight danced over polished metal, sending light skipping about the small cell as he handed Sol the helmet. "Happy birthday."

Sol stared, speechless.

"Well," said Grall with a smile, "go ahead and put it on."

With reverence worthy of a sacred vessel, Sol did as he was told. Sharply angled cheek guards nearly touched the nose guard framing his eyes in steel. A row of sharp, finger-length spikes ran down its midline starting at the forehead, each one shining the bright red that had been forged into the steel.

Grall gave the helmet a whack and a twist. "How's it fit?"

Sol finally found his voice. "Perfect."

"I had the smith add some extra padding. That way you can take it out as you grow."

"You had this made for me?"

"That's no hand-me-down boy, that's the real thing. I heard that one of the smiths was an armorer on the outside. I wasn't sure he'd be too keen on the idea but it turned out he jumped at the chance. Said it was a waste of his talent to be stuck making chains and repairing cages all day. By the looks of that helmet, I'd say he was right."

This time they both jumped at the rap on the door. Sol's eyes went wide as a rather fat guard stepped inside.

"I'll bring him out," Grall said sharply.

Confused and eyeing Sol's helmet, the guard backed out while mumbling, "Yes, Sir."

Grall grabbed Sol by the shoulders. "You'll be fine. Stay calm, ignore the crowd, and remember what I told you." He guided Sol out the door and passed him to the other guard with a nod.

Sol was led to the entrance of a long dark tunnel. As they made their way up the sloping passage, he considered Grall's words. He thought about Oci and about the other women that had helped raise him. He thought about the smith, so happy to take up his art and craft the helmet he now wore. He thought about Grall, a guard and a friend. He thought about his mother. As these faces crossed his mind he felt a part of himself change, felt it harden. *This is my home. They are my family. I fight for them.*

The passage ended at a large wooden gate. Sunlight and sound trickled through the slight gap under the door. The fat guard drew two swords. One he handed to Sol, the other he kept. Sol tested the weight of the weapon. It was a short sword and a little pommel-heavy, but the blade was straight and sharp. He twirled it and the guard stepped back, his own sword raised defensively.

Sol lowered the weapon. "What's your name?"

The guard looked over his shoulder as if Sol might be addressing someone else. "Ramsey," he answered suspiciously.

"Ramsey, will you be here when I get back?"

"*If* you get back," Ramsey corrected.

Sol knelt at the foot of the massive gate. He bowed his head and closed his eyes. The dark passage shook with the roar of the crowd, smelling strongly of dirt, blood, and urine. He ran his fingers over the polished metal of his new helm and nodded. "I'll see you then."

2.

The Coliseum throbbed.

It was as if the massive structure had a pulse, a pulse with a name. The thousands of spectators that packed the stands had enjoyed the earlier carnage but it was now time for the main events; time for the champion fighters to emerge from the bowels of the Coliseum to be pitted against man or beast. The sandy floor was already stained with the blood of the fallen and the throng chanted the name of the one that they would have add to it.

Sol, Sol, Sol.

The name repeated slow and steady, almost somber like a funeral march. Amplified by the deep stone bowl of the Coliseum, the sound was deafening. Blocks away babies awoke crying in their cribs as the surrounding city shook with it. Down in the lowest dungeons carved into the living stone beneath the Coliseum, fighters stirred in their bunks. The animal handlers backed away from the massive cages, whips cracking, trying to subdue the beasts driven mad by the sound. Ladies of society high in their shaded luxury boxes covered their ears while casting disparaging looks down upon those from whom the chant sounded, but still it continued.

In the whole of it there was only one that was oblivious to the throb. Crouched in the dark at the foot of the gate between the Coliseum floor and one of the many tunnels that lead to the dungeons, the gladiator himself was too deeply immersed in concentration to give any heed to the din. It likely would have been lost on him, anyway. After all, for the thousands who chanted his name, this was all a spectacle of pleasurable entertainment. For him it was a matter of survival.

The armor clad figure rested on bended knee in the dirt awaiting the opening of the gate, a ritual he had picked up in the years since that first fight. The two guards standing a dozen paces behind him had given him no weapon this time, so he held his empty hands clasped on his thigh. His head was bowed and eyes shut tight as he contemplated the first crucial moments after the gates opening.

It was true that Sol was strong, but others were stronger. He was fast, but others were faster. There were those that were smarter or even better trained for combat, although not many. Sol was a successful fighter for a number of reasons but one thing stood out: adaptability. He had the uncanny ability to take in a situation at a glance, decide what tools were available to him, and act without hesitation. It was something you couldn't teach and few had it.

Sol knew from experience that the first few moments after the gate opened were the most crucial of the fight. Many questions had to be answered and answered fast. Man or beast? How many? Armed with what? What's the available cover? These questions and more had to be answered, answered well, and usually answered at a dead run to have a chance at staying alive. Each time he emerged from the tunnels he faced a new challenge. The lone rule of the Coliseum was that the crowd got what the crowd wanted. And since the crowd demanded novelty the promoters went to great lengths to satisfy.

Exotic animals were brought in from the far corners of the constantly expanding Empire. Many times they were pumped full of stimulants or narcotics before entering the arena, making them crazed and unpredictable. Elaborate battle scenarios played out complete with detailed props and scenery. With a different horror awaiting him each time the gate opened, a fighter could take nothing for granted. Every appearance had to be approached with an open mind so as not to be caught off guard.

Sol's pulse quickened and his jaw clenched as he heard the sound he had been waiting for. The huge wrought iron chains that opened the tunnel gate clinked and whined as the slack was removed and the first trickle of light shone under the solid door. Seconds later the crowd cheered as the object of their chant ran out into the light of day.

He was tall and lean, perhaps leaner than he should have been. The life of a slave was a hard one, but he was strong and as he ran his sinewy muscles rippled under his armor. A brightly polished silver breast and back plate strapped together at the sides and shoulders covered his torso. The long chain mail shirt he wore under his breastplate draped over buckskin shorts secured by a wide belt. He had on high leather boots with shining shin guards that flashed in unison with his forearm guards as he ran. And covering his shaggy blond hair was his signature spiked helmet. The rest of the armor had been pieced together over time having been taken from various foes: a shin guard here and a pair of boots there. Sol had done his best to hammer out the dents and polish every piece to its utmost. Right now the shiny helm pivoted right and left as Sol surveyed the field at a sprint.

Eight roughly cut blocks of stone, each nearly twelve feet tall, had been evenly spaced a dozen paces from the Coliseum wall, three each down the sides and one on each end. On the wall side of each block a different weapon hung on mounted brackets. As Sol ran for the spear on the nearest block he saw that three other doors had opened at the same moment as his.

He recognized the figure at the opposite end of the oval as the massive Frorian fighter K'nal. He was clad only in high boots and a loincloth, and like all his kind he was covered in fur so white as to have a nearly bluish tint. The heavily-muscled giant stood head and shoulders over any other fighter and probably weighed twice as much. Sol knew little about Frorians, except that they were from a frigid wasteland far to the south and they were known for their exceptional strength.

He didn't recognize the other two fighters that emerged from each side, but by their wide-eyed hesitation he suspected they were relatively new fighters, here only to add to the body count.

Sol quickly reached the first block. Grabbing the long-shafted spear he continued running toward the next block. Again he surveyed the field, looking for something he'd missed. A four-fighter standoff wasn't grand enough. Being a crowd favorite had its perks but it also meant the promoters took special care to think up the most complex scenarios just for you. This was just too simple.

No sooner had the thought crossed his mind than a loud scraping sounded from the center of the arena. The four fighters paused to watch as a large hidden door in the ground parted down the middle, exposing a steep sided pit to the crowd above. Then a different scraping sounded as the floor of the pit started to rise to the surface and revealed its contents. Emerging from the dark to the thunderous roar of the delighted spectators raised the largest head Sol had ever seen.

Of the thousands of people watching the beast rise, perhaps only the Frorian from the frigid south knew what he was looking at. In his language it was called a "Dybuk" or quite literally a "demon of snow". The massive animal stood as tall as K'nal at the shoulder and sported four razor-sharp, hand-sized claws on each foot. Protected by long white fur and thick layers of blubber, Sol didn't see that the animal had much of a weak spot.

"Ah", Sol said to himself as he resumed his sprint to the next block, "that's more like it."

Reaching his goal, he watched the Dybuk lumber toward one of the newer fighters. The brave fool had crouched down behind a block with a crossbow and was currently trying to add a third arrow to the two already stuck harmlessly in the beast's thick hump of back blubber.

"Oh, good idea, piss it off!" Sol shouted sarcastically across the arena. Unfortunately the arrows seemed to be doing exactly that. As he watched, the monster charged its assailant with surprising speed, pinned him to the ground, and bit his upper torso, promptly tearing the man in half.

The crowd cheered.

Sol ducked behind the second block and quickly put on the weapon: skykes; long, curved, serrated blades whose base strapped to the underside of the forearm. Each had a hole for the fingers where the hilt met the blade, making the weapons move and feel like mere extensions of one's arm. A skilled skyke wielder could hold off a small group of trained soldiers. They had always been a favorite of Sol's.

With the skykes strapped securely to his arms and the spear he still carried, Sol judged himself as well-armed as he was likely to get. He looked down to the far end of the arena and saw K'nal with a short sword strapped to his hip and a massive double-bladed battle ax in hand. He stood much as Sol did, at the ready with a stone block between himself and the Dybuk who was, at the moment, testing the tall arena walls for a place to escape. The huge creature paced up and down a section, sent some chips of rock and sand flying with a healthy swipe of its paw, then moved down the wall.

The remaining new fighter seemed to deem the beast sufficiently distracted to risk an attack. Brandishing a narrow blade nearly as long as himself, he quickly closed the distance to the restless Dybuk, who turned to meet its attacker head on. The small fighter dodged a paw swipe and slashed the beast across the face, rendering one eye useless. The now infuriated monster charged the fighter, swinging at him only to miss again as he dived to the side.

Sol, who had slowly been working his way toward K'nal, was impressed. The little guy was shifty and certainly very fast. If he was able to slay the Dybuk unscathed, Sol would have a difficult time surviving a three way brawl involving speedy and the white giant.

Yet again the lone rule of the Coliseum raised its ugly head. It wasn't enough that having been forced to fight, the gladiators also had to survive a raging, half-crazed beast likewise fighting for its own survival. After the beast was dead they would likely have to be the last one standing out of their own ranks. The crowd got what it wanted and the crowd always wanted more blood.

At the moment the crafty fighter was using his speed and size well. Dodging and ducking, he worked his way into where it seemed he might have a chance at the beast's throat. With a final diving roll he crouched with his sword poised for what could be a deathblow.

The blow never came.

As the fighter pivoted on the balls of his feet his back foot slipped just slightly, enough that he had to delay his attack a fraction of a second to correct his balance. The minor misstep was all the Dybuk needed to land a paw swipe and send the fighter flying. With a sickening crack the small but brave fighter hit the wall then slumped down into the dust, dead.

The crowd cheered.

Sol made a decision. The small figure now being dismembered by the Dybuk had been a skilled swordsman. If he was going to make it out of the arena today he would need help. Turning to the Frorian who was now only a dozen paces away he pointed first to himself and then to K'nal.

"Together," he said, loud and firm.

K'nal nodded gravely. They both knew that they would need the other to kill the beast. They also knew that if they succeeded they would have to fight each other, thus making their brief partnership tricky at best.

The Dybuk stopped venting its rage on the dead fighter and turned its attention on the remaining two. They stood their ground side by side as the beast started its charge toward them. Sol positioned himself and heaved his spear. The throw went badly. Due to the nature of the skykes he hadn't gotten a proper hold as he threw. The Dybuk slowed only slightly as it sidestepped the spear and continued its charge.

K'nal frowned down disapprovingly at Sol, who could only manage a sheepish grin before the giant turned and charged toward the beast. As he ran he dropped the ax and drew the short sword from its sheath. The two snow-white forms met with a fury of swinging claw and steel. The exchange was rapid: a parry from K'nal, a Dybuk dodge and swing, a lunge from K'nal. The Frorian was having a tough time getting to the creature with the short, broad blade and the Dybuk seemed to have lost most of its depth perception when it lost its eye. It was aiming its swipes poorly; sometimes long, sometimes short. The two disadvantages quickly came to a head as the Frorian stepped in a little too close, meeting a paw that would have fallen short.

K'nal's great form flew through the air and landed between Sol and the snow-demon, his sword clattering off at an angle. The beast charged toward the fallen fighter and Sol charged without hesitation toward the beast. He sprinted over the discarded ax then hurtled over the dazed but conscious fighter. The space closed fast.

In the same instant the snow-demon raised its paw to strike, Sol hit the dirt in a feet-first slide. He skidded directly under the surprised animal and rolled to his back, lashing out with both arms. The razor sharp skykes sliced deeply into the back of the Dybuk's forelegs, severing muscle and tendon. Howling in pain the beast stumbled forward, its legs unable to support its considerable bulk. Sol scurried to crawl out from underneath, but not quickly enough. The great Dybuk toppled, pinning the fighter's legs to the ground, trapping him under the writhing creature.

Sol lowered his forehead to the sand. He could have let the Dybuk tear into the downed Frorian and then struck the distracted beast with relative ease. Putting himself between K'nal and the monster was the decent thing to do, but decency didn't keep you alive.

He looked up at the cheer of the crowd to see K'nal walk slowly to the head of the beast, the massive ax in hand. Sol watched as he paused and said something to the distressed animal. Then in one fluid motion he swung the ax up over his head and with a powerful downstroke he buried the blade deep into the Dybuk's skull. The once mighty beast twitched briefly and then lay still in a growing pool of its own blood.

The crowd cheered.

Sol struggled again to free his lower half from the dead weight of the animal but it was no use. He had helped topple the beast, this was true, but now he lay trapped and helpless. He watched K'nal walk over and collect the spear he had thrown.

The crowd suddenly grew silent.

"At least I'm not in pain", Sol said to himself. The fallen Dybuk hadn't crushed his legs and besides, K'nal wasn't known to be cruel. Hopefully his death would be quick.

Sol lifted his head and looked up at the Frorian who now stood with the spear just out of reach of Sol's skykes. A thoughtful frown creased the giant's flat, furry face as he looked down on Sol.

Moments passed.

The Coliseum was still and quiet. Some wanted to hear a heady comment of victory from the usually stoic K'nal. Still more wanted to hear Sol beg and plead for his life. Some just wanted to hear the deathblow. Finally, they all heard something entirely unexpected.

K'nal bent down slightly and glared into Sol's eyes saying only one word, "Together."

With this he slid the blade end of the spear under the lifeless Dybuk and began to heave the dead mass off of Sol's legs. The spear shaft bowed and the strain showed on K'nal's face, but slowly the weight shifted until Sol was able to pull his legs free with great difficulty.

He staggered to his feet, the feeling returning to his legs. He turned to face K'nal, skykes at the ready. The giant again held the bloodstained ax he had just wrenched from the Dybuk's skull. They stood a mere dozen paces apart, neither one ready or willing to make the next move.

Moments passed and then slowly the crowd began to awaken from its stunned silence.

Such acts of selflessness and nobility had long been absent from this arena. Gladiators fought for their survival without conviction or principle. Most people had only heard of such deeds in fireside stories told to them as children. Life was hard and it wasn't long before ideals gave way to reality. Every spectator there knew that today they had witnessed something special.

Out of the silence a new chant slowly grew. Although quiet at first, it soon pulsed with the same intensity Sol's name had.

"Both", it said, "both…both…both…"

The lone rule of the Coliseum was simple: the mob gets what it wants. For once the masses wanted both gladiators to live to fight another day.

Sol unstrapped the skykes and K'nal dropped the battle ax. They looked each other in the eye and then each with a brief nod, turned to walk back to their respective tunnels, victorious.

"That was quite the performance," Slink hissed from the dark hallway outside Sol's cell door. "I would have put the situation to better use than that half-wit Frorian, though. Not killin' a trapped man, thas just stupid."

The guard had the ever-annoying habit of silently "slinking" in and out of the shadows without being detected. It had earned him the nickname which fit the lanky, long-haired, rather greasy guard so well that everyone had long since forgotten his real name. With his ratlike face and matching disposition, Sol had never felt anything but disgust for the slimy little man.

The gladiator lounged in his bunk without giving any sign of surprise at Slink's sudden appearance. "*You* would have never made the main event. Besides, I didn't think you were allowed see the tournaments".

Slink scoffed with annoyance, stepping into the lamplight. "Of course I didn't *see* it. I didn't have time. But I heard all about it. Sounds like I was almost rid of you."

"No such luck, I'm afraid. I'm not even too beat up this time."

A wicked smile creased the guard's pale face. "Shame your spoil's 'bout used up."

To the victors went the Spoils. By "used up" Slink probably meant that the girl wasn't new to the Coliseum. Sol could only guess her condition.

"That is a shame. I could have used a little extra attention. I think I've earned it." Sol had an almost legendary reputation amongst the guards as having never turned down a spoil, no matter how injured or tired either of them was. The guards snickered amongst themselves at what they assumed to be Sol's motives. He let them think what they liked. It suited his purpose.

Slink grinned again. "This one's seen better days. In fact, I'm doubt she'll have anything left for you after I give 'er a go."

At that a gloved hand reached out of the darkness and clenched Slink's shoulder. "I have personally counted every bruise and scrape on that young woman," came a gruff voice, "and if there are any additions after you fetch her, you'll pay dearly," Grall warned, stepping into the light. The contrast between the two guards was striking. While Grall's uniform was impeccable, his brightly polished chainmail vest hanging neatly over his merlot shirt and his matching pants tucked into the high leather boots, Slink's uniform, with its dirty chainmail, untucked pants and stained shirt could only be described as disheveled. Grall stood straight and walked with an even stride. Slink slouched and shuffled. In short, Grall was everything the other guard should be.

Sol smiled as Slink nearly jumped out of his skin. "Dammit Grall! You 'ave no right to interfere."

The truth was that as Captain of the Guard, Grall had every right. He shoved Slink up the corridor. "Why don't you politely escort Sol's young lady back here and then slink back into whatever hole you came out of."

Slink paused and opened his mouth as if to reply, only to shut it again before scurrying off to do as he was told.

Grall turned to Sol who stood to greet his keeper. "He thinks he's the only one who can pop out of a shadow," Grall said.

Sol stood head and shoulders above Grall, though the guard was still broader in the chest. Time had added girth to Grall's waist, but despite the flecks of gray that were finding their way into his hair and beard, no one with any sense would doubt the capabilities of the powerful Captain of the Guard. Sol reached through the bars and clasped Grall's hand at the wrist.

"I can't stay long," Grall said. "I just wanted to stop in and tell you you're an idiot."

Sol blinked, "What?"

"You heard me. I saw that stunt you pulled today." Grall frowned, "Sure it worked out alright in the end, but fighters like

K'nal are few and far between. It could have easily ended differently. What you did was stupid and reckless," he paused and then smiled, "and downright decent of you. Made me proud."

With that he turned on his heel and walked down the corridor saying over his shoulder, "Try and get a little sleep tonight…idiot."

Sol lay back down as Grall disappeared around the corner. Praise from the old guard was rare. He wasn't unkind; he just played his cards close to the vest. Grall's words left Sol with rare warmth.

He also found that despite Slink's warnings he was excited for tonight's visit, though not for the reasons Slink imagined.

Most of the fighters took great pride in the spoils they bedded. Quantity was definitely boasted about far more than quality. The number of women you accepted into your cell was directly related to how long you managed to survive. Then of course there were boasts of sexual prowess with most fighters swearing that their spoils begged to come back to them again and again. In reality many of the fighters treated the women terribly. Rape was the norm and beatings were common, sometimes even to death.

Sol could never comprehend why a man whose days were filled with blood and death would choose to bring that into his cell at night.

But then again, Sol rarely slept with one of his prizes.

It wasn't that they weren't desirable. Women were sent to fighters based on "freshness", as Slink put it, and based on their looks. The newest and most beautiful women went to the best fighters. Consequently, Sol had some of the most beautiful and exotic slaves in the region pass through his cell. The Empire was constantly expanding, and as a land fell under the Emperor's control its resources and peoples were dispersed throughout. Even though as a rule they were a little worse for wear, he knew he was welcoming the daughters and wives of fallen nations into his cell.

That was one of the reasons his sheets stayed clean most nights; there were two others.

The first was fear. Despite their vast differences, every woman that came to meet him had that in common. It was in their eyes, in their voices, and in the way they moved. Some struggled valiantly against it, some were overcome by it, but they all shared it.

And who could blame them? Their stories were awful. All of them torn from their families, some even forced to watch them die. They were taken from their homes, beaten, raped, passed from soldier to soldier, only to be sent as a sex prize to men like himself whose entire existence centered around death for spectacle.

Sol also had his own fears to contend with. He knew of his father and what he had done to his mother. Having been begot through such violence, he feared he was destined to repeat it.

The second reason he so seldom shared his bed was the opportunity that these women presented him. Where other fighters saw orifices to be used for pleasure he saw an opportunity for a kind of brief escape. Because of course he did want something for the small bit of comfort and rest he could provide. He wanted to know more of the outside. He wanted their stories.

Sol knew almost nothing of life outside the Coliseum except that which he had learned from the women forced into his cell. He wasn't sure why Oci and Grall had always been so reluctant to speak of the world, but he suspected they were only trying to protect him. Why fill the boy's head with dreams of a world he would never see? In truth, the omission only fueled his desire to learn.

Sol sighed and rolled onto his side. He had seen the outside world once. Living your whole life in one building seemed an absurd impossibility to most. Since he was almost sure to die within the Coliseum walls at the hands of another fighter, to Sol it seemed a fate impossible to avoid.

Though the Coliseum was a year-round venue, gladiator fights were far too expensive to hold constantly. Subsequently, fighters were only brought in from the various gladiator schools for the four seasonal festivals, each lasting a month with the exception of the spring festival, which was extended as a result of falling immediately after the week of the Emperor's birthday. During the rest of the year the Coliseum held chariot races, plays, executions, or any variety of other spectacles. As a result it was always manned by dozens, if not hundreds, of slaves.

Sol's situation was different than most. The majority of the fighters were criminals. Condemned to die in the Coliseum, they were the few with enough potential for providing entertainment that they were assigned to a school rather than executed outright by hanging, beheading, fire, crucifixion, or any number of other methods currently in use. Their fate was the same in the end but a good fighter could buy himself precious time, even netting himself a degree of fame in the process. A handful of fighters, having been skilled or lucky enough to make it through a tournament, left the Coliseum to return to the gladiatorial school where they lived and trained, at least until the next tournament.

Sol had no such escape. While surviving a tournament bought him just as much time as anyone else, his time was that of a Coliseum slave. Rather than training in a school, he was confined to manual labor in the tunnels. The cycle of slave and gladiator had continued unbroken for six years now.

Looking back over that span a lot had changed. At first he had been an unknown. There had been no chant; he had just been the lanky kid with the fancy helmet. But soon spectators took notice that the helmet stuck around, festival after festival.

Sol looked around his small cell. His living accommodations had certainly changed in the last six years as well. After his time in the Pit, sharing cells with other fighters had been little better. His bunkmates kept him constantly on guard. Many a sleepless night he had spent with his head buried in the mattress trying to ignore the muffled cries of a spoil being raped. In time he had earned a private cell in the lower tunnels. It was anything but roomy but it served him well enough. The rectangular room had a single barred door allowing him to see out into the hall. It wasn't much of a view; the corridor turned after about ten feet.

A previous occupant had carved a few cubby holes into the stone walls which Sol had enlarged over the years. One held the lamp that provided the feeble light by which he lived. The others were mainly for show, his possessions being few indeed. He had collected some creature comforts such as a softer, warmer blanket and a little nicer bed. His floor was partially covered by a thick rug and he had even been given a thin, fraying curtain that he could hang in front of the door for a little bit of privacy. His prized possessions were stashed in a single cubby at the head of his bed. Guarded by the troop of soldiers Grall had carved him so long ago, here lay a couple blocks of wood, several partial carvings in various stages of completeness, a few finished carvings, and most importantly, his carving knife.

For a slave to have a weapon in their cell was unheard of. Every precaution was taken to keep the slaves defenseless. Cooks were searched before leaving the kitchen and rooms were torn apart on a regular and random basis. Fighters were especially closely watched. Men had been killed for trying to sneak in an arrowhead or dagger from the fighting floor. Conversely, guards had been killed when smugglings had succeeded. As a gift from Oci, Sol knew that the small knife was a supreme show of trust from Grall. As such he treated the knife, and carving itself, with reverence. Even if none of his carvings ever looked quite right, which even he admitted they didn't, it was his only hobby and he cherished it.

He rolled onto his back, settled his head on his pillow, another luxury, and decided a nap would do him good. Who knew how long Slink would be? Besides, Grall had told him to get some sleep. Even if the girl had seen better days, as Slink put it, Sol doubted he would get much rest that night.

It seemed like he had barely closed his eyes when he was awakened by the sound of footsteps approaching down the hall. He didn't sit up or even open his eyes. He was lying on top of his blanket, wearing plain wool pants and long sleeve shirt with heavy socks to keep warm. It was cold in the dungeons.

The foot of his bed was pointed away from the door, so he didn't see the two come in, but he heard the footsteps stop and Slink's whiney voice. "Brought you a lil somthin'. I'll just leave her here and be off."

"Fine," Sol replied. He heard the cell door open and close but he waited until Slink's steps had died away down the hall before slowly sitting up. He kept his movements small and slow and his face blank. A smile meant different things to different people and he didn't want to scare his guest any more than she already was.

He looked at the woman standing in the corner by the entryway. The lamp that lit the small cell sent light dancing over the sequined outfit they had put her in. The guards always dressed the women in an assortment of racy little costumes kept just for the purpose. This one had seen better days; small to begin with, it had been torn several places, leaving even less to the imagination.

Slink was right, she didn't look to have much left. She was tall, almost as tall as he was, and far too thin. Her pale cream skin was covered in bruises and her sharply-angled face misshapen with swelling. Sol could hear her breath coming ragged and labored. She swayed as if ready to faint and he wondered how she was managing to keep her feet.

Almost on cue her saw her knees start to buckle. He rushed forward to try and catch her only to receive a jab to the nose. He stumbled back, holding his face. The woman slumped against the wall, eyes wide. Between rattled breaths she spoke to him in a harsh language he didn't understand. He stepped back further, trying to calm her with low, even speech, no doubt equally incomprehensible to her. A coughing fit racked her body. Sol approached her again only to fall back when she lashed out. The exertion was too much for her. Wheezing and holding her side, she fought to keep her eyes open but lost consciousness, her head drooping and a trickle of blood coming out the side of her mouth.

He hesitated before approaching again. It was impossible to know if her cough was a result of the broken ribs betrayed by the bruising on her side or something more nefarious. Sol eyed her over with apprehension. The poor girl whimpered in her unconscious state, goose bumps visible even in the dim light of the cell.

Finally Sol moved toward her again, this time without resistance. He lifted her head slightly and saw that she was still alive, though he doubted it would be for long. Her breaths were short, her skin almost transparent. Taking her into his arms he lifted her all too easily and moved her to his bed, wrapping her in his blanket. With his small ration of water he cleaned her face before trying unsuccessfully to get her to drink the rest. She had been beautiful once, even with the abuse that was obvious. He wondered who she had been, sad in the knowledge he would never learn.

With a sigh he lay down on the floor and wrapped the rug around him, preparing for a cold, quiet night.

3.

Sol knew before he opened his eyes what the silence in his cell likely meant. Several times during the short night he had awoken to the Spoil's coughing fits. Each time he lay helpless as spasms racked her frail body. Even when the fits subsided her breath came in a rattled wheeze. The morning's absence of sounds likely meant the lack of any breath at all.

He knew he should probably get up and check on her but he held back, still wrapped in the rug on the floor with his eyes closed. Opening his eyes meant having to deal with the reality of the situation, something he really didn't feel like doing. So he laid there, still and quiet, trying not to think about whom she may have been, what she may have wanted to do with her life, where she came from. Given her foreign language and exotic appearance, he guessed she came from the western wilds. She certainly knew how to throw a punch, perhaps she had been a warrior of some kind. If only he could have spoken to her he might have been able to ask.

Realizing that he was failing at not thinking about her, he finally opened his eyes and rose to his feet, not entirely pleased by the throb in his head. Moving slowly over to the bed he found his suspicions confirmed; the girl had not made it through the night. She lay there peacefully, her serene face showing no trace of her difficult end.

The body in his bed coupled with a wicked headache did not constitute a good start to his birthday. He had thought himself lucky to have his birthday fall on an off-day, one of the few breaks in the bouts dedicated to the logistics of the tournaments. During the off-season, when Sol was just a regular slave, there were no days off. He had hoped today might be one of rare leisure. Now he wondered if labor might not be a welcome distraction, if not just an excuse to get out of his cell.

He heard the door rattle and turned to see Slink poke his head in the door. "You done with 'er yet?"

Sol sighed. "She's dead." There didn't seem to be anything else to say.

"Bloody 'ell!" Slink exclaimed, stepping in the rest of the way. "Gave 'er a real go, did ya? Rode the life right out of 'er!"

"Shut up," Sol snapped. "I didn't touch her. She was sick."

Slink recoiled. "Sick eh? And you shut up with 'er all night. I might be rid of you yet!" he cackled.

Sol glared. "Just shut up and get her out of here."

"Me? If she was sick as you say, I ain't haulin' that carcass anywheres."

"Fine. Go get someone else to do it."

"Listen to you givin' orders! Maybe I'll jus' leave you two love birds in 'ere all day." With that Slink slammed the door and stormed down the hall.

Happy as he was to see Slink go, Sol dreaded the possibility that the guard's crude sense of humor might include actually following through with his threat. The last thing Sol wanted was to be stuck in his cell all day with the dead Spoil. He moved over to the far corner of his cell and sat slumped down against the wall. It wasn't long before he heard footsteps and the door opened again. He was surprised to see Grall come in with an old, ratty blanket in hand.

"I heard what happened," was all he offered. Without further explanation he moved to the side of the bed and began to lay the old blanket on the floor. Sol moved to help and together they lowered the body from the bed to the blanket. Sol felt a swelling of gratitude toward the old guard. That Grall had come down to see to the body himself was an especially generous act considering his rank. They rolled up the body and Grall hoisted it easily over his shoulder before carrying it out the door. There were no formalities for a dead slave, the body was simply removed.

After a time Grall returned carrying a tray with the morning meal. He passed Sol a plate before joining him on the edge of the bed to eat. The meal progressed in a heavy silence and it wasn't long before Grall finished. Sol still stared blankly at the strips of dried meat and the side of porridge on his own plate.

"Eat. You need your strength," Grall prompted.

"I can't." Sol set the plate on the floor and rested his head in his hands.

Grall set a hand on the fighter's shoulder. "This kind of thing happens. Don't let it get to you."

"It doesn't get to you?" Sol's voice was hoarse.

Grall removed his hand. "I'm not saying that. I'm just saying you've gotta shake it off."

They sat quietly for a long moment before Grall spoke again. "This place gets everyone eventually. You've known that your whole life. Spoils have it pretty rough. They come and go almost as often as…"

"Fighters?" Sol offered knowingly.

"Yeah, fighters."

"You're Captain of the Guard," Sol said with a slight tremor. "Can't you do something?"

Grall shook his head, his eyes downcast. "That's the way it is. I can't change it any more than you."

Not for the first time Sol wondered if Grall was as helpless within the system as he let on. He suspected not, but he didn't feel like pressing the issue. There were some things best left unsaid, so again they sat in heavy silence, each lost in his own thoughts.

Eventually Grall stood. "I'd better get on." He walked to the cell door and stopped. "I've arranged for a little visit today."

Sol raised his head from his hands. "Oci?"

Grall chuckled. "Like I had any say in the manner. Shameful the way that woman henpecks me. A guard brow beat by a cook!"

Sol smiled for the first time that morning.

Grall let himself out. "Happy birthday, kid," he said back over his shoulder as he walked down the hall.

Sol again lowered his head to rest in his hands. He knew Grall was right; a dead spoil was nothing new. He shouldn't get worked up. And to ask Grall to do something, to somehow fix the problem, it was unreasonable. In their own way the guards were just as much prisoners in the Coliseum as the slaves. That's just how it was.

Grall walked slowly down the corridor away from Sol's cell, rubbing his temples with his calloused fingers. Hauling dead spoils around certainly wasn't his preferred way to start the day. If it hadn't been for Sol he wouldn't have even considered it. But it wasn't the morning's duty that troubled him, it was Sol's question.

The kid was right; he was Captain of the Guard and he probably could do something. He could find a way to slip the Spoils a little more food or to dispose of one or two of the more sadistic guards. It would be a huge risk; the Empire had spies everywhere, even here. Then there were the frequent inspections he and his men were subjected to. Any breaks from protocol would be one hell of a gamble and in the end it probably wouldn't do any good. The

Coliseum was still a one-way ticket regardless of how long you lasted within its walls.

It wasn't any of those things that stayed Grall's hand though. Had risk and futility been the only factors he would have acted long ago. After all, it wasn't just this morning that he struggled with these feelings. Every day he questioned whether he was doing the right thing. But there was nothing for it; he had made his decision long ago.

Grall leaned against the cool stone wall of the corridor and sighed, remembering another morning many years before.

She was late.

Grall stopped pacing to once again peer out the barred portcullis for some sign of his wife and son. Meeting through the closed entryway was far from ideal, but with security being what it was this was the best they could manage. Security colored everything they did in the Coliseum. Every care was taken to minimize personnel in and out. When a shipment arrived, the crates changed hands at this single entrance rather than inviting the transporters inside. For a visitor to be allowed inside was rare indeed.

Seeing no sign of them he resumed his pacing. He was becoming increasingly flustered, fearing a repeat of their last scheduled rendezvous. Then he had waited in the same fashion for several hours before a runner appeared with word that Marie wasn't coming. Instead she requested that they reschedule for today. Angry but without any recourse, he had accepted. It had now been nearly a year since he had seen his family.

Similar anger began to rise as he paced. He knew damn well how hard this was for him; he could only imagine how hard it was on her. He cursed himself every day for ending up in this place, separated from his only son. To raise a child alone on the meager salary that he was able to send had to be hard. But that didn't give her the right to keep the boy from him. He was doing the best he could.

The sight of long red hair working through the crowd melted those feelings away. She was beautiful, as always. Tall and elegant, he had always thought she should have been a dancer. He straightened his uniform and ran a hand across his recently shaved chin, hoping he was presentable. She approached with a smile, a red-haired boy in tow. As they reached the gate Grall leaned in to welcome her.

She did the same but pulled away after a quick kiss. "Hello, Grall."

"Hello, Marie," he answered, disappointed by the brisk greeting. He noticed that she smelled differently than he remembered. "How are you?"

"I'm fine."

"It's good to see you. You look lovely."

"Thank you," she said quietly.

"Hello, Grall," his son mimicked, wanting to be included in the grownups' conversation.

Breaking into a big smile, Grall knelt to address his son. "Hello there, Thadius. You must have grown three inches since I saw you last."

"I'm the tallest in my class," Thadius agreed, "but everyone calls me Thad."

"Okay, Thad. Are you doing well in your classes?"

Thad nodded. "I can count to a hundred!"

"That's impressive! What else do you learn?" He had a million questions to ask. He wanted to know everything.

"We learn all about the Empire and how great the Emperor is and about animals and letters and all kindsa stuff!" Thad replied excitedly.

Grall frowned in mock seriousness. "And are you good for your teachers?"

"Yes, Grall," he answered with practice.

Grall chuckled. "If I call you Thad, you have to call me dad. Okay?"

Thad looked up to his mom. She glanced hesitantly at Grall. "I think Grall is fine."

Grall stood; this time his frown was real. "He's too young to call me by my first name. He should call me dad, don't you think?"

Instead of answering him she turned to Thad. "How about you go wait for me at the café?"

Grall couldn't believe his ears. "What are you talking about? You just got here!"

Thad looked at Grall, then back to his mom. "Will you get me a sticky bun?"

Marie nodded, turning the boy's shoulders toward a group of umbrella tables down the street.

"Please don't do this," Grall pleaded.

"Go ahead," she told the boy, patting him on the rump. "I'll be there in a few minutes."

"Bye, Grall!" The boy waved over his shoulder.

"Goodbye, son," was all Grall could muster. He stood, dumbstruck, watching Thad fade back into the crowd. His stomach dropped with the distinct impression he had just seen his son for the final time. Wanting some kind of explanation, he looked to his wife. He found her watching him, her cheeks streaked with tears.

"Why?" he asked simply.

"I'm sorry, Grall. We can't keep doing this. It's going to confuse him."

He tried to keep his voice calm but without success. "Keep doing what? Confused about what?"

"He a growing boy," she answered. "He needs a father."

"He has a father!"

She shook her head, sobbing. "You're not there. He needs someone to be there for him."

"You don't think I know that? I hate this as much as you do."

She nodded. "I believe you. But that doesn't change anything."

He stood dumbstruck for a moment. "So what are you saying?"

Her eyes dropped. "I've found someone. He's not you but he's there. And he's kind and he can provide for Thad and me." She paused. "He's asked me to marry him."

Grall slumped as if punched in the gut. "So that's what this is all about. You're in love with someone else."

"I didn't say I love him. Besides, you don't know what it's like," she pleaded. "When you came to this place it was like you died. People sent flowers and now they treat me like a widow. I grieved. Then to see you like this, once or twice a year separated by a metal gate, it's like you're a ghost."

"And you need a man of flesh don't you," he said coldly.

"It's not like that," she implored. "I'm so alone."

"And I'm not?"

She shook her head. "This isn't what I wanted."

It was quiet for a long moment. "You can't keep my son from me," he demanded in a low voice. "It's wrong."

"It's what's best for him."

"Says who?"

She didn't answer immediately and he realized her focus had shifted to behind him. He looked over his shoulder to find one of his fellow guards jogging up the long tunnel. "We're not done. Don't go anywhere," he commanded before turning to address the guard. "I asked not to be disturbed."

"You're needed," the guard said, out of breath.

"What for?"

"Hell if I know," the guard answered, annoyed. "I was just told to get you right away."

"It'll have to wait."

"Grall," Marie chimed in, "you should go."

"I said we're not done here," he answered without turning.

Her voice was filled with a deep sadness when she replied. "Yes, dear, we are."

Recognizing the finality in her statement he moved to the gate, reaching out for her. "Please, Marie. Don't do this," he pleaded. "I love you."

She stepped back out of his reach, tears flowing anew. "And I love you. I hope you believe that." She smiled sadly. "Goodbye, Grall."

It was his turn to cry. "Don't go," he begged. He was trapped. All he could do was watch, helpless, as she, too, melted back into the crowd. "Marie, please!" he cried to her. "Marie! Marie!" he yelled again and again. She didn't answer, she didn't come back.

His family was gone.

He slumped down to the ground with his back to the gate. He would never see his boy again. Thad would grow up with a substitute father. Another man would teach him about life. He would play games and learn about fighting from someone else. Eventually there would be dating, breakups, then a wedding and grandchildren. And he, the boy's true father, would fade from memory, forgotten in his Coliseum prison.

A muffled cough brought his attention back to the guard, obviously embarrassed by the intimate scene he had just witnessed. Still Grall sat. He suddenly wondered if it was worth getting up, worth continuing on this way. His family had been what drove him. Every morning when he awoke to the Coliseum walls, it was the thought of his wife and son that got him out of bed. But now they had left him. He would never see his son again.

He shook his head, refusing to accept this fate. Maybe Marie would come to her senses. Maybe in time Thad would seek him out. There was even the slim chance that if he survived long enough and worked hard enough that someday he could retire. Then he could leave this wretched place and find his family. He couldn't let himself be forgotten. He sat for another long moment and then slowly stood. "Lead the way," he said.

He had to keep going. He vowed that he would do whatever it took to make it out. Someday, he would see his son again.

Grall wiped a tear from his eye, the memory of his son's last visit as painful as that day so many years ago. With a sigh he straightened and returned to his duties.

Sol still sat with his head in his hands when a familiar voice approaching from down the hall brought him to his feet. Oci prattled on to her escort Slink as he led her in. Though they lived in the same building, the fighter and the slave quarters were set about as far apart as they could get in the Coliseum complex. As a result, he hadn't seen Oci since his last birthday and the sight of the aging cook brought a genuine smile to Sol's face. Sol was concerned to see the white-haired figure, as round as ever, enter his cell with a slight limp. He greeted her with a hug, noticing that despite her girth she felt frail in his arms.

"There's my little darlin'," she said with her always present smile. "Happy birthday!"

"Lil' darlin'?" Slink mocked.

"Shut up." Sol shot a threatening look at Slink before turning back to Oci. "It's great to see you. How are you?"

"Oh, I make out. I heard about your last bout. I always knew that Frorian was a good 'un."

Sol nodded. "Good thing, too. I almost missed my birthday."

Oci nodded in kind. "I remember it like yesterday. I always liked your mother. She –"

"Never let this place get to her, I know," Sol finished for her with an awkward smile. He didn't like having such a private conversation with Slink in the room.

"Why don't you get out of here?" He glared at the guard.

"If I go, she goes. She ain't even suposta be down 'ere."

"Just do as you're told so Grall doesn't beat the tar out of you."

Slink stepped threateningly toward Sol. "I'd like to see 'im try!"

Sol met the step so that the two stood nose to nose.

"That's enough!" Oci's voice rang with an authority that made each man fall back a step.

"Slink, dear," she continued sweetly, "I only get to see this dumb oaf once a year. Can you please wait down the hall for a few minutes?"

"Dumb oaf?" Sol asked, but was silenced with a look from Oci.

Slink shrugged. "Well, if ya put it that way." He handed Oci a small package Sol hadn't noticed him carrying before retreating down the hall.

Once he had rounded the corner Oci turned back to Sol. "You should be nicer to Slink."

Sol scoffed. "That creep? Why?"

"I'll have you know he has it just as bad as us, if not worse with how the other guards treat him."

"Because he's a creep."

"He's not a creep," she argued. "He's just..." Oci struggled for the right word.

"Slimy?" Sol offered.

"Awkward," Oci corrected with a disapproving look.

"Pfff. What's Slink ever done for anyone but Slink?"

Oci raised an eyebrow. "Oh, you might be surprised."

"Try me."

"Fine." Oci handed him the small package. Sol opened it to find his yearly birthday cake.

"My cake?"

Oci nodded.

"Slink makes my birthday cake?" he asked with a grimace.

"No, you slow boy! I made the cake. I swear, if your sword was as slow as your wits –"

"What then?" Sol interrupted.

"Every year since you were 6 years old I've made you a yellow honey cake with strawberry frosting. You've never once wondered where I got the honey or strawberries? You helped me in the kitchen for years. Did you ever see either of those things lying around?"

"I never thought about it," Sol admitted. "You get them from Slink?" It was hard to believe. Sol had known the guard most of his life and he'd never seen him go out of his way to help anyone. Not that anyone ever wanted his help. He was thoroughly disliked by guard and slave alike.

"That's right," Oci nodded. "Every year he smuggles them in. No easy task, mind you."

Sol sat on the bed, box of cake in hand. "Why?"

Oci set a gentle hand on his leg. "Because I ask him to, dear," she said softly.

"Yeah, but what's in it for him? Do you make him a cake too?"

Oci hesitated. "Well, yes, some years when I have extra. But that's got nothing to do with it," she added quickly.

"Right." Sol rolled his eyes.

"That's not the only thing," she huffed. "He does all sorts of little things for me."

"Because you cook all sorts of little things for him," Sol continued stubbornly.

"But he doesn't have to do errands to make me cook. He's a guard, even if no one treats him like one. He could make me do anything he wants but he doesn't."

"Because he's got no backbone."

Oci threw up her hands again. "Fine! If you need to hate him so badly, you go ahead." Tears rimmed her eyes. "The one day a year I get to see you and all you want to do is argue!"

Sol quickly stood and hugged her. "I'm sorry, O, you're right. Slow wits and all." He steered her toward the bed where they both sat down. "I promise I'll be nicer to Slink, okay?"

Oci smiled and wiped her eyes. "Good. Now, Grall told me about last night and he's right. Nobody's made of stone but you have to let things like that go as quickly as you can. They'll eat you alive if you don't."

He hung his head. "I know. It's just…hard."

"You bet it is. I don't want to know a man that doesn't think so. But you have to remember," Oci's eyes dropped, her voice lowered, "her pain is over now."

Sol noticed the change. "O, is there something you're not telling me?"

She waved the question off, smiling again, "No, dear, I'm fine."

Sol took her hands gently into his, noting again how thin they felt. "Oci, tell me."

She tried to pull away but to no end. She sighed. "I fell again. I've always been clumsy and you know it."

"Are you okay?"

"Oh, I'm sore enough, especially in the mornings. Got some pretty good bruises, too, but I get around all right most days."

Sol frowned. "Most days?"

"Well, some days, not that many mind you, I just can't seem to get up the energy to get out of bed."

"How often? What do you do? Do the guards know?" Sol knew what happened to slaves who couldn't do their work.

"It's fine," she said to comfort him. "It's only been a few times and one of the others has always covered for me."

"But what's wrong?" Fear had found its way into Sol's voice.

Oci's always present smile softened. "I'm tired, dear," she said quietly. "I've been in that kitchen for almost thirty years now, most of my life. I work every day from sunup to sundown and sometimes longer. I've seen some good things," she winked at Sol, "but I've also seen plenty of bad." She slumped slightly. "I'm worn out."

Sol looked at the woman who was more his mother than the woman who bore him. He knew what she was saying but he couldn't accept it. Not today. He shook his head, unsure what to say. Thankfully, she saved him the trouble.

"Don't you worry, though," she chirped, straightening up. "You'll still get a few more birthday cakes out of me yet." The warmth returned to her smile.

They chatted a while longer before Slink came to take her back to the kitchen. They talked about the old days and Oci caught him up on all the latest Coliseum gossip. He teased her about the quality of her cooking and she even let him share a little of his cake with her. It was a good visit. But even as Sol watched Slink lead her out the door, promising all the while to visit sooner this time, he wondered how many visits they had left.

"Two visitors in one day. Aren't we special?" Slink sneered as he opened the door to Sol's cell.

"Fairly special, yes," Sol agreed with hesitation. Having already seen Grall and Oci that morning, he couldn't guess who else would want to call on him. A visit by a stranger meant that someone had bribed a guard into smuggling them in for reasons unknown. Given the considerable risk and cost involved with such an excursion, the motive was usually extreme. In Sol's experience a visit usually involved either a wealthy woman passionately smitten with a fighter or a formerly wealthy man hell-bent on avenging some perceived wrong, usually having to do with a mislaid wager. In either case these rare events were to be handled gingerly.

"Don't get a big 'ead," Slink chided.

A flamboyantly dressed figure stepped in behind Slink. "He's so top-heavy as it is it's a wonder he doesn't fall over."

Sol feigned insult, relieved. "Why Vance, you know better than I the difficulty of staying humble in the face of an adoring public."

Vance nodded. "Indeed. Of course, I've always found humility to be overrated."

"Humility and modesty," Sol replied, eyeing the visitor's outfit. "Is that all silk?"

Vance ran a graceful hand down his bright red tunic, exquisitely detailed in gold stitching. Pants of the same make were tucked into the top of his highly polished black leather knee-high boots. Coupled with his fine bone structure and pale complexion, the effect was stunning. "This old thing?" he chuckled. "One does try."

The two men turned to Slink, still standing to one side of the doorway with an unintelligent look.

"Poor thing," Vance assessed, looking the guard over. "Like a eunuch in a brothel."

"Eh?" Slink chimed, obviously confused.

"You can leave now," Sol offered.

"I'll leave when I'm good and ready!" Slink barked. A long silence followed with both of the men looking expectantly at the guard. "Right." And with that he turned for the door.

Something poked at the back of Sol's mind. "Slink, uh, thanks."

Slink halted, looking still more confused. "What?"

Sol glanced at Vance who had raised an eyebrow at the little scene. "Thanks," he repeated.

Slinks eyes narrowed. "Right..." he said slowly before backing the rest of the way out the door and scurrying down the hall.

Vance questioned Sol with a raised eyebrow.

"I..." he started to explain, "don't ask," he finished.

"Very well," Vance conceded with a wry smile.

Vance was Sol's lone contact outside of the Coliseum. He had visited a handful of times on an irregular basis since Sol started participating in the bouts. The visits all went the same; some playful banter leading to a few questions about the bouts punctuated with a small gift. As benign as they seemed, Sol had come to regard a visit from Vance as a sort of omen. Change always seemed to follow in his wake. Even more, Sol had the feeling that Vance knew about it; his questions were leading, like hints to a riddle. The last visit, several years ago, had included queries about Sol's grappling technique. Shortly after, it was announced that that year's spring festival tournament would be completely weaponless.

Try as he might Sol was never able to glean more than small bits of information. It was a dynamic that frustrated Sol; someone from the outside swooping in as he pleased to tease him with allusions about his future. He toyed with ideas of rebellion, of not participating in the next visit but instead boycotting the conversation. In the end he had to admit he enjoyed the visits. They were like a game, each player trying to score a little more knowledge about the other. Sol had tallied some points. He had learned that Vance was a rather famous bard and that he had a son. Plus Vance, although guarded, was as charming and charismatic a character as could be found. Omen or not, Sol was happy to see him on his birthday.

"How's the boy?" Sol asked, sitting on the bed.

"As headstrong as ever. Chip off the old block, really," Vance replied distractedly, searching the small cell. "Haven't they given you a chair yet? I'll have to speak with someone on my way out."

"My sincerest apologies, Sir, that my humble accommodations don't fulfill your every need," Sol offered with a mock bow.

"Not at all, Sir," replied Vance, returning the bow. "Although I'm not a minimalist myself, you've managed to pull it off nicely." He took a seat next to Sol on the bed.

"I feel it gives the room an open, airy feel. Plus, I don't entertain often."

Vance flashed a mischievous smile. "That's not what I hear. Word on the street is that you host a veritable parade of the fairer sex."

Sol shrugged. "People will talk."

"Indeed they will. It must be something, really, to have women delivered to your door," he said wistfully.

Sol flinched at the memory of the last such delivery. Vance noticed and tactfully added, "Though I'm sure it isn't as ideal as it sounds."

"Not exactly," Sol answered with a sad smile.

"But I am sure that as a senior fighter," Vance recovered with a flourish, "you must welcome some of the most exotic creatures in the land into your humble abode."

Sol conceded with a nod.

"Lantanians?" Vance asked.

Sol nodded.

"Acacians? Typheese?"

More nods.

"Frorians?" Vance asked with a slight raise of his brow.

Sol shook his head. "No. Exotic is one thing, Frorians are another."

"Quite right. What do you know of them?"

"Frorians?" Sol stretched out at the head of the bed. "Not much. They live far to the south in a frozen wasteland beyond the Empire. I know they're huge and I've been told that they don't have any…uh, anything below the belt," he chuckled. "I don't know how accurate that is though," he added quickly.

Vance nodded casually. "I believe they keep the hardware, as it were, inside. Frigid temperatures aren't kind to the extremities. They're not human, after all."

"I figured as much. They do speak our language, though."

"Some of them," Vance confirmed.

Sol eyed his companion. "You seem to know a little about them."

"Of course!" Vance replied. "It is my responsibility to know a little about a lot. I will have to concede, though, that you have a bit more firsthand knowledge as of late. Did you two have that moving performance planned or was it spontaneous?"

"Who? K'nal? That was our first and only conversation, one word long."

Vance leaned in with a hungry look in his eye. "And what word was that?"

Sol smiled. "Sorry, friend. That's between fighters."

Vance straightened indignantly. "Of course, Sir. I wouldn't dream of meddling in the affairs of those whose fates intertwine on the Coliseum floor. I merely sought to share in some small piece of the experience. It was, after all, a spectacle to be remembered."

"You enjoy the bouts? I thought they might be too pedestrian for you."

Vance dismissed the poke with a wave of his hand, "I enjoy all human drama. On occasion the Coliseum delivers. The real question is why did you put yourself between that beast and the fallen giant?"

Sol shrugged. "I've been thinking that over. And why did K'nal do what he did? Or rather why didn't he do what he could have?" He paused. "I don't have a good answer. There just wasn't anything else to do."

Vance hopped suddenly to his feet with a satisfied smile. "I thought as much. My dear Sir, it has been a pleasure, as always." He fished around his pockets producing a solid chocolate horse, presenting it to Sol.

"A birthday present for me?" Sol asked coyly.

Vance perked up even further, his face lit with a genuine smile. "Is it really your birthday? That's wonderful. I'm honored to have shared it with you." He extended his hand.

Sol took it, slightly in awe of the odd character in front of him. Vance called to Slink and the guard let him out and led him away, all the while Vance chastising him for the lack of proper furniture in a senior fighter's quarters. Sol could only smile, shake his head, and wonder what changes his personal omen would bring this time.

4.

Lysik groaned as he caught himself staring yet again at the tiny bubbles rising up through the mug of ale sitting on the bar in front of him. He drained the remainder and then turned to survey the room once more before retiring. The piano tune "Fair Country Maid" hung in the smoky air, an already tired jingle made even more so it having been played twice already that evening. Lysik sneered at the piano player, who took no notice of him or much of anything else. The old man played the scant few songs he knew for the few meager coins he received, nodding dumbly to requests that would never be played. Occasionally the owner would storm out from behind the bar and threaten to throw him out on his ear if he didn't learn some new material. The regulars knew it was all for show. The piano-man worked only for tips and besides, folks visited the dingy bar on the edge of Fort City expected cheap liquor and dark corners, not entertainment.

Lysik would have preferred the Fox's Den, a more reputable establishment in the heart of the city, but they knew him there and that could make things difficult. They knew him here too, in fact; the assassin and his daggers were known throughout the Empire. The difference here was that nobody particularly cared. He looked around the bar, noting no new faces in the gloom, then stood to leave, disappointed by the evening. Turning from the bar he heard a rough cough behind him. He turned back to see the bartender wiping the same glass he'd been wiping all evening. "Tab's due, Crow."

Lysik's lip curled. "Is that right? And how much do you expect for this swill?"

The bartender frowned. "You don't have to drink if you don't like it," he said sharply.

A mask of mock indignation settled on Lysik's face. "Why, Tom, could it be you don't appreciate my patronage? Would you throw me out on my ear like you threaten that dimwit on the piano?" He leaned his thin frame across the bar so that his hooked nose nearly touched the bartender's. "You wouldn't do that to me, would you, Tom?"

There was a long awkward moment when neither man moved. Sweat began to bead on the bartender's brow. He flinched when Lysik's hand moved suddenly. Lysik pinched Tom's cheek hard, smiling playfully. "I know you wouldn't. You like me too much. Why else would you have given me such a delightful nickname?" He leaned back and patted his chest, "Crow. That's very clever. Tell me, Tom, why Crow?"

Tom squirmed, obviously uncomfortable. "Er, your nose," he said lamely.

"My nose?" Lysik prompted, this time without any trace of humor. His hand moved to the long dagger displayed prominently on his belt. "What about my nose?"

The bartender's eyes strayed to the dagger. More than once Tom had been forced to clean up his bar after its use. On one occasion, he had even seen the second matching dagger residing in the assassin's boot. Lysik had been outnumbered five to one. There had been a lot of cleaning up after that day.

"Well, not so much your nose as your face," he tried to explain as Lysik's fingers toyed with the hilt of the dagger. Tom continued quickly, "I mean your face is like bird's, like a noble bird's, like an eagle."

Lysik's hand relaxed but did not move from the dagger. "Then why Crow?" he hissed.

"Well, can you picture an eagle in this dump?" Tom asked, forcing a sad smile. "To bring in eagles I'd have to stop serving swill."

Lysik laughed and slapped Tom hard on the shoulder. "That is clever! Crow it is, then." He turned his back on the visibly relieved bartender and felt slightly better about the evening. Watching old Tom sweat wasn't his ideal entertainment but it was better than nothing.

Moving to leave, he again stopped short of the door. A new face had entered the bar while he was distracted with Tom and was now sitting in a dark corner booth. She was young with straight black hair. Bright red lipstick contrasted starkly with her snowy skin, as did the equally scarlet bow tied around her arm, marking her trade. Lysik smiled as his evening's prospects improved drastically. He moved to the booth, pleased to see she sat alone. He greeted her with a nod and sat down.

"Sorry, darlin'," Lysik winced inwardly at the sound of her high, squeaky voice, "I'm spoken for this evening. Care to make plans for tomorrow?"

He leaned across the table and took her hand. "Such beauty in such a place is rare indeed."

She pulled her hand away, "I'm meeting someone," she said shortly. "But I'd be happy to meet you here some other evening," she added with a sweet smile.

He sat up straight. "I'll double it."

"What?"

"Whatever you're receiving for the evening, I'll double it."

The girl eyed him suspiciously. "Why?"

Lysik flashed his most charming smile. "I'm used to getting what I want and I want your company," he said simply.

The girl hesitated, looking around, "But I'm meeting someone," she repeated.

Lysik also looked around dramatically. "I see no one here worthy of your time, save myself."

He could see her start to waver. "Double?" she asked.

"My offer still stands." It mattered little how much she expected. He would have promised to triple her rate if he wasn't sure it would scare her off.

She offered her hand back and smiled seductively. "Then I am all yours."

Standing and taking her hand, he helped her toward the door. "Yes," he replied, "you are."

Old Tom shook his head as he watched the two walk out. "Shame," he said to no one, "she's awfully young. Wrong place at the wrong time, I guess." With that he went back to wiping the same glass.

Lysik's nose had nothing to do with the nickname. The bartender knew the old saying:

A crow may follow death or precede it, but they're never far apart.

The same could be said for Lysik.

The warm water felt good as he washed his tired hands. He poured some more from the steaming kettle the porter had brought him into the wash basin. The clean, clear liquid blended with the blood-infused water, diluting its crimson color. To the side of the washstand the morning suns shone through the room's lone window onto a chair draped with his discarded clothing, bloodstains drying into a rusty brown. There had been a bit of a stir when he emerged from his room during the night, in the same blood-spattered garb, to request fresh towels from the inn's night desk. He hadn't considered how his appearance might disturb the elderly innkeeper. Half asleep, the old fool had cried out at the sight of him, inviting more than one guest to peek out of their doors to discern the source of the ruckus. The realization of who the gory visage was shut the old man up quickly enough. Lysik had casually returned to his room, towels in hand, secure in the fact that his reputation had once again preceded him.

He dried his hands with one of the clean towels and then moved to the bedside table, which was crowded with a myriad of different colored bottles. Shuffling through the bottles, he selected a dark blue one that he held up to the light, inspecting its precious contents. Only a few spoonfuls of the syrup remained. "A trip to the apothecary may be in order," he said to himself. He replaced the powerful paralytic, setting it neatly beside a gruesome tray of shiny metal blades, not yet cleaned after the night's use. Picking up a larger green bottle, he carefully poured some of its sweet smelling contents onto another clean towel before turning to the bed to survey the night's work.

The girl lay naked; her ruby red lips still shone in stark contrast to her pale skin, but now so did the dozens of thin strips where the skin was absent, painstakingly removed by Lysik's skilled blades. The recessed ribbons decorated the girl's torso like the striped coat of a jungle cat. Each strip was uniform and perfectly parallel to its neighbors, revealing the surgical precision to which Lysik had honed his craft, forever polishing his skills as the Empire's top interrogator. He rubbed the salve-soaked towel over the wounds, assuring no infection would befoul his work of art. Though the salve had to sting horribly, the girl made no sound or movement, save a slight widening of her darting blue eyes. He looked into those eyes and smiled, noting how their color matched that of the bottle containing the serum which so perfectly stole her mobility while at the same time leaving all sensation.

His hand grazed ever so gently over one of her bare and as of yet unblemished legs, goose bumps rising in the wake of his fingers. "I'm going to go get some breakfast. I'll be back in a few hours. Then we can continue."

The girl clenched her eyes shut, the strongest reaction she could muster in her current condition.

"But you're unfinished," he answered in response to her silent protests. "We can't have that, can we?"

Her eyes went wide and then clenched shut again.

"I know the problem, you're lonely! Perhaps I can round up a companion for you, another girl to chat with. Would you like that?"

Her eyes opened and closed rapidly, tears streaming out their corners.

"Then it's settled. You just relax and we'll be back before you know it."

Wearing a clean set of clothes and a wide smile, he quietly exited the room, looking forward to a hearty breakfast.

The girl lay in the bed, her motionless form betraying nothing of her inner turmoil; the battle she waged with her body in a vain attempt to coax movement out her lifeless limbs. In her heart she knew the futility. If the liquid in the blue bottle was able to steal her mobility during the horrors of the night, there was little hope it would fail now. She just wanted the pain to end. After a time she gave up, knowing he would soon return to prolong her agony.

And by the sounds of it, this time she would have company.

5.

"Now remember what I told you," Grall said, strapping on Sol's shin guards during their usual pre-bout routine. "You stick to what you know and you'll prove those promoters right."

Sol hated promoters.

There wasn't a day that went by during which he wasn't reminded how little control he had over his own life. Nothing made that lack of control more apparent than someone, whom he would never meet, throwing his life into turmoil hoping to sell just a few more tickets to patrons bent on seeing him kill or die.

And the things they came up with. "Come see Sol, Son of the Coliseum, clean up the streets of Astrolia!" Months later, Sol had learned that particular idea came from a promoter who had come to the aid of a bureaucrat friend. Apparently the official's office had been inundated with complaints from Astrolia's elite concerning certain undesirable components of the city's population. Soldiers had spent days rounding up every beggar and transient unlucky enough to get caught up in the sweep. Men and women, young and old, many blind or crippled, were given clubs and dumped into the Coliseum in large groups to fight trios of well-armed senior fighters. The resulting slaughter had done little to reduce the city's surplus population and had left Sol sleepless for nearly a month.

Then there was the now infamous "Fifty Fighters, No Weapons, Last Man Standing!" day of horror. As it turned out, even the mob has its limits. By the end of nearly five hours of abhorrent brutality, when Sol stood alone, the great Coliseum was nearly empty. Apparently seeing a man decapitated with a sword is entertaining but seeing a man bludgeon another man's face in with the lower leg physically torn off of a third crosses a line. Sol had never spoken of that day since with anyone and he never would.

Much to Sol's chagrin, both of those fateful fights had closely followed a visit from Vance, and the meetings were laced with subtle hints and clues Sol found impossible to discern except in hindsight. A trend, it seemed, that looked to continue once again.

They finished putting on Sol's armor and exited his cell in silence with Grall in the lead. Sol carried his signature helmet and followed, trying to use the pre-bout routine to clear his thoughts. Between Vance's hints and Grall's news about the upcoming fight, Sol's mind was anything but at ease. They reached the holding cell all too quickly, Grall offering his customary, "Good luck," and quick pat on the shoulder before leaving.

Sol sat on the hard wooden bench, relieved to have a few minutes to compose himself. The sensation was short lived. A few moments later the door opened to admit the hulking form of K'nal. Squeezing his way into the small cell, the furry Frorian sat on a second bench directly opposite Sol. The space was so cramped their knees touched, or rather Sol's knees touched the giant's shins. The two gladiators silently eyed each other in the dim light. The tension in the small cell was palpable.

Sol had a nagging feeling he should say something but he had no idea what. What could he say to a Frorian? He knew nothing of K'nal's background or Frorian customs. What if he said something that offended the giant? Part of him wanted to thank K'nal for his actions during the Dybuk fight but a larger part worried that the gesture would be taken as a sign of weakness. Looking at the way his companion filled the small cell, all muscle and fur, he suspected that weakness wouldn't be well received.

More to break the silence than anything else he finally settled on a simple, "Uh, good luck today."

With no discernible change in his expression, K'nal looked his companion over. "And you," was his baritone response.

The silence resumed.

Sol sat contentedly, thinking things could have gone worse and waiting for their turn on the Coliseum floor.

Sol hated promoters, but even he had to admit that this time they had something. K'nal's selfless act during the Dybuk fight on the opening afternoon of the Emperor's birthday week had struck a real chord with the people. The city was abuzz and the promoters smelled a new selling point. Fighters being thrown into pairs or groups was nothing new but the teamwork had always been short-lived, usually only lasting until the opposing teams had been vanquished before the crowd demanded the comrades turn on each other. In the short time since the Dybuk fight, something new had been taking shape.

Now when two fighters were paired it was conceivably for life, however long that might be. Rather than fighters being randomly thrown together minutes before an event, pairs were being assigned in advance based on complementary fighting styles and experience levels. Bards had been hired to tell grand tails of camaraderie and brotherhood between partners. The stories were rubbish but the results were something else. The spectacle of seeing a man fight not only for his own life but for the life of another drew crowds the size of which the Coliseum had not seen for years.

Successful pairs fought as a team, not out of some new-found sense of altruism, but out of necessity. The rules of the game had changed. A fighter's life rested not only in his own hands but now also in the hands of another. More importantly, the constant threat of a fighter's partner suddenly turning on him had been stripped away, leaving as close a thing to trust as could come of such circumstances. A fighter could now make a riskier move with the knowledge that since his partner's fate was intertwined with his own, it was in his partner's best interest to defend him and keep him alive.

A subtle dance played out with each new pairing; each fighter testing just how far the other would go to keep him alive. Not far enough and they fought with hesitation. Too far and the unnecessary risks added up very quickly indeed. Successful pairs figured it out quickly.

Against the promoter's better judgment, Sol had been paired with K'nal. Their concern, and not an unfounded one, was that pairing the two most senior and successful fighters tilted the field in a way that would make choosing opponents difficult. In the end they had been given no other choice. Since the movement had started with the two, the crowd demanded that they stay together.

Now in their inaugural paired bout only a week after the Dybuk fight, they looked ready to prove the promoters right. Sol and K'nal ran out from the tunnel to find themselves pitted against another pair of seasoned fighters billed as "the fastest swords in the Coliseum". Being from one of the larger fighting schools, Sol knew the two dark-skinned brothers by reputation only. They were young, younger than Sol, and built in a similar tall, lanky fashion. Each wielded a flat-bladed scimitar and wore loose-fitting black and red robes.

The two pairs met at the center of the Coliseum floor to the roar of the capacity crowd. The action was immediate as the brothers sought to press their advantage in blade speed. With a blur of twirling robes the two pressed in, one high and one low. K'nal and Sol were forced on the defensive, each giving ground to a brother's blade. Still the two pressed, alternating attacks at a blistering pace. The tactic continued to pay off as K'nal and Sol were once again driven back. The brothers' speed left no time for either fighter to mount a counter, giving the robed figures every advantage.

But the advantage was short-lived.

Forged by the heat of the battle, the two fighters' styles meshed before the crowds eyes. Sol's speed and agility nearly perfectly complemented K'nal's strength and power. Likewise, K'nal's handiwork almost perfectly complemented Sol's footwork. Parry after parry, defense after defense, the two fighters' separate rhythms became one. It wasn't long before the brothers were on the defensive, quick thrusts and parries from Sol's short swords clearing the way for devastating swings from K'nal's massive claymore.

The brothers responded admirably, losing ground but keeping their wits. Though it seemed impossible, they increased their pace further still, a blur of steel keeping the powerful pair at bay. In the end it wasn't their blade speed that failed them; it was their focus, which was, understandably, trained on K'nal's two-handed claymore. The six-foot blade crashed into the brothers' defenses at a rate no human fighter could have matched. It took all the brothers' considerable skill to keep it from cutting them into kindling. Unfortunately for them, this gave Sol all the opportunity he needed to follow the Frorian's attacks with lightning-fast thrusts from his short swords. The crowd erupted as first one and then the other brother hit the sandy Coliseum floor.

K'nal and Sol lay their weapons on the ground, prepared to retire for the day in victory. Moving back to their tunnel, K'nal stopped Sol with a massive hand on his shoulder. "Something's wrong."

Sol could feel it too. Anticipation still hung thick in the air. A low grumble grew in intensity and mixed with the applause. The crowd wanted more.

The two fighters weren't the only ones to notice. In the Coliseum tunnels the organizers scurried to find the means to pacify the mob. Plans changed and "improvise" was the word of the moment.

Sol and K'nal had started to move cautiously back to their abandoned weapons when two doors opened on either end of the fighting floor, admitting four more fighters. The two pairs had been scheduled to fight each other but were now instructed to work together to fight Sol and K'nal. The gladiators scrambled for their weapons as the quad closed, forming a box around them. There they remained, Sol and K'nal back-to-back circling one direction, the quad spaced evenly around them circling the other direction, no one willing to make the first move.

Eventually one of the quad caught his companions' attention enough to gesture a strategy. The quad split back into the original pairs with the obvious intent to divide and conquer. Two short men, each with a broadsword and a small shield, approached K'nal, while Sol was left to deal with two brutes wielding axes. If the tactic was designed to separate the pair it failed miserably. K'nal stood tall, heaving the massive claymore in continuous wide arcs while Sol crouched low, darting back and forth between the oncoming pairs.

One of the shielded pair timed a charge at K'nal's back only to have the white giant abruptly pivot back on his swing with inhuman strength. The fellow was just able to get his shield up before the claymore shattered it, sending him sprawling back into his partner. At the same moment the axemen charged Sol, both partners' heavy war axes raised high. The big men chopped down only to have Sol duck quickly to one side, parrying the ax of one man across the body of the second thus leaving both vulnerable. A simple backward spin and Sol's short swords raked across the backs of both men.

The quad fell back, the axmen grimacing and the short fellow with the shattered shield with one arm hanging limply by his side. It was a short reprieve. Again they charged and again they fell back, this time with the other short fighter bleeding badly from a wounded thigh. Finally growing impatient, the quad charged the pair full bore from opposite directions. Standing back to back, Sol and K'nal met the charge in a spinning whirl of sharpened steel. The action was furious but brief, with Sol's sword piercing the throat of the last of the quad before the body of the first to fall even hit the ground.

The crowd erupted. This time no grumbling accompanied the thunderous applause that followed the fighters as they retired to the tunnels and as the Coliseum throbbed with the crowd's roar, all the promoters heard was the sound of coins pouring into their coffers.

Sol eyed the woman Slink had left in his cell. The guard had assured him that this one was much *fresher* than the last. He wasn't real sure why Slink made an extra trip down to his cell after every bout simply to announce his evaluation of that night's Spoil, but for once, rather than a grunt or growl in response, Sol had attempted something a little more civil.

Over the last few days he had been trying to take Oci's words to heart. The results of his pleasantness had been most entertaining. Always paranoid, Slink seemed to take Sol's newfound kindness as an attempt toward subversion. The encounters had thus far left Slink edgy and irritable. Sol on the other hand couldn't help but be rather amused by the situation. Plus, he had to admit it was nice to put the insults and threats aside for a while. In a way, Sol figured that perhaps he owed it to Slink. Though crude, the guard had never treated him particularly unkindly. Plus, Oci was right; the other guards treated him horribly. Slink always seemed to have a new black eye or busted lip. He didn't deserve that. And after all, Sol had known Slink most of his life.

Rather than a heartfelt talk, the result of Sol's most recent attempt at conversation had been typically unproductive. It ended with a very nervous Slink scurrying down the hall, murmuring all the way, "This un'll do better for ya. Much fresher, much better."

The young woman standing before him certainly appeared to be in better shape than his last spoil. Sol, on the other hand, was a good deal more sore this time around, a fact that worried him. He was barely through the Emperor's birthday week and he had the whole of the Winter Festival to look forward to. Things seemed to get a little harder every season. He tried to remind himself that he wasn't that old but at the same time he couldn't forget how quickly the Coliseum could age a person.

The woman was small; short with a petite frame. She was slim but not the skeletal-skinny the ladies in the luxury boxes worked for and the slaves in the tunnels couldn't avoid. She had generous hips and relatively long legs for her short stature. Long, curly chestnut-colored hair hung down over her face as she stood with her arms crossed, head down. Even in the dim light Sol could see the bruises on her thighs and arms. He could also see the goose bumps.

He stood up slowly so as not to startle her. Taking the blanket from his bed he handed it to her.

"Here, it's cold down here. You're not exactly bundled up."

She took the blanket without lifting her head and quickly wrapped it around her, covering the sheer outfit she had been provided.

Sitting on the edge of the bed, Sol spoke gently, "I'm not going to hurt you." He wasn't sure she could even understand him. "I won't even touch you without permission. My name is Sol. What's yours?"

"You won't touch me?" She was trembling, "You'll keep away?" It was obvious she didn't believe him.

"Yes, I'll give you plenty of space", he replied as he moved to the far end of the bed. "Please, sit down."

She stayed put but looked up slightly. Sol still couldn't see her face.

"They say you're an animal. They say you've bedded more women than any man here. They say you've bedded a Spoil for every man you've killed. They say that's a lot."

He liked the way she spoke; soft, but with a certain melodic force.

"They say all that, do they?" he mused with a grin. "And if it's true would you hold it against me? Would you deprive me of the only nonviolent personal contact a fighter can hope to receive? Does bedding a woman each time I survive stepping out into the arena make me an animal?" It was a harsh question but he kept his voice soft and even.

She raised her head a tiny bit more. "Raping even one woman makes you an animal."

Sol could hear from the pain in her voice that she knew this from personal experience. No one made it all the way to his cell undamaged. Somewhere along the way they were always used, sometimes violently, sometimes often.

"I agree", this time his voice had a slight edge, "but I've never raped anyone."

Her laugh was cold and sarcastic. "So you're telling me you bedded all those women with only charm and good looks?"

"I'll take that as a complement," He paused and then said, "but I never said I bedded all those women."

She hesitated. "What do you mean?"

"Oh, after every fight I accept a woman into my cell, that's true enough. But rarely have I accepted one into my bed, and never unwillingly. Will you sit down now?"

She took a small step forward with her head bowed and her arms crossed, then she stopped.

"Then what *do* you do with these women?"

"If I don't move, and you sit down and tell me your name, I'll show you."

She hesitated again but then moved to the foot of the bed and sat stiffly. Finally, she lifted her head and looked him in the eye. "Korra. My name is Korra."

Sol's breath caught in his throat. She was beautiful, no doubt. She had high cheekbones and nicely tanned skin but that was not what gave him pause. Her eyes; he had never seen eyes like that. They were hard, fierce, ice-blue eyes that seemed to look into him rather than at him.

He blinked. "I'm Sol."

"You already said that," she replied. "You also said you would show me something if I sat down."

He smiled. "To the point, aren't you? Well, there's really nothing to show. I just wanted to talk."

"What do you mean?" Korra scoffed as she asked again. "You just want to talk? Like, nice weather we're having?"

"That's as good a place to start as any", Sol replied with a smile. "Was it nice today? I was a little busy in the Coliseum, but now that you mention it the ground wasn't muddy so it must not have rained this morning. Not that we get much rain around here, anyway. It's always hot and dry. Can I ask you a question?" he asked abruptly.

"Yeah", she said with hesitation.

"Does snow hurt?"

"What?"

"Some of the others have talked about frozen rain coming down as snow. I've thought about it and it seems that balls of ice falling from the sky would hurt like hell."

She didn't reply but just glared at him instead.

Sol flushed a little with embarrassment. "I've seen ice, you know. When I was a kid working in the luxury boxes they used to ship big blocks of it down from the mountains south of the city. We'd put it into drinks and the cooks would make slushies for the ladies."

He stopped but she still didn't reply.

"So it probably hurts when it snows, right?"

Finally she answered, "Is this some kind of a joke? You bring half-naked women into your cell and then play stupid? To what, mess with their minds?"

Sol looked away but he couldn't keep the bitterness out of his voice, "I've never been outside of the Coliseum. I've never seen snow. I've never seen a lake or an ocean. I've never seen a starry night or a sunrise. Other than the beasts that try to eat me I've never seen a wild animal, unless you count the rats that share my home. All I know of the outside world I'm told by half-naked women brought to my cell against their will. Now, we can either sit and talk or sit in silence. Or maybe", Sol scowled, "maybe you'd prefer I live up to your expectations and force myself on you."

"You've really never been outside?"

Sol shook his head.

She looked into his eyes for a moment and then seemed to decide something as her expression softened. "Frozen rain is called hail and it does hurt. Snow is more like little pieces of frost that fall when it's really cold out. I've lived placed where it piles up so high you have to dig trenches in it to get from building to building."

The conversation progressed from there. Sometimes it flowed and they sounded more like old friends meeting over coffee than two slaves locked in a cell. The conversation was light; they each smiled and even laughed on occasion. Other times it halted completely and they would sit in cold silence until a new subject was breached. They spoke of many things, everything from Sol's years in the dungeons to Korra's attempts to describe certain wild animals, several of which Sol was sure she was making up at his expense.

Well into the night the subject came back to who Korra had been before her capture. Usually this was brought up much earlier but while Sol had repeatedly tried to steer the conversation that direction, she always took it someplace else. Even now that the topic had again been brought up she hesitated. "Talking about far off cities and the creatures I grew up around is one thing," she said. "Discussing my past is, well, a bit more complicated."

Sol had been expecting this line of reasoning as it often came up. He had learned that the best thing was to be blunt. "You're worried about your family. I understand." He kept his voice and expression soft. "The thing is that if you're here, they've almost certainly been taken. When the Empire takes a city or a province it's over quickly. They kill who they don't want, take who they do, and put everyone else to work. Just hope that your people have skills enough that manual labor isn't their lot. Besides," he counted the reasons on his fingers, "I've got no one to tell, I wouldn't anyway, and every bout there's a pretty good chance I won't live to see the next."

He sat silently, letting his words sink in. She bowed her head for a moment and then much to his surprise, looked up and regarded him an expression of frustrated pity.

"And you accept that?" she said.

The question caught him by surprise. Frowning, it was his turn to ask, "What do you mean?"

She gave a quick sigh. "You accept that this is it? That this is your life? That you'll never be anything else? You'll fight and kill until someone faster and stronger comes along and kills you. Have you given up all hope of escape? All hope of freedom?"

All Sol could manage was a blank, confused stare. The frustration faded from her face but the pity remained. "It isn't that you've given up on freedom, is it? You haven't lost hope. You never had any to start with."

Sol didn't care for the tone in her voice. He was used to fear and respect – but pity? "Don't act like you feel sorry for me. Who are you? You're someone's prize. My prize, in fact. And until you grow old and your looks fail you, if you aren't beaten to death before then, that's what you'll be." He was a bit shocked at the coldness that had found its way into his voice but he continued, "Hope is for the recently captured. But let me assure you, it dies quickly. Soon you'll realize that there is no hope because *no one's fighting back*. Oh, every land that falls to the Empire puts up a fight, but in the end, the more they resist the more of their own people they sentence to death."

He was starting to get angry. He was tired and he didn't feel like justifying himself. The fact that a small smile had creased her lips didn't help the matter.

"Now you're smiling? You find this amusing? Or perhaps you just think that you're different and that you'll never lose hope." His face became hard, his voice forbidding. "Well I hate to break it to you but you will. Some morning after some fighter has had his way with you, you'll hear some guard talking about some slave province, your province, and any hope you had left will drain from you."

He knew his words were harsh but he felt the need to shock this woman into seeing the reality of the situation. In the long run it would be for her own good. Much to his surprise, she didn't seem fazed in the least. Still cuddled up in the blanket with her back to the wall she replied, "And that's where you get your information from, isn't it? Boastful guards and traumatized women? I realize you've got nowhere else to get your news but did it ever occur to you that maybe you weren't getting the full story?"

Sol had been ready with a scathing rebuttal to what he had imagined her reply to be but yet again her answer stumped him. "No," he answered, shocked into blunt honesty, "but why would the women, or even the guards for that matter, make the effort to lie to a fighter like me? I don't matter."

"It's not that they lied so much as they repeated the falsities told to them. Information is power. The Astrolians censor and filter information very carefully, coercing some, killing others, so that no one that would dare disagree with them has a voice to do so. Did you know that the first people they kill when they invade a place, after those in power of course, are the teachers and priests? Tribal elders, storytellers, bards, anyone whose life is dedicated to the sharing of knowledge is systematically butchered, all in the name of controlling what information reaches the ears of the people."

"Why?" It was the only thing Sol could think to ask.

"Think about it. What's easier, quelling an uprising of rebellious slaves or making sure that the only information to reach those same slaves convinces them that a rebellion would be futile to begin with?" She became more animated as she spoke. "Subjugate the people through misinformation. Dash their hopes of freedom by allowing no news of hope to reach their ears or," she paused, "*their eyes*. Didn't you ever wonder why no slave is allowed to read? There is no better way to spread information than through the written word *and* if everyone can read and write it's impossible for the Empire to control the spread of information. Believe me," she said with pride, "there's a lot more going on out there than you are in a position to hear about."

His anger abating, Sol's curiosity was now getting the better of him. "But you are? In a position to know more, I mean."

"Well," she said with a sad little smile, "I was, anyway. Perhaps I should start at the beginning."

Korra's forehead creased in thought. Then she sat up straight and clasped her hands in her lap. "Okay," she nodded "tell me about the Astrolian Empire."

Sol frowned. "I thought you were going to tell me about the Empire."

Korra nodded again. "And I will, but it's late and I want to see what you think you know. This is educational for me, too. I get to see what news reaches the heart of the Empire."

Still a little puzzled, Sol took a moment to collect his thoughts. He was beginning to feel more like the slow pupil with the tutor than he cared to. When he spoke, he chose his words carefully, "Now, if you keep in mind that you've already discredited my only sources of information, I'll tell you what I've been told. The Astrolian Empire, as I know it, is old, vast, and very powerful. Through conquest the Empire is constantly expanding in every direction, welcoming those lands that accept their fate and crushing those that don't. When a state or tribe resists, the struggle is short and the retribution swift. While the lands that voluntarily join have a relatively painless assimilation, those that resist are dismantled, their people butchered, and the survivors scattered as slaves.

"As we discussed before, I've had many women into my cell, so while I know very little about the Empire overall, I know a good deal about the carnage inflicted upon the conquered lands. Every woman that comes to me has a story and despite the differences between who those women were and where they came from, the stories of how they came to me are always the same. I've never known freedom. I've been the property of the Empire my whole life. Listening to those women's stories of death and suffering upon their introduction to slavery, I sometimes wonder if I'm not the lucky one."

Korra closed her eyes and bowed her head, resting her face in her hands. For a long moment the cell was silent, then she raised her head and spoke, "A lot of what you've said is true, or at least partially true. But like all the best propaganda, it's been twisted and laced with lies. There is one thing I need you to know before I go on. I'm about to dump a ton of information in your lap, but there are things I'm going to have to leave out and there may be some questions I just can't answer."

Sol began to protest, "I've already said I've got nobody to tell and..."

She cut him off, "I know what you said but my situation is far more complicated than you realize. The soldiers that captured me and the guards here, they haven't figured out who I am. They think I'm just another slave and if they find out I'm not, it'll mean more than just the end of my life. I'm sorry but I just can't risk it. Either you accept that I can't tell you everything or I tell you nothing."

Sol, now even more curious, had little choice but to nod reluctantly.

Korra continued, "The one thing you said that was completely accurate concerned the ordeals those women went through before coming to you. The Empire is ruthless when it moves into a new land. People are resources to be used or discarded as they see fit. I have no doubt that because of the number of testimonies you've heard over the years, you probably know this better than almost anyone that hasn't actually been through it, so I won't speak any more of that. The twist on this particular part of the story is that whether a state surrenders willingly or is taken by force, the resulting atrocities are the same. There is no such thing as painless assimilation."

Sol stopped her. "That doesn't make sense. If a country was violently dismantled and their people butchered whether they surrendered or not, no one would surrender. They would all fight to the last man, using up their resources and destroying the land the Empire wanted in the first place. It wouldn't benefit the Empire in any way to fight those who have already surrendered."

Korra blinked. "I think I've underestimated your grasp on things, but you're right and I couldn't have said it better. It wouldn't make any sense to march an army into a state that's already surrendered. As you said, in the long run it would be self-defeating. Instead, when a land surrenders the Empire welcomes it with open arms. Treaties are signed, there are parades and grand speeches using words like 'partnership' and 'trust', and for a while everything is just as good as it was before, maybe better. Then, after a time, things begin to change. The differences are subtle at first. Maybe money finds its way into local official's pockets and a few Empire-friendly pieces of legislation pass. Maybe there's a tax hike or tariff put on local goods. In time the taxes, tariffs, and embargos slowly crush the local economy. There are protests. The protesters are arrested. There are executions. This leads to riots. Martial Law is imposed. Soon there are soldiers in every town, in every home. During this whole process the public is manipulated into believing that the Empire is acting for the good of the people. The taxes are for public works projects, the arrests to quell a small number of dissidents, the soldiers are there for protection. And then of course it's too late, the Empire can take whatever and whoever they want and the people can do nothing because there are soldiers everywhere."

"I know firsthand, if you look at a province who accepts the Empire after ten years, you can't tell it apart from one taken by force after the same amount of time. And of course the expansion of the Empire moves faster than the decay. The Empire moves on to the neighboring province after a year or two while the first province still appears relatively prosperous. The next province sees the destruction of the state that resisted on the one side and the mirage of prosperity in the state who surrendered on the other. Which do you think they will choose?"

She finished with a mischievous smile, "Which is where we come in."

"We?" Sol asked.

Korra nodded. "Earlier you said that there's no hope because no one's fighting back. You're wrong. There *is* hope and people *are* fighting back"

She began to speak again when Sol held up his hand to interrupt her, "I hear footsteps, someone's coming."

Korra bowed her head. "Well, I guess our time's up. Will I be able to see you again?"

Sol nodded. It wouldn't be the first time he had invited the same spoil back into his cell. "I can request you, it is my right, and I'll try to put in a good word for you with the guards. You won't be spared your visits to other fighters but they might be able to help you avoid sadists and maybe even give you a night off."

She nodded and held out her hand. "You've been nothing but a gentleman and I thank you." Then she smiled. "I'll put in a good word with the guards for you, too. After all, you've got a reputation to maintain."

6.

A copper piece clinked down into Telain's tarnished tin cup and the slumped-over pile of rags that was the beggar mumbled a gruff 'Thank you'. He raised his head slightly and watched the fat trader waddle away, a large full purse swinging heavily from his belt. It wasn't the fact that the trader could afford more charity than he offered that chided Telain. It was that this particular act of generosity had not been for his, the recipient's, benefit. He had seen the group of women the trader had pretended not to notice; the same group of women that now bustled around the trader, praising his generosity. The man had just bought social standing for less than a loaf of bread.

Telain brushed off the distraction and turned back to the task at hand. He focused his well-trained ears on the talk of the people that passed around him. It still amazed him how little attention people paid to the destitute. Men and women stopped to whisper within arm's reach of the beggar, their conversations hushed, lest their fellow pedestrians eavesdrop. He was a man in plain sight, yet invisible. Over the years this social invisibility had served him well just as he, in turn, served his master. He had been the one that had made contact with General

Shadon, looking to take advantage of a few choice pieces of information he had gleaned off the streets. Shadon had seen potential in the situation and taken it a step further, making him a full time spy, even charging him with the recruitment of other beggars for the same task. He now made weekly reports comprised of what the General dubbed "grumblings", mainly the Empire-related complaints of the populace. The grumblings were usually petty and random: an overtaxed merchant, a cheated trader. Most people were far too scared of retribution to make any complaints outside of their homes. He dutifully recorded it all for Shadon to decide what grumblings and which grumblers required further attention. As a result of the occasional *further attention*, most were smart enough to keep any grievances with the Empire to themselves.

A few days ago, something changed. He had been playing his part in the market district on the far side of Astrolia when he noticed a gradual increase in grumblings. More than that, the grumblings had become more focused. Instead of scattered economic or political complaints, the sentiment was one of defiance with a subtle undertone of rebellion. The whole scene had a different feel and smell to it than usual and tying the thread of all these conversations together was a single man.

He closed his eyes and concentrated. It wasn't long before he heard what he was listening for, bits of hushed talk: *only a slave, defiant, survival*. The talk was more concentrated here, he was getting closer. Like a salmon to its spawning grounds he had navigated the meandering tributaries of talk through the city in search of its source. He moved quickly out of necessity, lest the concentrations of discontent diffuse and make tracking even more difficult.

He picked up his cup and moved against the flow of the crowd from which the grumblings came. He stayed in the shadows and out of sight as much as possible. Panhandling was against the law in all of Astrolia but it was rarely enforced in the outskirts of town. Now as he moved into the heart of the city, it was in his best interest to stay unnoticed. The official papers he carried would ensure his timely release should he be picked up by the authorities but such encounters were an inconvenience he tried hard to avoid. He became sure of his destination well before he reached it. The talk flowing from the Coliseum was thick with grumblings no longer whispered but spoken freely; he had never seen anything like it.

His efforts eventually lead him to a large crowd at the main gate of the Coliseum. There, perched on an overturned wooden crate, was the source of the grumblings: a single bard. One of the many that had been hired to promote the gladiatorial bouts, this one was young and good looking. Telain settled himself inconspicuously in a shaded corner and examined the orator. The young man was tall and thin, with a strong chin and a contagious smile. He moved with fluid energy and spoke with conviction. He addressed the crowd not as someone telling a story but as someone living one. The crowd listened in rapt attention as the entertainer turned the wooden crate into a stage.

"I speak to you on this day of a mere slave," the bard said. "A slave the same as the poor soul that shovels in the stables. No different than the wretch that toils in the field. A slave! Less than any free man. Less than you, less than me. I speak to you my friends of a slave, but not just a slave, a fighter. A gladiator! Born a servant of the Empire, nay, of the Coliseum itself. A man that has never known a day of freedom, has never set foot out of the walls before which you stand. And yet a man who, at times, knows freedom the likes of which few of us will ever glimpse: the freedom of equality. For what is the Coliseum if not the great equalizer? Be you a noble in a box or a peasant on a bench, the draw of the Coliseum knows no class. It is the same! Combat! Again I ask, what is the Coliseum if not equality? What is a title on the Coliseum floor? Can you wield the word 'Duke' at a foe? Can you shield your flesh with a bloodline? No. On the Coliseum floor a slave is equal to an emperor! And on the Coliseum floor no man is equal to Sol. Begot in these walls, raised in their depths, Sol, Son of the Coliseum! A slave of the Empire. A slave that has not merely survived in the Empire's meat grinder, but thrives in it. For just as the Coliseum is equality it is most surely oppression. A place men go, nay, are sent to die. Sent from throughout the Empire to perish for your viewing pleasure. And why not? It is their place to die as surely as it is your place to cheer. For once the Empire declares it a man's fate to enter these walls, so too is it his fate to die. Yet some persist. Some defy their fate and live day to day, month to month, year to year. Their very survival is an act of defiance! Defiance against the Coliseum itself, against its purpose. And no man has survived longer than Sol."

Telain watched the ebb and flow of the crowd. As the speech continued individuals and small groups joined the crowd and left. Due to the constant addition and subtraction of the listeners, the crowd never really grew or shrank, it just changed consistency. At times it was a fluid flowing mass whose members wouldn't actually stop, but just slow down for a time. Other times the crowd congealed as listeners halted to take in the oration.

It continued for hours and as the day waned, so too did the crowds. Telain remained still and watched the young bard struggle to right his overturned wooden crate of a stage and drag it back to the fruit vendor from whom he had borrowed it. The remains of the crowd gave him a wide berth knowing, as Telain did, that the bard was a marked man. In these days, backroom whispers often wound up drawing the attention of the Empire. The young bard's bold sermon was apt to bring down a firestorm that would surely engulf the man and anyone close to him, so the dispersing onlookers understandably kept their distance.

Since settling to observe the oration, Telain had been musing over what the bard's motives might be, unable to account for the apparent naivety of the speaker. His smile was easy and his step was quick; the gravity of the situation seemed to weigh little on the boy's shoulders. Telain couldn't say the same. He felt the burden that the bard's actions now forced upon him and as he gathered himself to follow the boy he felt something else: anger.

Had the bard applied himself in the right circles he might have made something of himself; he certainly had talent. Now he had thrown that away and for what? Noble words? What could he possibly expect to come from today's performance? Did he expect a single voice to make a difference? He had to know that the Empire would get wind of the dissidence radiating from the heart of its own capital. The bard's punishment would only reinforce what happened to those who speak out. Whatever the boy's cause, he would only hurt it in the end.

And Telain knew he had to report the situation. It was his job and if he didn't get the report to Shadon, someone else would. Then there would be questions and possibly repercussions. There might still be, anyway. It was probable that given the brazenness of the breach there would be expectations that he resolve things himself. He knew others in his lot that would love the chance to distinguish themselves with quick decisive action. However, he was a spy, not an assassin.

Telain again weaved his way in and out of shadows as he followed the young man, being careful to remain far enough back to avoid detection. He needn't have bothered; his quarry was oblivious to the tail. He followed the bard away from the Coliseum past the villas and mansions of Astrolia's elite. Telain likened the city's class topography to that of a mountain's. The tallest buildings resided at the center of the city: theaters, courts, and the great Coliseum. The wealthy were drawn to these and their large residences clustered around the city center. The status and wealth of the inhabitants decreased with the distance from the heart of the city, as did the size of the buildings. He continued to follow the boy downhill until he turned into a neighborhood of modest dwellings.

Telain noted the house the bard entered and then quickly moved on. He decided he didn't want to know any more about the bard or his family. Whatever the youth's motives were they mattered little now. He had done his job and that was enough. Anything else would just make things more difficult.

Besides, his type weren't usually weren't encouraged to linger in neighborhoods.

Lysik worked his way up the long stone stairway to the top of the tower and Shadon's office, cursing the General for his burning thighs as he climbed. The man could choose any office in the Empire but he picked the top of the highest tower in Fort City. And because Lysik relied on Shadon for employment he had to stay close, whittling away his time in this dreadfully boring place waiting for orders. He hoped that this summons would result in work somewhere with a bit more color.

He heard quick footsteps descending the stairs above and saw the same runner that had been sent for him this morning rounding the corner. Stopping dead in his tracks, the already pale youth whitened further at the sight of the assassin. Lysik continued up the stairs until he was even with the boy. "Good morning, son."

The boy's eyes widened at the casual address. "Good morning, Sir." He flinched as Lysik placed a hand on his forehead.

"My dear boy, you don't look well. Are you ill?" Lysik asked with mock sympathy. The boy recoiled from his hand. "Maybe that's why you scurried off so quickly this morning at the inn." He smiled wickedly. "You should have stuck around. We would have loved the company." The boy flushed and stammered something inaudible as he squeezed by, scurrying down the stairs without looking back.

Lysik continued his ascent and then paused to knock respectfully before entering Shadon's office. The General was sitting at his large desk and he motioned for Lysik to take a seat in a chair along the wall. The chair, Lysik realized, was one that usually sat in front of the desk. In its place there was a young man, a captain by his uniform, standing stiff and uncomfortable with dark circles lining his bloodshot eyes. Shadon continued to shuffle through papers, making both men wait.

Lysik didn't mind the delay; it was all part of the drill with Shadon. Being made to wait quietly was a show of power and he respected that. To pass the time he looked around the office. The furnishings were of high quality but not ostentatious. The rugs were thick and soft but simple in pattern and design. The desk was large and made from the finest hardwoods, but not ornately carved. The chair Shadon sat in was high-backed dark leather but obviously well used. Matching bookshelves neatly lining the walls were filled not with trinkets or trophies but with books and scrolls. The walls were draped with thick tapestries to keep in the heat from the large stone fireplace but otherwise devoid of art. A new visitor might think that the portraits behind Shadon's desk were ornamental but the assassin knew better. They were sketches of high ranking members of the resistance and some of the most wanted individuals in the Empire. Several new additions had been included since he last visited Shadon's office, one especially catching his eye. The drawing was that of a woman, young and beautiful with curly hair and bright eyes.

The young Captain shifted on his feet and grimaced. Still Shadon concentrated on his papers. Lysik smiled to himself and continued his inspection of the room, noticing the highly polished suit of armor that stood to one side of the fireplace. Complete with a short sword, it had in fact been Shadon's own armor. The only object that passed for ornament in the whole office was a small bronze statue displayed prominently on the corner of the desk. The figure was that of a gladiator with a sword raised in victory and spiked helmed head held high.

The utilitarian atmosphere of the office mirrored that of Fort City itself. It was an old city built within thick stone walls dotted with tall towers and a single fortified entrance. Life here revolved around the Army and its soldiers. Farmers grew crops to feed them, tradesmen made wares to sell them; it was an industrious place. It was, in fact, the historical nexus of the Empire, although now the city was in its southeastern corner. Conquest after conquest had originated here, expanding the Empire to the North and west. It sat at the natural corner of the continent where the cold, deserted badlands to the South met the towering Stony Mountains to the East. Although the capital city of

Astrolia sat leagues to the northwest, the great Fort City was still, in many ways, the center of the Empire.

The contrast between Fort City and Astrolia was stark. Where Fort City was utilitarian and functional, Astrolia was a place of pomp and show. Despite the hordes of people housed both within and outside of its walls, above all Fort City was just that, a fort. Fortified with massive walls surrounding fields and pastures, shops and churches, armories and smiths, Fort City was a self-contained entity that could survive siege for months, if not years.

Astrolia, on the other hand, produced nothing and consumed everything. While it was true that a soul could find and buy any trinket, delicacy, device, or diversion there, every wonder the massive city boasted had to be shipped in from near or far. Without constantly clear shipping lanes, the city would wither and die. Centered in the heart of the ever-growing Astrolian Empire, the wealthy inhabitants saw no need for concern. Further, aside from the palace guard, the Capital housed only a single regiment of specially-assigned city soldiers, a unit separate and distinct from the general army. The Emperor insisted that barracks were an eyesore and that too many soldiers would imply some nonexistent weakness. As always with Emperor Dionus, it was all about appearances.

Lysik was distracted from his musings by Shadon's sudden address of the young Captain. "Perhaps I'm getting soft in my old age," the pause that followed left little doubt he thought no such thing, "but I am willing to give you one more chance to instill a sense of discipline in your men, Captain." Shadon spoke calmly but with an unmistakable edge to his voice. "Should you fail, the least you will lose is your command. You are dismissed."

The tired Captain gave a quick, "Thank you, Sir," and salute, then he turned and left.

Shadon stood and walked to the window. Lysik saw him frown as he watched the Captain stumble slowly to the barracks. "The boy's exhausted."

"Sympathy? Shadon, you *are* getting soft," Lysik teased.

Shadon shot him a sharp look. "Sympathy has nothing to do with it. Exhaustion is intolerable." He continued to himself, "I'll need to schedule more night drills to condition the men."

"What did he do? The Captain, that is?"

"He didn't *do* anything. A fight broke out in the barracks amongst his men yesterday."

"Boys being boys, nothing more," Lysik replied.

Shadon raised an eyebrow. "Most of my predecessors would have agreed with you. I. however, see things differently. The Army is mine and I control what's mine. The incident between the two new recruits may have been nothing or it could be a symptom of discontent within the ranks. Even worse, and what I suspect, is that it's a sign the Captain had lost the respect of his men. This is unacceptable." The General returned to his desk, inviting Lysik to return the chair to its usual station with a gesture. "The two men have been flogged, at what they thought was their Captain's orders, while the rest of the unit watched. Then the Captain joined me here for a night of discussion."

Lysik shrugged. "The Shadon of old would have whipped him alongside his men and then had him demoted."

"Perhaps. But now instead of a desolate broken man I have a very grateful, very motivated captain. My leniency is not motivated by compassion but by reason."

Lysik nodded his assent.

Shadon frowned. "The runner I sent for you this morning, however, will need to be dealt with."

"Whatever do you mean?"

Shadon raised an eyebrow. "When reporting to me his success in tracking you down, the boy seemed most agitated." Shadon sat back in his large leather chair and regarded Lysik critically as he spoke. "He took it upon himself to inform me that you were entertaining a guest at the Kay Club." He paused long enough to allow Lysik to pick up the thread of conversation and explain himself. Lysik sat silently, a slight smile on his lips.

"He stammered on for some time about the state of the room." Again the General paused. "The state of your person upon answering the door."

Still Lysik sat silently.

He jumped as Shadon pounded the desk in front of him. "Damn it, man! Do you have any idea what a bother it is to clean up after you? The least you could do is refrain from parading around the Kay Club covered in blood!"

"I wasn't parading–" Lysik started but Shadon cut him off.

"Who was she?"

"Who was who?" Lysik replied with another smile, and then quickly answered after seeing the look of warning in Shadon's eyes. "Some whore. Nobody of consequence."

"No? And what about her people? With the number of whores and bar maids that have gone missing since you've taken up residence, someone could raise an army of angry family members."

Lysik brushed the concern aside with a flick of his wrist. "I'm just staying sharp. Interrogation is an art, you know. Besides, that's one less bottom feeder distracting your men and spreading disease. I'm doing you a favor."

Shadon sighed. "I suppose that's one way to look at it," he conceded. "I sometimes wonder whether you're worth the hassle."

Lysik sat up straight, finally serious. "Have I ever failed you? Have you ever given me something I couldn't handle?"

There was a tense pause before Shadon answered. "No, not once." He seemed to relax slightly, then leaned back again into his chair. "Which is why you're here. I have need of your…talents." He picked up one page of many from his desk. Lysik held out a hand but then let it fall when Shadon made no move to give him the paper. "Every week I receive hundreds of reports from all over the Empire. I trudge through economic ramblings from my men in the treasury, conflicting rumors from my men in society, and conspiracy stories from my men on the streets." He wore a pained expression. "In short, I struggled through rubbish composed by those who, though they may be competent spies, can't write worth a damn." He turned his chair back toward the window, his expression almost wistful. "But one day a week I get a brief reprieve, a report straight from the Capital by special runner from my man Vance."

Lysik perked up at mention of the Capital. He didn't know the man but that wasn't a surprise, considering Shadon's vast network of spies.

Shadon continued. "I discovered Vance while he was embedded in an infantry unit in the North. Even his accounts of the mundane seemed vibrant and engaging. I commandeered him immediately and employed him in a station more deserving of his talents." He turned his chair back to face Lysik, "Do you follow the bouts?"

"Bouts?"

"The gladiatorial bouts of the great Coliseum of Astrolia! I would have wagered you a fan, given your...*tastes*. They're my one leisure. I'm far too busy to attend but once a week I sit down with Vance's report to catch up on the bouts."

Lysik suppressed a grin. He had never heard the General so animated. The effect was odd to say the least.

"Do you know that at first I didn't believe him?" Shadon asked, not waiting for an answer. "How could I? The reports were so grand. One fighter in particular, the battles seemed impossibly exaggerated." His eyes settled on the statue on his desk. "It vexed me greatly," he said quietly, suddenly somber. "By Vance's descriptions my brightest captains would be hard pressed to match his feats, and he is a mere slave. Eventually, I took an unannounced trip to the Capital for the sole purpose of verifying the reports. What I saw astounded me."

Shadon stood and began to pace behind his desk. Lysik got the feeling Shadon felt the need to explain himself for some reason. Since he had never known Shadon to make a mistake, the chance of a confession intrigued him.

"I seriously considered pulling the slave from the Coliseum and finding him an appropriate post in the army, perhaps as a trainer or even a captain. In the end, I decided against it for the same reason I kept you out on your own."

Lysik was surprised to hear himself included in Shadon's reasoning. He had never considered that the man might direct any thought his way, outside of the occasional mission.

Shadon continued, "The army has a way of smothering talent. Organizing a massive fighting force requires conformity. New recruits are mashed and beaten into a preformed mold. The result is a reliable soldier who does what he's told without question or initiative of his own. The army is a homogenous and uniform mass that smothers opposition with numbers, not ability. Real talent gets lost in the mix."

"Shadon," Lysik interrupted with a grin, "I'm flattered."

Shadon raised an eyebrow, "You should be. I have the resources of the entire Empire at my disposal. Do you really think I engage your services simply because you make yourself convenient?" He paused as if he expected an answer. When none came he continued, his voice sharp. "No, your messes wouldn't be worth cleaning up without substantial return, a fact that I expect you to keep in mind."

"As I was saying, I decided to keep the slave in the Coliseum, for my own entertainment if nothing else. Now I am forced to question that decision."

Lysik leaned forward, genuinely interested. "What could a slave hundreds of miles away have done to move you to regret?"

Shadon snickered. "The slave? Nothing. He merely continues to exist. No, it's the bards that have caused the problem and one bard in particular." He picked up the page again and handed it to Lysik. "This is an account from one of my men in the Capital, Telain."

Lysik struggled over the report. He could read, but not well. Shadon waited impatiently for him to finish. Finally he looked up. "That's quite the speech. Who is he?"

Shadon shook his head. "That's why you're here. I don't know anything about him, if he speaks for a group, or what he hopes to accomplish. I need you to find out."

Lysik's brow furled. "Your spies are obviously all over him. Why do you need me?"

Shadon nodded. "True, he is being watched, but getting answers through observation alone will take time we don't have. This bard, foolish though he may be, has struck a chord with the people. He's dangerous. Telain's a good spy but he doesn't have the stomach for this kind of work. I need you to go to the Capital and get me answers. That's your first task."

"And the second?" Lysik prompted.

Shadon sighed. "The second means an end to the best part of my week. The simple fact is that too much damage has already been done. The people see this gladiator as something more, a symbol or some other nonsense. He needs to fail them."

"Can't you just have him killed in his cell?"

Shadon shook his head. "He's a borderline folk hero as it is. The last thing I need is to create a martyr. It needs to happen on the Coliseum floor."

"How?"

Shadon concentrated on the statue. "I'm going to leave that at your discretion. Whatever you decide, it needs to be public. The people need to see him fall."

Lysik frowned. "I'll get your information from the bard, and anything else you want for that matter, but I work in close quarters, you know that. Arranging some kind of grand public spectacle to topple a hero isn't really in my repertoire." He shrugged. "Perhaps that would be best left to someone else."

Shadon regarded him coldly for a long moment. "Perhaps you're right. There are dozens of would-be assassins chomping at the bit to enter my services, most with far less baggage than you and all with enough sense to know that when I lay out an assignment it's not their place to question my reasoning."

Lysik realized his mistake and fought to correct it. "And wise they would be to not forget their place, as it most certainly would be for me not to forget my own. I merely intended to point out an alternative. It was foolish of me not to realize that you have no doubt already considered it. I shall leave for the Capital at once to see to the bard and the gladiator." He breathed a sigh of relief when Shadon assented with a nod. "Is that all?" Lysik asked.

Shadon's expression sharpened again. "All? I warn you not to take these tasks lightly. I have a personal interest in this. You would do well to not fail me." He turned back to the statue, his voice low. "Now go."

Lysik stood and took his leave in silence.

7.

Sol looked up from his carving at the rattling of the cell door, a little surprised to see Grall let himself in.

"Aren't you a little early?" He had expected Grall to bring him his gear and lead him to the holding cell before this afternoon's fight, but that wouldn't be for hours. Plus, the guard carried no armor.

"Yeah, a bit. I just wanted to check in," Grall answered unconvincingly.

Sol could tell by the hesitation in his voice that there was likely more to it. He decided not to press though; the old guard would tell him in his own time.

"Whatcha workin' on?"

Sol tossed him the carving and watched as Grall looked it over. "It's supposed to be a Dybuk," he offered when it became apparent that no recognition was forthcoming.

"Of course," Grall bluffed. "Saw it right away."

Sol smiled knowingly and chuckled. "I bet. I can picture the beast in my mind but there seems to be some kind of blockage between my brain and the wood."

"Well, I wouldn't say that." Grall frowned thoughtfully, turning the carving over in his hands. "I think you're getting better. To be honest, it looks kinda like a squirrel."

"Really?" Sol asked with a raised brow. "Is a squirrel a lot like a Dybuk?"

"Oh, sure," Grall answered quickly before changing the subject. "Actually, I had a reason for coming down early." He chuckled. "That Spoil of yours, the small one with the curly hair, she's a handful."

"Korra?"

"That's her. I don't know who she thinks she is but you better watch out when she puts her mind to something. I haven't been tongue-lashed like that in a long time."

"Oh no." Sol hung his head. Didn't that woman know anything about self-preservation?

Grall nodded. "Yup. I had half a mind to throw her into the Pit and let her blow off some steam in there. Almost did, too. The thing is, she was so intense, like what she was asking was the only thing in the world that mattered." He shrugged. "What can I say? I gave in."

"So what was she asking for?"

Grall grinned. "That was the other thing. I thought since she was beggin' to have me take a message to you that she had really taken a liking to you."

"To me?"

Grall nodded. "But then when I finally agreed to take the message…" he trailed off.

"What? What does she want?"

The old guard looked at him like he wasn't sure he believed what he was saying. "She wants you to convince the Frorian to ask for her after today's bout."

Sol stared, incredulous. "But…K'nal…why?" he stammered.

Grall shrugged. "Beats me. Damndest thing I ever heard." He tossed the carving back to Sol. "But I do know that the look on your face was worth the trip." He belly laughed as he let himself out.

"Thanks for nothin'!" Sol yelled at the closing door.

He couldn't believe it. He had been left on a cliffhanger at the end of their first meeting and had waited patiently for days to continue their conversation. Now she wanted to spend the night with the Frorian instead of him. And worse yet, she expected him to play matchmaker. He had a good mind to ignore the message just to hear her explanation. What possible motive could she have to request K'nal? She couldn't be *interested* in him could she? He wasn't even human!

No. He wouldn't do it. A rain check was tricky business in the Coliseum. There was no guarantee that either of them would be alive to make their next appointment. She would just have to accept it.

He returned his attention to his carving, trying to push the matter out of his mind and imagine what a squirrel must look like.

"Are you gonna do it?" Grall asked as he dumped Sol's armor onto the bed. The guard had returned at his customary pre-bout hour, still chuckling about his earlier visit.

"Do what?" Sol asked.

"Set up the Frorian and the Spoil!" Grall answered impatiently.

Sol shook his head. "Nope."

Grall chuckled again but thankfully asked no further questions on the matter, electing instead to help Sol into his armor like usual. They walked to the holding cell in silence, Grall leaving with his customary good luck wish and pat on the shoulder. This time K'nal was already there, giving Sol his turn to squeeze uncomfortably onto the opposite bench.

Again the two fighters sat in tense silence. Sol wondered if all Frorians were this quiet. He pictured a group of the white giants sitting in an ice cave together without speech for days on end. Heck, for all he knew, K'nal might be considered chatty.

Finally, without much forethought, Sol spoke, mainly to break the silence. "Uh, this might sound a little weird," he started lamely, "but I have been asked to make a rather odd request."

K'nal nodded without a word.

"Well, there's this Spoil…you know Spoils, right?" Sol had no idea if the guards took spoils to the nonhuman fighters.

K'nal nodded again.

"Right, well for some reason one of them wants you to ask for her after this bout." He waited for some reaction from the Frorian. When none came he continued, "Her name is Korra."

Much to Sol's surprise, K'nal did not debate, he didn't laugh, and he didn't even request an explanation. He merely said, "Very well," in his deep, dignified sort of way and returned to silence. Sol could only join him and wait for their time on the floor.

When their time came, it wasn't the rare cloudy afternoon that had the two gladiators gazing skyward. Four wooden poles towering as tall the Coliseum had been erected in a straight row down the center of the fighting floor and draped with a massive net. Weighted against the wind by sandbags, the net extended all the way down to the stone wall separating the floor and the stands, effectively enclosing the floor in a net tent. Sol and K'nal jogged to the center of the arena, each armed with a long, barbed spear and a small, round hand shield, and turned circles as they scanned the enclosure for what they would face.

"See anything?" Sol called out.

"Nothing," K'nal answered.

They stopped between the center poles, listening for a sound that would signal the opening of a gate or door by which their foe would appear. Moments passed and still they waited. The whole Coliseum was oddly quiet, far quieter than it should have been. The hair on the back of Sol's neck began to stand on end. By now he would have expected the crowd to be voicing their displeasure at the sluggish pace of the action. Their silence troubled him. It was as if they knew something he didn't. A quick glance betrayed the worry on K'nal's usually stoic features and confirmed the Frorian felt it too.

A flicker of movement out of the corner of Sol's eye caught his attention. He squinted up at the top of the enclosure, trying to determine the source of the motion. "There!" cried K'nal, pointing to a different point high in the netting. Before Sol could look the movement had stopped.

"What did you see?"

"I do not know, but I suspect our opponent will come from above."

An excited murmur ran through the stands, hinting that K'nal was on the right track. They continued searching the nets until finally Sol spotted the source of the movement. One of the sandbags, placed there to keep the nets in place in the wind, stretched out a pair of wide, leathery wings.

"The sandbags aren't sandbags!" Sol warned his partner. "What are they?"

K'nal shrugged. Soon, more of the not-sandbags were flapping their wings. They were too high in the netting for the fighters to get a good look but their size was obvious. Sol guessed that if they stood on the ground, the tawny-colored creatures would be able to look K'nal in the eye. Suddenly one and then another of the beasts released their hold on the netting and began gliding in slow circles around the top of the enclosure, slaloming between the poles. The crowd was also stirring, ready for the entertainment to begin. As the creatures dove closer, Sol was able to see scaly skin and long beaks that sloped back into elegant crests extending from the back of their heads.

Sol hazarded a brief moment to marvel in the beauty of the sight. Though he had rarely seen them, birds were his favorite animals. He loved watching the graceful forms of vultures soaring in the hot air high above the Coliseum or pigeons working over the trash left in the stands. He realized that with their scaly skin instead of feathers and leathery membranes that stretched from their upper appendages to their sides rather than wings, what now circled overhead was more like a flying lizard than an actual bird. But nonetheless, the sense of freedom the creatures imparted and the elegant way they cut through the air left him breathless.

The moment of serenity was short-lived as the crowd finally got what it was waiting for. One after another, the flying lizards started to dive lower and lower toward the two fighters. As the distance narrowed, Sol could make out more details such as rows of needle-like teeth lining the beaks and strongly curved talons adorning the hind feet. Soon the fighters were being barraged with bursts of air from the powerful downbeat of leathery wings. Sol and K'nal closed ranks, crouching back-to-back, spears pointed skyward and shields raised defensively.

"How many?" Sol shouted over the increasing ruckus from the stands. Despite their bulk, the creatures swooped and soared with surprising speed. With their constant aerial acrobatics it was difficult to discern exactly how many of the beasts they faced.

"Eight. Perhaps more," K'nal answered.

"They couldn't have given one of us a crossbow," Sol complained. While the spears were useful for keeping the sharp teeth and claws at bay, he knew that mounting an offensive would prove difficult. They couldn't risk chucking a spear and being left defenseless, and with the numbers stacked against them if either one of them fell the other would no doubt be quickly overwhelmed. The fighters stayed on the defensive, adjusting shield and spear to counter each dive as it came. For the moment, the constantly shifting barbed points kept the creature's dives coming up short; the lizards kept pulling up just shy of the sharp tips. But with each adjustment, Sol could feel gaps open up in their defenses. There were simply too many angles for two fighters to defend.

The lizards started to increase the frequency with which they dove and began squawking loudly. The gladiators poked at a pair that came in almost simultaneously and were able to turn the force of the creatures away, only to have a trio follow with equal intensity. K'nal's spear dissuaded one and Sol repelled another, but the third slipped through with its feet balled into fists and aimed at Sol's head. The nimble fighter was just able to get his shield up, the blow sending him sprawling onto his back and numbing his shield hand. Dazed, Sol scrambled to his feet, trying desperately to renew his post at K'nal's back. He knew that if the first of the three had made contact, the other two would have had an open shot at the Frorian.

He returned to K'nal. The giant crouched lower, laying a heavy hand on Sol's shoulder to persuade him to do the same. At the same time the Frorian lowered the tip of his spear. Sol noticed and did likewise, suspecting what he had in mind. The lizards closed and the fighters held, luring the creatures in. Just as the lizards banked, inches above the lowered spear tips, both fighters lurched upward, driving the spears home. K'nal's aim was true. His spear tore through the creature's torso, but the beast's momentum toppled the Frorian.

Sol was a bit less fortunate; his spear sank deep into his target's muscular haunch. Much to his dismay the barbed head held fast and before he had time to react, he was dangling from the spear's handle while the lizard struggled to fly away. He cried out to K'nal but the Frorian had his own problems. The giant had successful wrenched his spear from one dead creature only to have two more come screaming in from above.

A squawk from Sol's immediate right demanded his attention and prevented him from seeing K'nal's fate. Kicking out wildly, he planted his heel squarely on the top of the head of a lizard that soared in from the side. He heard a loud snap and the creature's leathery wings folded across its back, sending it plunging to the ground with a broken neck. At the same instant, the force of the blow ripped the spear from the first creature's haunch, sending a spray of blood and Sol plummeting back to the Coliseum floor.

Sol landed hard, the impact knocking the air from his lungs. He struggled to his hands and knees, gasping for breath and searching desperately for his partner. The Frorian was close by. He had his spear sunk into one flapping and flailing beast while another lay dead at his feet. K'nal had paid for his progress, though. A deep cut stained a crimson diagonal streak across the snowy fur on his back.

A sudden gust from above was all the warning Sol had of another lizard descending upon him. With almost no time to react, all he could manage was to roll onto his back, the shaft of his spear extended in both hands defensively across his chest. The speed of the move saved him, as did the spear. Instead of raking across his back, the clawed talons gripped the spear's wooden shaft. Sol's muscles strained and the wooden handled bowed, threatening to snap and send the beast toppling onto him as he fought to keep the creature at arm's length. Then suddenly the weight was gone and instead of pushing, Sol was holding on as the winged lizard rose into the air, he and his spear in tow.

Perhaps this lizard was a stronger flyer than the one Sol had just fallen from, or perhaps it was that this beast was more comfortable carrying its human cargo, rather than having it dangle from a wound. Regardless, the beast rose with relative ease and Sol was soon dangling near the top of the towering net tent. Panic would have overtaken most fighters but Sol kept his head, searching for an opportunity in the insanity. He could see thousands of faces turned up to see the spectacle and far below, appearing only slightly less massive from the great height, K'nal wrestling one of the beasts with his bare hands, the two halves of his broken spear lying off to the side. The powerful Frorian was obviously struggling. Despite his own predicament, Sol felt for his partner. He should be fighting at his side.

Anger overcoming fear, he kicked up at the lizard. "Stupid bird! Brought me up here, now what?"

As if to answer the lizard let go.

Sol fell, spear in hand; the grandstands were a slow motion blur. The rushing wind stung his eyes and forced tears to stream across his temples. For the first time in his appreciably perilous life, Sol knew he was going to die. He wondered if the crowd would cheer. He supposed he should be afraid but as the Coliseum floor rushed closer he felt strangely at peace, like he had always imagined flying would make him feel.

The serenity ended abruptly when Sol hit not the floor but the back of another diving lizard. Caught unaware, the helpless lizard's shoulder bones snapped loudly, broken from the impact of the mid-air collision. This time there was no sensation of slow motion as the pair plummeted in a tangled mess. Sol scrambled, trying desperately to put the beast between him and the ground. The impact was sudden and violent and the lizard crumpled into a motionless heap, sending Sol sprawling off to the side.

He lay face down near the wall, conscious but dazed. Blood ran freely from his nose and every breath brought a sharp pain to his left side. He couldn't tell the extent of his injuries but he knew he couldn't stay prone on the sand. Surprised to find himself still clutching his spear, he used it as a brace to struggle to his feet. The effort sent his head spinning. He tried to orient himself, expecting a new attack at any moment. Five of the creatures lay dead in the sand: three of K'nal's and two of his own. Another one of his huddled off to the side, bleeding badly from its wounded haunch. A quick survey revealed three more lizards, one of which was circling near the top of the tent.

The other two were on the ground in the far corner, their backsides to Sol. He was amazed to see that they used their finger-tipped second wing joint to walk on all fours. Surprisingly mobile, they were attempting to corner the unarmed Frorian using their long, needle-lined beaks to cut off any escape routes. The Frorian appeared to have been having an equally tough time of things. One of his massive arms hung limp by his side, its white fur blood soaked and dripping in the sand. Still he stood tall, snarling and swinging his good arm like a club whenever one of the lizards got too close. Sol couldn't understand the creatures' hesitation. Why didn't they simply rush K'nal and end it? On closer inspection, Sol noticed both lizards sported sizable gaps in their rows of teeth. Even two-to-one and unarmed, any foe facing K'nal had good reason to hesitate.

Despite his valiant efforts, the creatures were slowly driving K'nal back. It wouldn't be long before he would run out of space to retreat. Seeing the white giant stand defiantly against such odds, Sol knew he had to act. He broke into a jog, grimacing against the pain but pleased to find such movement possible after his fall. As he ran he hoisted the spear up into a throwing position. Instead of running directly toward the trio he angled to approach the skirmish from the side. Neither the creatures nor K'nal paid him any notice, their focus was trained on each other; K'nal had finally run out of room to retreat. With the giant's back set firmly against the Coliseum wall, the creatures pressed in with snapping beaks. Spectators leaned forward in their seats in anticipation of the kill.

And a kill they got.

Both of the lizards charged K'nal with maws agape. Determined not to go down without a fight, the Frorian desperately swung his fist at the nearest lizard. Just as he made contact, so did Sol's spear. The combined force smashed the lizard sideways into its companion, the spear head going clean through the first and into the second. Both animals writhed in agony but their thrashing only condemned them further. Connected by the spear protruding through both their bodies, a jerk by one tore the spear through the other's flesh and vice-versa.

Sol stopped to admire his handiwork as K'nal ducked away from the doomed creatures. "Better throw this time, huh?" he yelled with a smile.

If he had expected gratitude from the Frorian, he was disappointed. What he got instead when K'nal turned from the spectacle of the lizard kabob was the closest thing to fear he had ever seen his partner display. "Drop!" K'nal bellowed.

His trust in K'nal saved him. Without hesitation he hit the dirt, only to have his helmet knocked off by the outstretched talons of the forgotten last lizard as it zoomed past. He spit out a mouthful of sand and looked for K'nal. What he saw ranked as one of the most daring moves he had ever witnessed. As the lizard wheeled near K'nal to make another pass at Sol, the Frorian pounced. Grabbing the tip of the pivot wing in the vice-like grip of his good hand, he planted his feet and braced hard. The lizard's momentum spun the pair in a full circle, the pirouette threatening to topple K'nal. Only his considerable bulk managed to keep him grounded. Suddenly anchored, the lizard hurtled violently into the sand, its neck snapping on impact.

The crowd cheered.

Sol stood and picked up his helmet before walking over to K'nal. The giant had released the lizard but hadn't moved away from its still twitching form. He stood watching it, his face expressionless. Sol joined him and together they saw the broken creature take its last breaths. Even in death its long limbs and sinewy muscles spoke of unmatched grace. Never before had he seen something that looked so out of place in the Coliseum.

"I tire of killing beautiful things," K'nal said quietly.

Sol nodded, just able to hear him over the roar of the crowd. "Do you want me to pop that shoulder back in for you?"

"No. I will tend to it later."

With that the two fighters turned and walked silently off the Coliseum floor.

Sol turned the figure over and over, his fingers running over the whittled wood and trying to feel out his next cut. The figure taking shape under his knife had a feminine quality to it with long, flowing curves, but it wasn't necessarily that of a woman. He was trying a new approach. It seemed that when he worked against the wood, trying to bend it to his will, it never wanted to cooperate. This time he would try and let the wood speak for itself and see what came of it.

Last night's spoil seemed to think it was a good idea. Actually, she seemed quite taken with the notion, likening the wood into some grand philosophy on life. Sol attempted to explain that he wasn't a very good carver and that it was just wood, but the girl was persistent. She insisted that his new carving technique was all about taking what life gave you. In the end, he figured that she was probably just saying what she needed to hear and he humored her. After all, there was no harm in it and it seemed to please her.

Actually almost anything seemed to please her. Tall and blond with small hips and a generous bust, the Spoil named Aura seemed determined to make the best of the situation, a notion that struck Sol as nonsensical at best. Rather than quiet despair or screaming terror, Aura could probably be best described as bubbly. She smiled and chatted on and on about nothing at all, as if she needed to fill any silence with the sound of her sing-song voice. A casual observer might have thought she was actually enjoying her time in the Coliseum.

Sol however, was not a casual observer. He saw the way her smiling eyes darted nervously around the room. He noticed how any attempt at a meaningful question was deflected by the steady stream of pleasant chatter. Then there was the constant movement, always tapping her foot or twirling her long blonde hair around her fingers. After a few hours of this behavior with no sign of it waning he had resigned to his bed.

To his considerable surprise, Aura had other ideas. Not only did she join him in bed but she made it very clear that she intended to fulfill her duty as a Spoil. Out of respect for her fragile state of mind Sol tried to tactfully decline, but again she was persistent. After what he considered an appropriately respectful amount of time, he relented. She was, after all, quite attractive and she showed such enthusiasm – who was he to deny her? Afterwards, she stayed with him in bed and he learned that, ironically enough, she also talked in her sleep.

He had awoken this morning to find her standing at the bars of his cell door, chatting away to no one. She continued to talk even when Slink came for her, casting a lewd smile at Sol before guiding her away with more bodily contact than was necessary. He felt bad for her but he was also glad that the rest of his off-day would be considerably quieter.

As he carved he thought about Aura, and about how people handled, or didn't handle, captivity. It had always fascinated him. Since he had never known anything but captivity, in a way he had never known it at all. These walls were his home. But he knew that for everyone else the Coliseum was a prison. It was interesting to see in what manner people coped with entering his existence. In fact, he had made sort of an informal study of it.

After reviewing his experience, he had concluded that there were basically two broad groups of captives: copers and breakers. Aura was a breaker, an individual that just couldn't handle confinement and eventually drifted down the road of madness. Each person's path along the road was different. Most breakers went through stages of denial, anger, and depression. The character of emotion within these stages ranged from subdued to violent. Likewise, the nature of their eventual insanity varied greatly. Some breakers went stark raving mad, while others simply shut down. Suicide was frequent and even those that hung onto life seemed to do so with less vigor and conviction.

Copers, on the other hand, found some way to hang on. It wasn't necessarily that they stayed whole; far from it. This simple truth was evidenced by how many copers eventually transitioned into breakers. No, it was that copers found some thing, some routine or means of release, that let them cope with the monotony, loneliness, and despair of being a slave. Again, these mechanisms were sometimes anything but healthy. Some captives found their release in violence, a trend not uncommon in fighters. There was definite irony in the reality that without the release of violent combat, some fighters likely wouldn't be able to survive the Coliseum as long as they did.

As a fellow slave, it was the copers he tried to surround himself with. Oci was a good example. Sol was of the opinion that the borderline obsessive way in which she mothered every person she came across, whether they wanted it or not, was her way of maintaining her sense of self. He had little doubt that she was a nurturing person by nature and had most likely been a mother figure to most of the children in whatever little town she came from, but the extent to which she would do so within the Coliseum was something else entirely. Sol remembered one instance where Oci had talked a guard into letting her see to the wounds of an unruly fighter, only to have that fighter turn on her, beating her badly. The guard, who looked upon the large cook as a mother figure, would have killed the fighter if not for Oci's insistence that it was she who hadn't approached the situation properly. Not a day later Oci was back in that fighter's cell, bruises and all, trying to convince the brute to let her help. Eventually he had, and yet another surrogate child was added to Oci's always growing brood of misfits.

Sol cursed to himself as he cut a little too deeply with his carving knife, removing more wood than he had intended. Frustrated, he tossed the carving aside on the bed and rose to stretch his legs. Today was to be one of quiet rest. He didn't have another bout scheduled until tomorrow and he didn't perform his usual duties as a Coliseum slave during the month or longer tournaments. Grall would be off supervising repairs or personnel transfers and Slink, who had already made his morning appearance, probably wouldn't stop in again until it was time to deliver his evening meal. Today was his.

He realized he was pacing and stopped, noting how his lack of movement left the dimly-lit cell quiet as a tomb. Suddenly he felt very alone. He found himself hoping for Slink to come down and assign him to a work detail. Even Aura's inane babble might be welcome, if only to break the silence. Thinking of the Spoil gave Sol an idea.

He cleared his throat, feeling rather sheepish. "So, ah, guess I've got some time to kill." He realized he was whispering and tried speaking up. "That K'nal was really something yesterday. I bet the promoters are working double time trying to come up with a way to kill us off after that performance."

The harsh likelihood of the statement hung awkwardly in the quiet of the cell. "Nice," Sol muttered, deciding that he wasn't very good at conversing with himself. Aura's constant stream of words had made it seem easy. As he returned to the silence of his bed and his carving, he conceded that very ease was likely the problem.

8.

"Stop stalling," the assassin hissed.

Telain peeked around the corner of the building from the alley. "I'm not stalling. It's in our best interest not to draw attention." It was a lie; he was most certainly stalling. Every informant and spy in the city knew of Lysik's arrival. There was little chance the two soldiers getting their early morning coffee from the nearby stand would interfere with the dangerous assassin on a mission from Shadon himself. Telain was simply trying to buy more time.

He wondered why he even bothered. As much as he disliked Lysik and their current chore there was nothing he could do about it. The young bard had sealed his own fate. Telain was only doing his job by reporting his activities. He had known the Empire would act, most likely without mercy. It made perfect sense to make an example out of anyone so brazen. What kind of fool drew such attention to himself?

It was a question that had haunted Telain in the weeks since he first witnessed the bard enthusiastically entertaining crowds with tales of the slave-hero. At first it was just a nagging tug at the back of his mind, easily brushed aside. In time the nagging grew into a harassing need to know more about the young man he had marked for death. Day after day, almost at the neglect of his other duties, he found himself tucked into dark alleys near the Coliseum, listening to the young bard's oration. Day after day the crowds grew, drawn into stories and declarations delivered with unsurpassed passion and conviction.

Telain listened to every line, every detail, looking for clues. More than once he had followed the boy home in the hopes of uncovering some secret driving force behind the infectious hope with which he spoke. He had originally suspected the boy or perhaps his family was part of the People's Resistance, the growing insurgent organization always pestering the Empire. Or maybe some specific perceived slight by the Empire drove the bard toward revenge. After weeks without anything to back up these assumptions he had been forced to concede that the young bard might be exactly what he seemed: a single voice speaking out for what he believed in.

It wasn't a comforting thought to the spy. On the surface this was far from a novel situation for him. His reports often required imperial intervention into people's lives, but greedy merchants griping about taxes or violent dissidents harassing a bureaucrat were one thing. A charismatic young man with a dream of freedom was quite another.

Having apparently had their fill of coffee, the soldiers moved on.

"All right, beggar, no more nonsense. Take me to him," Lysik pushed.

Telain could tell by his tone that no more delays would be tolerated. He stepped out of the alley and started down the now familiar path to the boy's house. The city was already bustling as the suns rose over the horizon and the two were forced to weave in and out of the paths of carts and pack animals on the way to market. Telain could only hope he had delayed enough that the boy's father, who rose and left the house early most days, would be gone. It was difficult enough knowing that he would be the fall of the son without condemning the father as well.

They stopped at the entrance to the neighborhood. "Third house on the left," Telain pointed, "the one with the rose bushes." Thinking his task complete he turned to go, anxious to be rid of the assassin. A firm grip on his shoulder stopped him short.

"Until I have the bard in hand, you're with me. Besides," Lysik grinned, "you wouldn't want to miss all the fun would you?"

Telain had no choice but accompany Lysik to the front door of the house. The assassin knocked politely but no one answered. He tried again, this time with more force. Still no one came to the door. Abandoning civility, he produced a lock pick and set to work on securing their entry.

A flicker of hope arose in Telain. Perhaps the father and son had learned of their persecution and left town. Depending on how much warning they had received, they might be a full day's ride out, maybe more. With a little luck they could elude capture for months, if not completely. Regardless, his involvement in the whole affair would be over.

The approach of a lanky youth from down the road extinguished all such hopes almost before they had begun. The young bard carried a bag of pastries, presumably his breakfast. Telain glanced at Lysik who was too focused on the door's lock and hadn't noticed the approach of his quarry. The bard was still far enough away that if warned, he might have a chance. Telain's heart raced; the moment of decision was upon him.

"There he is!" he shouted.

But it didn't sound like a shout. It sounded like a whisper. Rather than warn the bard he had alerted the assassin of the bard's approach. Telain's courage had failed him. His decision was made.

Lysik straightened, quickly concealing the lock pick. The bard drew closer and noticed the two strangers on his doorstep. Rather than turn and run he approached with an easy smile.

"Good morning!" He waved to them.

Lysik returned the smile, although his was decidedly more sinister. Try as he might, Telain couldn't force his face to mirror the friendly greeting.

"And a good day to you, young bard," Lysik chimed. "Just the man I wanted to see."

The three men met with handshakes. "What can I do for you?" the bard asked.

"I have a proposition for you. But come, let us discuss these matters inside. Perhaps you might even be good enough to share one of your fine pastries."

The boy frowned. "I'm afraid I only have enough for two."

"That's okay." Lysik patted the spy's shoulder. "My friend here was just leaving. Weren't you?"

Telain nodded, grateful for being excused but not trusting his voice to speak.

"Fair enough," the bard answered, his smile restored.

With that the two men entered the house. Anxious to put as much distance between him and the cursed residence as possible, Telain hurried away with his shoulders slumped, fading back into the shadows from whence he came.

The promoters had been right; the Coliseum was in a frenzy. Spectators had flocked from the far corners of the Empire to see the paired fights and elites that had long ago abandoned the Coliseum as "pedestrian" paid top dollar to pack its luxury boxes. Vendors roamed the aisles peddling food and souvenirs. Slaves readied the fighting floor, dragging off bodies and replacing props for the next round of bouts. Just below the Coliseum floor, the fighting floor was a flurry of activity. Keepers prepped newly formed pairs and handlers carted caged animals into staging positions. And in their customary routine, Grall lead Sol to the familiar holding cell to wait for the preliminary fights to finish.

The old guard dropped Sol off with his customary good luck wish. K'nal was already waiting there in silence. As the door closed behind Grall, the Frorian stood as best he could in the small room and held out his hand in greeting. Sol cautiously returned the gesture only to have the giant pull him into a very strong, very hairy embrace.

"The Lady Korra bids you hello, as do I, Brother Sol." Sol noticed he said "Lady" as a title, not a pronoun. Sol attempted to squirm and struggle his way out of the hug but without success; K'nal was far too strong. Finally, K'nal let go and Sol stumbled away, gasping.

"Lady Korra requests your company tonight. She has important matters to discuss."

Sol caught his breath. "Like what?"

"It is not my place to say. It is only my place to fight by your side and make sure that you survive. I humbly request that you continue to do the same for me," he added with a solemn bow.

Sol chucked nervously. "Don't bow. Of course I'll fight, I don't have a choice."

K'nal seemed to take this as a pledge of warriorlike devotion and reached to give Sol another smothering hug, but Sol managed to duck the big hairy arms. "Whoa, big guy, no hugging either. No bowing and no hugging, got it?"

K'nal frowned. "Very well, then sit. There are things that need to be said and we haven't much time."

His curiosity piqued, Sol sat across from K'nal, with their knees touching in the small cell.

"As I said, it is not my place to speak for Lady Korra."

Sol raised an eyebrow. "*Lady* Korra?"

K'nal continued, "But it must be understood, I back the Lady fully. Wherever the path we are on takes us, I will follow it to the end."

Sol wasn't sure if he was included in "us" or not. What he was sure of was that the Frorian was dead serious. He spoke with a solemn conviction that left little doubt.

K'nal leaned forward, looking Sol in the eye. "Do you understand?"

Sol could only nod. He didn't even come close to "understand" but what else could he do?

"Good. Now, the time grows near and I need to meditate upon our coming battle. I'm sure you do as well." With that K'nal closed his eyes and fell silent.

Sol sat staring at the silent hulk. He had a feeling this was going to be a long day.

"Now they give us crossbows," Sol snickered.

K'nal didn't respond; his concentration was trained on fitting another bolt into the unfamiliar weapon. The fur on his hands kept getting caught in the catch and, besides painfully yanking it out, it was playing havoc with his aim. Bows of any kind weren't commonly used in his frozen homeland. A throwing ax or spear was about the extent of the average Frorian's limited ranged arsenal. Today, however, he wasn't left with much of a choice.

The partners had emerged from their tunnel to find the Coliseum floor littered with wooden half-walls, large hay bales, and piles of sandbags. The obstacles created a veritable maze for the ten pairs of fighters participating in the bout, who were each armed with a crossbow and a generous quiver of bolts. In addition to their own, and the seemingly constant supply being shot in their direction by the other pairs, many of the obstacles were also adorned with a full quiver of bolts, thus assuring that no matter what difficulties the fighters might face, a lack of ammunition, and therefore a break in the action, wouldn't be one of them.

Currently the constant barrage was keeping most of the participants pinned down behind various pieces of cover. Upon entering the floor, Sol had managed to duck behind a wooden half-wall large enough to allow him to stand and maneuver in relative comfort, while K'nal unfortunately found himself behind a low row of sandbags. The white giant could barely move without exposing himself to the bombardment. Sol wasn't sure but it seemed that a disproportionate ratio of bolts were aimed their direction. Perhaps the other pairs sought to take out the most experienced fighters first.

Sol winced as a bolt grazed close enough to K'nal's head to ruffle his fur. "Just stay down. I have an idea!" He threw the crossbow's strap over his shoulder and braced his back against the heavy half-wall's supports. Planting his heels in the sand, he managed to budge the obstacle a few inches. Slowly Sol heaved the half-wall toward K'nal's position, angling his path in order to end up on the volley side of the sandbags. After a good deal of effort, he managed to get the half-wall positioned to shield K'nal.

"Thank you, brother," the Frorian said after abandoning his sandbags and joining Sol.

Sol peeked around the edge of the barrier to survey the field. His maneuver had not gone unnoticed. Another half-wall and a large hay bale were scooting across the floor, providing mobile cover and adding to the chaos. With all the obstacles there was no way to know exactly how many foes they faced or where they all might be.

A howl from behind a pile of sandbags betrayed one archer's position just before he staggered out into the open with a bolt buried deep into his thigh. His cry of pain was quickly cut short by another half dozen projectiles. Sol took advantage of the distraction to try and discern from where the fire was concentrated. At least three bolts had come from a single half-wall about twenty yards down the fighting floor. It seemed that at least two of the pairs had joined forces.

"Give me your crossbow and grab a couple sandbags," he ordered K'nal. The Frorian complied, happy to relinquish the weapon. Sol pointed to the barrier from which the bolts had come. "During the next distraction, chuck those sandbags at that half-wall and see if you can't knock it over."

Almost before he finished his request a distraction presented itself. The partner of the fallen fighter, realizing his vulnerability, was trying to make a deal. "I will fight beside any pair that would spare my life!" he offered from behind his barrier.

"Over here, mate!" a response sounded from a nearby hay bale.

"You'll never make it that far! Come over here, we're closer!" bargained a pile of sandbags.

Sol caught K'nal's eye and the Frorian shook his head. Evidently they shared similar feelings concerning the reliability of such alliances. Having a third or fourth join your cause was all well and good until the number of combatants started to wane. There was a threshold below which a pair could fend for themselves. At that point your new alliance became a liability; only one pair would emerge victorious, a fact that every man in the newly formed team would be well aware of.

The bargaining continued, now with a second hay bale entering the bidding. Sol gave a nod and K'nal gripped the tops of two sandbags in one hand. With a mighty heave he hurled his missiles at the barrier. Bolts whizzed over their heads, just missing the Frorian as he ducked back behind the half-wall. A loud crash followed by several shrieks of pain let them know that his toss had found its mark. Sol peeked around their wall to find the targeted barrier knocked flat to the ground and three bodies pin-cushioned with bolts lying nearby.

"Nice throw," he said.

One of the bolt-riddled bodies proved to still contain some life. The unfortunate soul was trying desperately to crawl behind a nearby hay bale but his legs had stopped working. Sol thought briefly about ending his suffering but instead trained his crossbow on a pile of sandbags near the hopeless fighter. As he had expected, an archer poked over the top and aimed at the prone figure. Sol loosed his bolt at the same moment as his target, both archers finding their mark with deadly accuracy.

"Nice shot," K'nal commented.

"Thanks. I think that makes five."

"Six." K'nal corrected. "The partner-less one doing the bargaining was taken down by the same pair he hoped to join. How many remain?"

Sol shrugged. "Hard to say. Are there any other barriers close enough for you to knock down with those sandbags?"

K'nal peeked around the half-wall and shook his head. "Only sandbag piles and hay bales."

"Well, we'll have to figure something else out, then." A movement out of the very corner of his eye caught Sol's attention. Without a word of warning Sol turned his second crossbow toward K'nal and fired. The white giant had no time to react, not even attempting to dodge as the bolt passed within inches of his shoulder, only to be buried in the chest of one of the pair who had just sneaked around a hay bale with their crossbows trained on K'nal's back. The second of the pair ducked back behind the hay bale and Sol quickly set to reloading both crossbows, cursing himself for having left one unloaded.

Hoping to take advantage of his distraction, a second pair ducked out from behind a barrier on the opposite side of the floor with their crossbows trained on Sol. An instant before they loosed their bolts the closer of the two caught an expertly thrown sandbag right in the chest. The blow knocked him back into his partner and left them both staggering out into the open.

Both men dropped soon after, riddled with bolts.

Sol had missed the whole scene. Trusting K'nal to hold up his end of the fight, he instead concentrated on the remnants of the pair that had started the flurry. Having reloaded both crossbows he trained his sights on the hay bale and waited. He didn't have to wait long. Just as K'nal launched his sandbag the fighter jumped out and fired, as did Sol. Sol missed badly but the other fighter didn't, his arrow slamming into Sol's head and knocking him onto his back.

The crowd cheered.

Certain he had taken out the famous gladiator, both the crowd and the other fighter's surprise were complete when Sol, still on his back, raised the second crossbow and fired again, his bolt lodging deeply into the fighter's eye. He was dead before he hit the ground.

Sol felt the dent on his prized helmet where the bolt had struck him and grinned. "If I ever get the choice of how to arm you," he teased K'nal, "I'm going with sandbags."

"I would prefer an ax," the Frorian replied, missing the joke.

Sol chuckled. "That's ten."

The action abated momentarily as the various combatants repositioned themselves on the field. Fighters ducked, dodged, and belly crawled into better positions, hunkering down in the hopes of letting the action come to them. Sol was eyeing a hay bale near the wall but K'nal had a different idea. Picking the heavy half-wall clean off the ground, the white giant motioned Sol to follow as he backed toward the Coliseum wall. With the rock wall to their back and a wooden half-wall to their front, they proceeded to circle the floor. The sound of bolts striking the moving barrier sounded like a flock of woodpeckers as the other combatants concentrated their fire on the daring maneuver. Sol tiptoed along nervously, expecting a projectile to slip under the barrier and pierce one of their feet at any moment. He was anything but sure of their current tactic but he stuck by the Frorian, trusting his partner.

His faith was soon rewarded. As they gradually made their way around the wall the other fighters' seemingly secure positions quickly became much less so. Suddenly exposed, the combatants had to choose between facing Sol's bolts and scurrying to find other cover. K'nal's impressive pace pushed the issue further and by the time they had made a half circuit, Sol had picked off two. One that he had missed and two more fell to the projectiles of others during mad dash attempts to relocate to different positions.

"That's fifteen," Sol counted.

K'nal dropped the barrier with a loud thud, panting with the effort. "Leaving how many?"

"Three, I think. Too few to flush by circling, but we should keep the pressure on."

K'nal nodded his agreement.

Sol peeked around the edge of the barrier; everything was quiet for the moment. "You see how there's sort of an aisle running down the center between obstacles?"

K'nal peeked and then nodded again.

"I think there's one behind the hay bale to the right and a pair behind that half-wall directly across on the left. Let's move this barrier down the middle of that aisle. I've got an idea."

Grunting, the pair pushed the half-wall forward, taking care so as not to tip it over. A couple shots thunked into the barrier but the effort was half-hearted. The half-wall had protected them fully thus far and shots were best saved for when they might count. Bit by bit they made their way up the aisle, the crowd urging them on in their effort. They stopped mere paces from the two hiding places, the three barriers forming a tight triangle.

Sol motioned for K'nal to squat down. Crossbow in hand, he took a couple steps back before charging forward. Using the crouching Frorian as a springboard he bounded over the top of the half-wall, landing on his feet directly between the enemy positions. The moment he hit the sand three figures stepped out and fired, one from behind the hay bale and one on either side of the half-wall. The crowd gasped and Sol dropped to the ground.

An instant later so did the other three.

So fast was the exchange that it took the crowd a moment to understand what had happened. A hush stole over the Coliseum. Only when Sol rose to his feet did a wave of comprehension break upon the stands. When Sol had landed he had planted his feet and used his forward momentum to continue falling forward, at the same time turning and firing successfully at the foe on the closer end of the half-wall. The three bolts intended for him were to be kill shots and therefore aimed high. His forward fall allowed all three to streak by just overhead. One skidded away harmlessly and the other two drove home into the torsos of the archers opposite one another. In effect, Sol had killed three archers with one shot.

The fighters left the floor to the crowd's raucous applause, every spectator thrilled to be present at a bout that would no doubt be talked about for years to come.

Slink lead Korra down the dark hallway to Sol's cell in silence. She was dressed in a little red outfit that had been mended one too many times. Even with a slight limp she walked tall just the same.

Slink tapped his keys on the cell door, "You sure you still want this one? She's 'bout used up, if ya ask me." Sol made no response, but as Slink shut the cell door behind her he had to agree that Korra definitely looked worse for the wear. Even in the poorly-lit cell, Sol could see the dark purple bruising over her ribs. She had a long cut along her hairline and a split lower lip. Her cheeks were gaunt and dark circles ringed her eyes. But those eyes were as clear and intense as ever and when Slink left the room she greeted Sol with a smile.

"*Lady* Korra," he said with a mock bow.

"I see you've spoken to K'nal," she said as she sat down next to him on the bed. "Don't mind him. All Frorians talk that way," she explained. "I've always found it kinda nice."

"You know other Frorians?"

Korra nodded. "In fact, I know K'nal's father. I met him when I was a child on business with my father. He was very kind to me. I never met K'nal outside of the Coliseum, though. He was away at the time enduring *Indok'var*."

"Indok'var?"

Korra nodded again. "It translates roughly into 'The Ordeal'. I don't know much about it but all Frorians go through it. Fasting, fighting wild beasts, all that good stuff. Do you have any food?" she asked abruptly.

Sol reached under his bed and produced a small bundle wrapped in an old but clean-looking piece of cloth. He opened it careful to reveal a hunk of hard cheese, a couple small strips of dried meat, a couple figs, and a hunk of stale bread. He picked a piece of mold off the bread before handing her the bundle. She accepted it greedily, not noticing the fighter quietly watching her devour the small meal. She noticed later, as she was picking crumbs from the cloth, and she turned away, obviously embarrassed.

"Sorry," she said. "I haven't eaten in a while."

He put a hand on her shoulder. "I guessed as much. I have a couple friends in the kitchen that can sometimes slip me some extra."

Their eyes met for a long moment and he could tell she was fighting it. Eventually the tears came, as he knew they would. He held her as the sobs racked her body. She held her battered side as she wept all the harder. Sol said nothing, content to let the weeping run its course. Gradually, the crying slowed and her body relaxed. Her breathing returned to normal and then deepened. She had fallen asleep.

He sat still, now with her head in his lap, letting her sleep. He knew that if he wanted cognizant answers to his many questions, he must first let her rest. He was exhausted too, so he tilted his head back and dozed. He slept longer than he intended but she was still asleep when he woke. He looked her over as she slept. The discoloration on her ribs was ugly but the ribs, while prominent, appeared unbroken. The strap of the skimpy garment had fallen off her shoulder, exposing a slightly bruised breast. Despite himself, Sol felt his body start to respond to the sight. He shifted to pull the blanket over her bare skin but with his movement she startled awake.

She scrambled backward into the corner like a trapped jungle cat, teeth bared and claws flashing. Her wide eyes darted about the room, frantically searching for her attacker. Striking out again and again she screamed, "Don't touch me, you fucking animal!"

Sol held up his hands. "Easy, Korra, it's me, it's okay," he said in a calm but firm voice.

She looked at him, seeing him for the first time and relaxed. "Sol, I'm sorry. I thought you were one of the others. I just…" she paused, looking pleadingly into his eyes. Again he could see she was fighting it.

This time Sol intervened. "Korra," he said stepping forward and grasping her shoulders, "it's me. You're safe here tonight. I've given you as much food and rest as we can afford. Now you need to tell me who you are, what you want with K'nal, and what I have to do with it all. And this time I need everything. I think you now have a better idea of how limited your time can be in this place. If you don't tell me what you have to say tonight, you might never get the chance."

The change in her face was immediate. Her eyes hardened, her jaw set. "I won't be able to tell you everything because there's too much to tell. I'll try to give you the important parts." Her expression softened again for just a moment. "Thank you," she said, lowering her eyes, "I don't know where you learned to be a gentleman in a place like this, but you are one."

Sol flashed a big, crooked smile. "I'll tell Grall you said that. He's always said 'A proper warrior must also be a proper gentleman'."

"Raised in the Coliseum with a guard for a father. The outside world's gonna be a real shock for you."

"If I ever see it."

"*When* you see it," she corrected. "But let's not get ahead of ourselves. I had better start at the beginning." She paused for a moment and seemed to gather herself. Taking a deep breath she held Sol's eye. After a dramatic pause she continued with an air of importance, "I am a high ranking member of the People's Resistance, captured on a mission directly from Captain Stolem."

She stopped, obviously expecting some kind of reaction. When none came she continued with insistence, "My father is Captain Ekard Stolem." Again she paused. "The leader of the People's Resistance and probably the most hunted man in the Empire." She waited expectantly. When still no sign of recognition came, she slumped down with her head in her hands. "That is depressing. Fighting for us, fighting against us, or not fighting at all, I thought everyone had at least heard of us."

Sol spoke up, his voice rising defensively, "I've already told you how I get my information. It's not my fault I –"

She held up her hand, stopping him. "It's not your fault, it's our failure. That's always been one of our fundamental goals. To let the people know that they have another choice, that compliance isn't their only option. There's no chance that people will join a cause if they don't know it exists."

"And what is your cause?" Sol asked.

"To stop the Empire and free the peoples of Astrolia," she replied in a matter-of-fact way.

Sol wasn't sure what to say. To him, the Empire was an all-encompassing, omnipotent entity. Taking down the Empire sounded about as possible as demolishing the Coliseum with a spoon. He replied the only way he could, "How?"

She smiled. "Well, that is the real question, isn't it? How do you take down an empire?"

Sol realized she was asking him. He leaned back and thought for a long moment. "Unless I'm seriously underestimating your numbers, and since I hadn't even heard of the People's Resistance I doubt that, you don't meet them head on, army to army, that's for certain. That leaves more subversive tactics: raids, assassinations, attacks on infrastructure, that kinda stuff."

She chuckled. "With almost no outside information, you summed up the militant half of our tactics pretty well."

"Tactics I get," he replied. "If I didn't I'd already be dead."

"True," she countered, "but you only got the militant half. You missed the equally important educational half."

"Educational half," he repeated

She nodded. "Spreading word of the resistance and making the people aware of all the misinformation they're being fed. Helping people to spread the truth, not to mention maintain their own cultures, by teaching them to read and write."

Sol perked up. "I can write," he said with enthusiasm. "Look." He hopped off the bed and crouched down in front of Korra. In the dirt that made up the floor of his cell he scrawled three crude but legible letters.

"S, O, L," she read. "You can write your name."

He nodded with pride. "A princess taught me that. She was from Banali, her name was –"

"Sanad," she finished for him.

"How did you know that?"

"King Danalso had only one daughter. You could have meant no one else."

"You knew Sanad?"

"*Knew*? Yes, I knew her. I'm the one who taught her to read and write over a summer we spent together. Her father and my father fought the Empire together. She was only two years younger than me," she said sadly. "I take it she never left this place?"

Sol shook his head.

There was a long silence.

"Sol," she said suddenly with a slight edge of panic in her voice, "we have to get out of here."

Sol was used to this line of talk. Almost everyone who came to his cell brought up escape at least once. "There's no way out," was all he said.

"Of course there is," she countered, ticking them off her fingers as she listed the options, "guards leave, prisoners are transferred, the dead leave."

Sol merely shook his head. "The guards that work the Coliseum live in the Coliseum. Most of them die on the job at the hands of the prisoners. There are a few that live to see retirement but it's so infrequent that it does us no good. And prisoners aren't transferred."

"Prisoners aren't transferred?"

"Nope, if you come here, you die here. The Coliseum is a death sentence. The condemned come to the Coliseum from the different fighting schools. Only a handful of fighters survive each tournament, a dozen or less. The few that do happen to make it go back to their respective schools until the next tournament. Except for me and K'nal, we stay here. So only a few well known individuals are taken out. That does us no good."

"What about the Coliseum slaves?"

"One-way ticket. This place leaves you good for nothing else. Even the cleaning staff, they're worked to death, or near it, and then disposed of."

Korra sat up. "The dead, then. I've thought about it a lot, we could fake our deaths. When they cart the bodies out for burial we can make a break for it. I have connections that…" she trailed off. Sol was shaking his head. "What?"

"There is no cart that hauls out the dead. There are no burials. That would be wasteful. The Coliseum wastes nothing." He let her chew on it for a minute. When he could see she didn't understand he elaborated, "As you know well by now, Spoils are fed next to nothing. The reason is because by the time one starves to death, they're used up anyway. That's efficiency. Fighters, on the other hand, stick around a little longer. A few of us do, anyway. And a fighter needs to be strong enough to lift a sword and put on a good show. That means meat. You don't think the Empire would use all the resources and expend the effort to ship in more provisions than absolutely necessary? Not with all that meat being carted out to be buried…"

Korra's eyes widened with understanding; the blood drained from her face.

"That would be inefficient," he finished.

"Spirits save me," she murmured, still wide-eyed. "They feed the losers to the victors."

"Or to the beasts," he added. "And then the beasts to the victors."

She seemed to grow paler still, "The jerky?" she asked in a hoarse whisper.

Sol nodded, and then dodged out of the way as she dived for the chamber pot at the end of the bed. Kneeling on the floor, she vomited violently into the vessel. Sol was glad it had been empty. He shook his head. Regardless of where the nourishment came from she still needed it, not to mention the hassle he had gone through to procure the extra provisions she was now heaving into his chamber pot. It was probably just Dybuk, anyway.

Still kneeling and gripping the pot she looked up at Sol, her face red and streaked with tears. "Can we tunnel?"

He kicked a depression in the dirt at his feet that bore his name, exposing solid rock.

She stood, quickly wiping her mouth. "We could fight our way out. Between you and K'nal we could –"

Sol interrupted, "So you *did* plan on including K'nal?"

"Do plan," she corrected him persistently and began to pace. "He's bonded to a High Council member and the Council rules the Frorians. If we can get him back to his people, he's promised to speak to the Council on behalf of the People's Resistance. They're already sympathetic to our cause, it's time they join it."

"So not only do you want to break out of the Coliseum, but you want to stroll down the streets of the Capital with a Frorian. Talk about drawing attention."

She punched his shoulder. "I'm not hopeless. I have connections all over this city. If I can get to them they can hide us, all of us." She continued to pace. "Although I have to admit I'm not sure how to make contact while being stuck in here."

Sol shook his head. "I understand how you're feeling. I want you to believe that. But there's no chance. This is the end of the road."

"No!" she screamed at him. "You're blind because you've given up! There has to be a way out!"

Sol shook his head. "I'm sorry."

She regarded him coldly. "Yes, you are."

He ignored the dig. "Listen, let's at least make the most of the night. Why don't you tell me a little more about your time with the Frorians?" He sat, patting the bed beside him, inviting her to do likewise.

Still glaring, she chuckled. "Still hoping for a bedtime story huh? I don't think so." She moved to the far corner of the small cell. "You disappoint me". She slumped down against the wall. "We're done. Don't ask for me again."

Sol sighed. She was being foolish but there was little point in arguing. If she preferred the treatment she received from the other fighters then that was her business. He stripped the blanket off his bed and tossed it to her. She wrapped it around herself without a word. Sol could only shake his head again, then curl up and go to sleep.

9.

"Okay, what's this all about?" Grall asked with a frown.

Sol could hear the agitation in the old guard's voice. He had a feeling that between demands from cooks, messages from spoils, and now being summoned to a fighter's cell, Grall was beginning to feel taken advantage of. Sol normally wouldn't request such a meeting but he needed to talk to someone. Korra had left his cell that morning as silently as she had spent the remainder of the night. It wasn't the first time that a spoil had given him the cold shoulder but this time something was different. Korra's words kept running through his mind. Was there some chance that she was right? Had he given up too easily? He had been stuck in his cell all day with her voice in his head.

"Come sit down, I have something I want to talk to you about." Sol gestured to the bed.

Grall didn't move. "Sol, I really don't have time for this. We're getting a shipment in this afternoon and all they'll tell me is that it's big, hairy, and smells like rotten cheese. I've got to figure out a way to combine two holding pens into one. I tell them, 'The walls are made of stone!', but do they listen?" He started toward the door and Sol grabbed his arm to stop him.

"Please, Grall, it's important." He gestured toward the bed again.

Grall sighed and moved to sit. "Okay, but try to make it quick."

Sol was still standing as he faced his mentor. He had spent the last several hours trying to figure out the best way to broach the subject. Sol was used to performing under pressure but at the moment he found himself wishing he was about to face another Dybuk. He took a deep breath. "When's the last time you were outside the Coliseum?"

Grall's brows creased. "Why?"

"Just answer the question."

Grall thought for a moment. "Well, how old are you?"

"Just turned twenty-two," Sol answered.

"Then just over twenty-two years."

"And do you miss it?"

The question struck Grall. He couldn't expect Sol to understand how much he missed his old life. He had never told the boy about his family, his son. He hadn't shared the worries that kept him up at night. Worries about whether his son remembered him, whether they missed him at all. The memories of his wife and son were his own blessing and burden.

Grall brushed the question aside with a flick of his wrist. "What the hell does that have to do with anything? I thought you said this was important."

Sol ignored him. "Do you miss it?" he repeated.

"It doesn't matter."

"Of course it matters."

Grall raised his voice. "No, it doesn't. There is no outside world for us, you know that. Why worry about it?"

Sol knelt so that their eyes were level. "What if there was? An outside world, I mean."

Grall shook his head. "Men drive themselves crazy with that stuff. That's why I've always told you to forget about it. It can only do harm."

"So you never think about the outside? What life could be like?"

"Never."

"But what if you could get out?" Sol pushed. Sol dared to use the word, only a whisper, "Escape."

Grall stood. He had outlived almost every other guard in the Coliseum. In a society where few lived to see sixty, Grall would be considered old on the outside at forty-eight. Inside the Coliseum's stone walls, he was ancient. If he could hold on just two more years he would be the first guard in a decade to actually retire. He cared for Sol far more than a guard should, but he had been forced to accept the boy's fate the day he became a fighter. He wouldn't risk his only chance to see his son again. "That's enough. I don't have time for games." He knew Sol too well. If he wavered at all, the headstrong fighter would jump all over him. He started toward the door.

Sol stood, blocking his path. "This isn't a game."

Grall's teeth clenched. "Yes, Sol, it is, and it's one you can't win. Believe me, I've played it a long time. My side always wins."

Sol held his ground. "Then maybe you're playing for the wrong side."

Grall looked up at the gladiator he had helped raise. "You forget your place," he warned.

Sol laid a hand on Grall's shoulder. "My place is with you. And what if there is a way out? With your help we could try. I've been talking with –"

Grall quickly raised a hand to stop him. He stepped back, away from Sol's touch. "Stop. If you tell me any more I'll have to act."

"But –" Sol began to argue.

"No, damn it!" Grall shouted. He ran his hand through his beard, composing himself. "No. Perhaps it's me that's forgotten my place. There will be no more visits from the kitchen, no more messages." He held out his hand. "And I want your carving knife."

Sol paled. "Grall, you know I would never –"

"Now," Grall interrupted.

"Grall, please," Sol pleaded.

The guard remained as he was, stone faced with his hand extended and waiting to reclaim Sol's symbol of trust. Sol's eyes dropped and he moved to the bed, fishing out his most prized possession from its cubby hole. He returned to his previous position. "This is uncalled for," he said as he placed the knife in Grall's open hand, handle first.

Grall slipped the short blade into his belt. "I'm going to go now," he said deliberately. "I am going to forget what you said here today. I strongly suggest you do the same. Now move."

Sol looked over the face he knew so well, recognized the set of the jaw, and knew the conversation was over. Dejected, Sol stepped aside. "Yes, Sir."

Grall left without another word. Sol watched him go, feeling any hope go with him.

"What is your name?"

The young bard's eyelids fluttered open. His cracked lips parted slightly but no sound came out.

Lysik positioned the eyedropper over one of the last remaining unmarred and particularly sensitive areas on the boy's sprawling, naked body. Minimal pressure applied to the bulb of the dropper loosed a few drops of the powerful acid, the liquid singeing and smoking the instant it made contact, burning away exposed skin. The boy thrashed uselessly against the restraints with his mouth opened wide in an equally futile scream. A harsh wheeze was the only sound to escape;

one of the assassin's potent serums had robbed the boy of all but whispers. Lysik allowed the acid to work for a long moment before wiping it away with a balm-soaked cloth. The bard stopped squirming at once.

"I'm growing weary of this game." It was true. The boy was proving particularly difficult to break. Lysik had reduced seasoned warriors to mindless drones in less time. The two had been repeating the same question and lack of answer for nearly twenty-four hours. Lysik knew now that he had underestimated his subject and that he had started off too gradually. But he had stopped being nice hours ago. The young man's resilience was admirable.

"I've been merciful with you out of respect for your talent as a bard, but you are trying my patience. You have one last chance before I put away the balm. After that there is no relief, only pain." Sitting on a stool next to the bed he inserted the long glass eyedropper into the large full bottle of acid, drawing in more of the liquid. As he had every time before, he removed the dropper slowly, allowing its sides to clink against the mouth of the bottle as an audible warning of the pain to come. The tactic seemed effective; the boy twitched with every deliberate *clink*. He once again held the dropper over the same spot as before, although this time the area was devoid of protective skin. Slowly, deliberately, he asked his question again. "What is your name?"

There was a long pause. Lysik sighed and started to squeeze the dropper's bulb.

"Detrik," the response was almost inaudible.

Lysik leaned down close to better hear the long awaited breakthrough. "What was that? Speak up."

"My name is Detrik," the bard whispered.

The assassin smiled and replaced the dropper into its bottle before setting it aside. "It's a pleasure to meet you, Detrik." He picked up a glass of water from the bedside table. "And since you're willing to be reasonable, you may have a drink." He held the cup up to the boy's parched lips and trickled in some of the liquid. The youth drank greedily but received only a small mouthful before Lysik set the cup aside. Then he helped himself to another glass of water, one that wasn't infused with the mild narcotic.

"Now that we have the introductions out of the way, we can continue." The truth was that he had known the bard's name before he ever laid eyes on him. It was all about control. He had gotten the bard to admit a simple truth about himself, one that he didn't want to reveal. Things would come easier now.

"You have caused quite the ruckus, Detrik. It takes real talent to strike such a chord with the public. You should be proud."

The bard nodded groggily.

"But your tales all seem to have one central character. Why limit yourself so? Who is this gladiator? Why is he so important?"

The bard shook his head. "He's nobody, just a slave."

Lysik picked up the bottle of acid and clanked out the dropper. "I don't appreciate being lied to. If he's just a slave, why pay him such attention?" He positioned the dropper. "Why is the gladiator important?"

The bard shook visibly, wide eyes locked on the dropper. "He's just a slave."

Lysik sighed and squeezed the bulb, sending the boy thrashing and wheezing. He waited a moment and then wiped the acid away, this time with a dry cloth. The burning would lessen but never really stop without the balm.

Tears streamed down the boy's face. "He's just a slave, just a slave," he repeated in his raspy whisper.

Lysik *clinked* out more acid and positioned the dropper. "You're going to have to do better than that."

A knock on the door stayed his hand. "I said I was not to be disturbed!" he barked.

He recognized the voice that replied as the guard he had set to watch the door. "I'm sorry, Sir," came the muffled answer through the door. "The bards you asked for are here."

"Excellent timing. Two birds with one stone," he said to himself. He squeezed the dropper, applying a liberal helping of acid to the boy's tortured body for effect. "Send them in!" he called to the guard.

The door opened to admit three individuals: one a pale-skinned, redhead youth; one a bent old man with a grey beard past his belt; and the last one a rotund black woman with bright red lips and hair to match. The three couldn't have varied more in appearance; the only thread that tied the trio together was their expression of horror upon seeing one of their own reduced to a thrashing, gasping mess of blood and scabs strapped to a bed.

"Spirits save us," the woman whispered and the old man turned away.

Lysik smiled at their predictable reactions. The only surprise came from the carrot-topped youth. His freckled face never flinched and his eyes never left the figure on the bed. Lysik wondered how well the bards knew one another. It mattered little.

"Take a good, long look," he commanded. "Keep this little scene in mind as you practice your craft. It's a good reminder of what happens to those that cross the Empire."

"You have no right," the redhead whispered, his face as hard as his youthful features would allow.

Lysik stood with the large bottle of acid still in hand. "What did you say?" he challenged.

The old man elbowed his young colleague aside. "He said that you're right, and I agree." He cast a look of warning over his shoulder. "This will serve as a very good reminder, one that we're not likely to ever forget." His bent figure bowed further in a show of respect. The youth held his tongue.

Appeased, Lysik set the acid on a shelf above the head of the bed. "Good, see that you don't." He motioned to the door. "Let's step outside for a moment. We have another matter to discuss and I don't want any more," he smiled and motioned at the still-thrashing youth in the bed, "distractions."

The woman gasped and the youth's eyes narrowed. The elderly bard laid a hand on the young man's arm, trying to prevent a situation that he may not be able to smooth over. Despite the tension, all three remained silent as they made their way into the antechamber, the old man guiding the youth with a strong hand. The pleasant smell of coffee and the bright candlelight illuminating the richly-decorated sitting room contrasted starkly with the sickly smell of the dimly-lit bedroom.

"Sit," Lysik commanded. The three moved awkwardly to an ornate couch, the bulk of the woman forcing the other two to scrunch together uncomfortably. A muffled banging from the headboard striking the wall sounded rhythmically from the bedroom marked Detrik's continued struggles. Lysik liked the effect. It would maintain the element of fear.

"You were brought here today to complete three tasks," he stood in front of the couch, ticking the jobs off on his fingers, "to witness, to destroy, and to create." He caught the eye of the redhead bard and smiled. "We've already taken care of the witnessing." The old man's fingers tightened around the youth's arm and the boy remained silent.

Lysik continued, "I'm sure you're all well aware of the dribble your fallen comrade has been spewing to the public. Your second task is to knock down the pedestal he has worked so hard to prop up."

The three exchanged confused expressions. "What do you mean?" the woman asked.

"This Gladiator your young friend has attempted to build up into a hero. He is due to fall. You and your fellow bards will prepare the populace for his descent."

"How?" she asked.

Lysik sighed. "You're the bards, you figure it out. Tell them he's grown arrogant. Tell them he's gone crazy. Tell them that he takes small boys into his cell at night. Tell them anything! Just make the stories good and make him bad." His expression changed to one of concern. "We simply want to make sure that when his time comes, the citizenry is ready to let him go." He knew they didn't believe his reasons but he didn't care. It wasn't their place to question his motives.

"Which brings us to your final task. To ease the public through this time of transition, we will provide them with another fighter on which to focus their attention. You three will have the honor of choosing the next fighter they are to admire."

"You can't just tell people who to cheer for! They have a choice!" the redhead blurted.

Lysik laughed. "So they do, my young fool, so they do. They can root for whomever they want, a fact that I'm counting on. It is choice that makes the whole thing legitimate. The power is in controlling what or whom they have to choose from. Given the option between an arrogant, half-crazed pedophile and a brave, patriotic rising star, who do you think the people will choose?" A shadow of understanding darkened the youth's face and Lysik let his question remain unanswered. "Now, I was told you were the three to make this happen." He fingered the handle of the long dagger at his belt. "Was I misinformed?"

The old man shook his head.

"No, Sir, we'll get the job done," the woman answered.

The boy remained silent, his expression softened in resignation.

"Good. Then get to work."

The guards moved to escort the three out, the bards more than willing to escape Lysik's presence.

Lysik watched them go. He wondered if he might not have to deal with the redhead at some point. The youth's idealism was apparent and whatever the connection might be, his affection toward his cohort in the bedroom was obvious. The last thing he wanted was to deal with this situation only to have it repeated by another fool and fighter. Perhaps this visit had been enough to turn the boy, though. His revelations on the illusion of choice seemed to subdue the bard well enough. Whatever the case, he had pressing matters to contend with. The potential dissident would have to wait.

He moved back to the door to the bedroom, suddenly aware that at some point during their conversation the pounding of the headboard had stopped. Perhaps the boy had passed out. An acrid cloud of smoke that came billowing out of the room when he opened the door suggested otherwise. Lysik stumbled to the nearest window, coughing as the vapors burned his lungs. He threw the shutters open and hung out as far as he could, gasping for breath. The rolling cloud forced him to stay in his awkward perch for some time to allow the room to clear. When it finally did he climbed back in, suspecting he knew the source of the disturbance but hoping he was mistaken.

A quick glance into the bedroom immediately quelled any hopes. Whether the banging of the headboard had been deliberate was hard to say. Regardless, what resulted when the bottle of acid fell from the shelf made Detrik's intentions irrelevant. Most of the young bard's upper half, not to mention that section of the bed, had been completely dissolved. Even the floorboards were being eaten away by the powerful acid.

Lysik cursed his own foolishness. The owner of the home he had commandeered would be compensated for the destruction, but the loss of potential information from the bard would be impossible to mitigate. Was the bard part of the resistance? Why this particular gladiator? Why now? Shadon had expected answers and Lysik was not looking forward to explaining why he wouldn't get them.

Detrik's last words echoed through the assassin's mind. *"He's just a slave."* Of course he was just a slave. All that effort for a meager truism. What a waste of time, not to mention another pricey trip to the apothecary. Lysik stared at the fizzling pool of debris and gore that used to be his prisoner. "He's just a slave," he whispered, shaking his head in frustration before turning from the room.

It had never occurred to him that the fighter's significance might indeed rest in the bard's final words; that the fighter's lack of identity was the very thing that drew the public's imagination. To the assassin, one man could never challenge the might of the Empire; it was impossible. But it was that very impossibility, as every bard knew, that made it such a good story. That the one man came from the lowest ranks of society made a good story even better.

Why was Sol so important?

He was just a slave.

It was morning and Sol was sitting alone in his cell, mentally preparing for that afternoon's bout, when Slink poked his head into the cell door. "You 'ave a visitor."

He briefly hoped that Grall had returned to talk things over but he could tell by Slink's tone and distracted look that something was out of the ordinary. His thoughts immediately turned to Oci. Had she fallen again? For her to visit again so soon almost certainly meant trouble. With a worried frown he stood to greet her, only to fall back when an unknown figure entered his cell. Slink's wide eyes met his own before the guard retreated down the hall, leaving Sol alone with the stranger.

Sol looked his guest over. Dressed in a plain tan cape and hood, the man slouched as if buckling under a great weight. The hood was pulled down low, revealing only an unshaven chin and cracked lips. Sol sat back down slowly on the edge of the bed. The figure silently stayed where he wa. As a slave, Sol knew better than to speak before spoken to, so he waited patiently, equally silent.

Finally, the man spoke. "Why do you fight?" he asked in raspy voice.

The question caught Sol by surprise. "What do you mean?"

"Why do you fight?" the figure repeated in earnest.

"I have no choice," he answered with a shrug.

"There is always a choice."

He thought this over. "True," he conceded. "I could die. I could choose not to fight, lay down my weapons, and die."

"You don't fight like a man who fights just for his life."

"Just?" Sol replied with a raised eyebrow.

"There are other things worth fighting for."

"Like what?"

The man sighed. "Like honor or family or home."

Sol leaned forward, trying to peer into the hood. Something about the man's voice was familiar, but the poorly-lit cell kept the stranger's face hidden in the shadows of his hood. "Noble words," he acknowledged, "but I am a slave and therefore without honor or home. And I have no family."

"So because you are told that you're the property of the Empire, you are without motivation besides that which is designated to you. You fight, you exist, because the Empire wills it. Is that right?"

Sol stood, trying to appear bigger than the stranger's words made him feel. "Who are you? What do you want of me?"

The figure seemed to buckle even further under his invisible weight. "I want to know," he started then seemed to lose his voice. When he spoke again his voice was raspy and harsh. "I want to know that my son didn't die for a pawn."

Sol eyed the man suspiciously. "Did I kill your son?" He silently edged closer to the figure, preparing himself for a fight. He had heard of grieving family members coming for the fighter who had bested their kin. If the hood and cape hid a weapon, he would be hard-pressed to defend himself. His only hope might be to close the gap quickly enough that he could take his attacker by surprise. Thankfully, the figure seemed not to notice his careful approach.

"My son died because of you," the man choked out. His hands went to his haggard face and he seemed to wrestle with himself before speaking again "No! No, he died *for* you."

Sol had heard enough. No man, deranged or not, was going to murder him in his own cell. He launched himself at the figure, pinning his squirming body against the wall. He reached for the hood, slim hands and fingers ineptly seeking to stop his advance. With a quick jerk he pulled off the hood and cape only to stagger back in shock.

"Vance?" Sol gapped.

It was Vance, or at least he used to be. The man before him bore little resemblance to the flamboyant fellow who had wished him a happy birthday a few short weeks ago. His hair was unkempt and his clothes were ragged. He was always thin, but now he could only be described as gaunt. His bloodshot eyes sank into hollowed cheeks and they grabbed and held Sol's own. They were filled with the sorrow and loss of a broken man.

"What happened to you?" Sol asked, grabbing Vance's arm in an attempt to steer him to sit on the bed. Vance jerked away, clinging to the cell bars.

"To me? Nothing's happened to me. It's my son. He's dead."

"How?"

Vance's hands flew to his face, covering his eyes in a vain attempt to block out the mental image. "My beautiful son!" he moaned. "Burned almost completely away! All that was left were his legs. They tried to tell me it wasn't him, but I knew. I know my own blood!" he choked.

"I'm sorry." Sol tried to comfort Vance. He couldn't understand why the distraught man was here telling him all this. "Who did this?"

Vance's eyes darkened. He looked down at his hands, twisting and wringing them as he spoke. "His name is Lysik. He's a mercenary of sorts, but unlike most that are in that line of work because it pays well. He does it because he likes it. He likes to kill. More, he likes to kill slowly. He's known for torturing his victims for days, sometimes weeks at a time, and when he's not killing for the Empire, he kills for fun."

Sol, who had killed more men than he liked to think about, recoiled inwardly at the description. To prolong a man's life only to more thoroughly enjoy his death took an appalling lack of conscience.

"That monster killed my son," Vance suddenly raised his head, looking Sol in the eye, "because of you."

"Whoa. I've never met your son or this Lysik. You have my sympathy but I'm not at fault here."

Vance shook his head. "You misunderstand me," he said wearily. "You carry no blame. That burden is mine alone. I raised him to question, to seek the truth of the situation. I encouraged him to be outspoken…" he trailed off, staring blankly into space. The room was quiet for a long moment. "He was a bard, you know, my son," Vance broke the silence with a small sad smile, "one of considerable talent, given his age. I suppose his talent helped condemn him. If he was inept, he wouldn't have drawn attention regardless of what he said."

"And what did he say?" Sol asked with considerable trepidation.

Vance regarded Sol for a long moment. "It's bad out there, outside the Coliseum. You're trapped by stone walls. People out there are trapped by fear. The Empire has eyes and ears everywhere. Believe me, I know. There is a minority, which I admit that I am a part of, who have connections, talent, or money enough that we do fine, but the average person barely scrapes by. There is no mobility, no chance at a better life, and should they complain too vocally they risk their lives, perhaps even the lives of their family. It's people like this who need hope. Don't you agree?"

Sol nodded, confused.

"Bards are essentially storytellers. Any bard can tell a story. Good bards tell the right stories. They have to be in touch with the people, they have to give the audience the stories the audience needs. People today need hope, they need a hero. Someone brave and daring. Someone who will stand up to the oppression. Someone who is everything they aren't." He paused and raised an eyebrow at Sol. "Someone like you."

"What?" Sol questioned, wide-eyed.

"For some time my son has used you as the central figure of his stories. Due to your prowess in the Coliseum most often he just relayed the details of your bouts, something I had a hand in. Originally you were a mere action figure, a slave and a fighter, nothing more."

"I *am* nothing more!" Sol interjected.

Vance continued without notice, "As time passed his skill as a bard improved. Simple blow-by-blow accounts of your bouts became boring for him. Rather than incorporating exaggerations and embellishments as I suggested, he began to weave in morals and messages. He said you were a symbol, that you represented freedom."

"I'm a slave!" Sol pleaded. "How can I represent freedom?"

Vance shrugged. "He saw something in you, Sol." He grunted as he lowered himself wearily to the ground. "And he wasn't the only one. He made others see it."

Sol held up his hands. "This is crazy. I'm no hero."

Vance nodded. "Perhaps not, but you fight like one. And you live while so many don't. You're unique, Sol, and people like that. You've caught the imagination of the mob," he held Sol's eye, "and you've caught the attention of the Empire."

Sol paused, trying to think. This was all too much. His life was changing too fast. "What does that mean, 'catching the attention of the Empire'?"

"Trouble." Vance chuckled ruefully and then elaborated, "It means that just as my son's rhetoric has been his own downfall, surely it will be yours as well. His stories have sparked something and it's spreading. People are tired of having friends and family disappear in the night. They're tired of living in fear. The streets are full of whispers and some even dare more than that. There have been skirmishes. The Empire's trying to stamp this out before it really catches but they may be too late already." He paused. "He's coming, Sol. He's coming for you."

"Who is?"

"Lysik. He's been sent to deal with this. He's taken my son and now he'll come for you."

"He's been sent to kill me?"

"He's been sent to deal with you," Vance corrected. "The crux of the issue is your popularity with the people. Killing you outright might simply stoke the fire. Lysik must try to bring you down before he kills you," he reasoned.

Sol could hear his heartbeat in his ears. "How do you know all this?"

Vance lowered his eyes and sighed. "I know. That's enough."

"Is it?" Sol questioned, raising his voice.

There was a long pause. When Vance raised his eyes again Sol could see the tears falling freely from them. "Yes," he choked.

Sol knew it would have to be. He could only guess how Vance knew what he did but it was obvious that the broken man sitting in front of him was paying dearly for any sins he may have committed. Sol had often wondered whether Vance constituted a friend; a handful of one-sided visits left plenty of doubt. "I'm sorry about your son," he said.

Vance's brow creased and he regarded Sol for a long moment. "I come bearing a death sentence and you console me." He shook his head and then grunted as he got to his feet. After picking up his hood he extended his hand. "He was right about you," he said.

Sol started to protest but Vance shushed him. "I'm sorry for any trouble my son and I have caused you. I doubt our paths will cross again. Good luck, my friend."

Sol's world was small, his acquaintances few, his friends fewer. Now he was losing one he had only just found. He felt a knot rise in his throat as he took Vance's hand. "Thank you, my friend. And good luck to you."

With that Sol's friend left him to his fate.

10.

The walls of the holding cell felt like they were closing in around him. Sol had sat waiting for bouts in this small room dozens if not hundreds of times, but never had it felt like this. The hulking form of the giant Frorian didn't help the sensation. Sol took a deep breath, trying to clear his head. He knew the cell was the same size it had always been. He tried to reason with himself, yet again, that nothing had changed. There was always someone out there plotting his end. Promoters from outside the Coliseum and fighters from within had been working for years to see him dead. This was no different.

Yet again the reasoning fell short. Promoters concocted scenarios featuring Sol's probable demise with an overarching goal of entertainment. Should the improbable happen, if the scenario failed and the fighter survived, it only thrilled the crowd that much more. In a way, it was in a promoter's best interest to see Sol walk off the floor to entertain another day. Then there were the fighters that challenged him. Each of these men was a discrete unit. A fighter fought to keep himself alive. Besting one assured that he would go on to fight another with the same motivation. These men were an unending stream, yet still individuals and not part of any movement or conspiracy.

Which was exactly what he now faced. This assassin, Lysik, had been sent for the explicit purpose of seeing Sol dead. There was no benefit for him should Sol live. It would only mean an increased effort to assure that his next bout would be his last. Or perhaps Vance was wrong and the added threat wasn't even on the floor. Perhaps he would return to his cell after surviving the coming bout only to find a dozen guards waiting to cut him down.

And there was still another divergence, now people were counting on him, members of the public whose lives were fueled by some kind of misguided hope that he apparently provided. It wasn't an entirely foreign concept to Sol. He had been fighting with others in mind for his whole career. The prospect of leaving Oci alone or of letting Grall down, these things fueled him. And there had always been fans. Like every successful fighter he had individuals that followed his bouts, people that considered him an object of entertainment, something akin to a race horse or their favorite chariot. That he might be considered something more had never crossed his mind.

In a way it angered him. In a place as awful as the Coliseum he had managed to carve out a decent life. He had loved ones and diversions enough to afford him some modicum of happiness. He never asked to be a symbol and he never wanted to be a hero. Vance's son and those that followed him had made him into something he wasn't. They had warped a simple gladiator into something more for their own purpose. And it would cost him his life.

"You seemed troubled, brother." He looked up to see K'nal regarding him with genuine concern. K'nal! Sol flinched at the realization that the Frorian was dead by association. The white giant with the noble countenance that had shown Sol mercy and respect would no doubt fall to Lysik's plot. Their partnership assured that their fates were shared. Yet another companion he would fail.

"I'm fine," he lied.

K'nal nodded but the concern remained. "I, too, have my doubts about today."

Sol eyed the furry face. K'nal certainly didn't look worried. It was an emotion Sol wouldn't have thought to ascribe to his partner. Even on the floor, K'nal was nothing if not stoic. Worry didn't seem to fit. It seemed far too human a trait.

Sol gave in. "Why's that?"

K'nal frowned, his brow creased. "I'm not sure your language has the words for it."

"This isn't your native tongue?" Sol had to admit that he had never contemplated Frorian linguistics.

"No. And with all due respect I find yours…cumbersome. I would say that something smells wrong about today but that is not right."

Sol looked away. He wasn't sure it was wrong. He had no way of knowing whether Lysik had a hand in what they would face today but if not, he would soon enough. They sat in silence for a long moment before Sol looked up. "Say it in your language."

K'nal frowned again. "It will mean nothing to you."

"Please," Sol asked.

K'nal nodded. A sound started to emanate from low in his throat. It slowly rumbled its way up through his chest before bursting from his open mouth. The sound was guttural and sad, like the mourning cry of some great beast. It echoed around the small cell, filling the whole of it. Sol's ears ached as K'nal dropped pitch and the tone reverberated in his chest.

K'nal was wrong. It was true that his words, if you could call them that, held no literal significance for his human companion, but their meaning couldn't be missed or ignored. The sense of foreboding they carried was the same that haunted Sol.

The sound ended and K'nal nodded. "It feels good to speak in my own tongue. Perhaps I have been mistaken. Perhaps today holds no menace after all."

Sol closed his eyes and hung his head, K'nal's optimism falling on deaf ears.

The Coliseum shook as the two Gladiators ran out of the tunnel into the blinding suns. Each carried the weapon he had been given, Sol a long halberd and K'nal a war hammer so large it seemed oversized even in Frorian's massive hands. The floor was devoid of props so the two continued to the center of the floor.

Sol felt the eyes of the crowd as he never had before. He scanned the stands for some sign of what was to come. He listened to the cheers, straining his ears for something out of the ordinary. He knew the futility of his efforts, the uselessness of searching for a face he had never seen, listening for a voice he had never heard. A sudden outburst by the crowd turned his focus back to the bout, realizing as he did that his inattentiveness may have already cost him.

Small doors had opened in the Coliseum floor, releasing a flood of what looked like fast-moving, slightly oblong balls of fur colored like a rusty nail. Sol could make out no distinguishing characteristics in the fur-balls. In fact, if it wasn't for the direction in which they moved, he wouldn't have been able to guess which end of the melon-sized creatures was head and which was tail. Hundreds poured out of the doors before closing to seal the creatures in with the fighters.

"What are they?" he shouted to K'nal over the roar of the crowd. K'nal shrugged, watching the herd of fur move in unison across the Coliseum floor, circling close to the stone walls in an apparent effort to escape. By their reaction he had a feeling that the spectators had already witnessed their new foe in action. He scanned the Coliseum floor again, this time noting several odd looking heaps piled up against the stone walls. His mouth dropped when upon closer inspection he recognized scraps of cloth, armor, and bone. They were the remains of fighters, completely stripped of skin and flesh. The fur-balls had skeletonized their predecessors.

"We're in big trouble!" he shouted to K'nal. So this was what Lysik had come up with. He was to be reduced to a pile of rubbish with the cheer of the crowd ringing in his ears. Sol glanced back up into the stands, willing his executioner to show himself.

A bellow from K'nal forced his eyes back to the floor. Two of the fur-balls had veered off of the pack and were bee-lining toward the Frorian. As they closed, he raised his giant war hammer and brought it down in the creatures' path with bone-jarring force. The nimble critters skipped to either side of the hammer, easily avoiding the blow. Sol moved to help, wielding the halberd at the leaping fur-balls. He was just able catch one mid-air with the razor-sharp blade but the other sailed by unscathed. K'nal howled as it tore into his shoulder, staining his snow white fur red with blood. The giant dropped the hammer and pounded at his tormentor with his fist. After a few blows the creature dropped motionless to the ground. Sol looked at the way the animal's long fur had parted, revealing a snow white undercoat similar to K'nal's. They weren't naturally rust-colored, he realized with horror. They were covered in dried blood.

Sol jerked the halberd away as K'nal reached for the weapon. "Give it to me!" the Frorian demanded. Sol stared in shock. He was part of it. The white giant was in on the whole mess. He would take the halberd and leave Sol defenseless to face the voracious fur-balls. Lysik had gotten to him. Sol had been a fool.

At the far end of the Coliseum the swarm had turned. Perhaps the scent of blood had gotten their attention. Regardless, they were headed right toward the pair. "Brother!" K'nal pleaded. "Together!"

The words struck home. Sol shook off the thoughts of betrayal and tossed the halberd to K'nal. The giant caught it and with one fluid motion brought the blade down hard on the handle of the war hammer, severing the head from the wooden shaft. He then brought the halberd's own shaft down hard over his knee, snapping it in half before tossing the two pieces back to Sol and doing the same to the hammer's handle. Sol understood the strategy at once. Both the weapons were far too large and cumbersome to defend against the speed and maneuverability of the horde that approached. K'nal's quick thinking might give them half a chance.

The two fighters turned to meet the swarm with their modified weapons raised and the fur-balls were on them immediately. The creatures broke like furry waves as the fighters tried desperately to stay free of their teeth and claws. There was little strategy to their defense. All they could do was to keep swinging and hope not to miss. Invariably, one or two of the little devils would make it through the blur of lumber and attempt to bury itself into one of the fighters, leading to one of the pair beating the other in an effort to dislodge the beasts, a sight the crowd found very comical. Fortunately, the animals turned out to be rather fragile, despite their ferocity; one good whack was usually all it took.

Regardless of how many fell, the swarm didn't fall back or didn't regroup, it just pressed on in a seemingly endless wave of teeth, claws, and fur. Soon the fighters were completely encircled and the onslaught wore them down. Sol's armor provided him a little more protection but K'nal was suffering. No longer snow-white, his fur was now a mosaic of his own red blood and the more purple blood of the creatures. K'nal grimaced, but despite his obvious pain the giant bore his wounds without complaint. Stoic or not, both fighters were tiring and the ring of creatures continued to press in. There just didn't seem to be any end to them.

Somewhere in the haze of battle Sol realized that in spite of how many they had already killed there was no growing pile of dead fur-balls at their feet. He managed to steal a glance to confirm that as each lifeless form dropped to the ground its companions would surround and devour it before the body even stopped moving. The observation seemed of little import until, out of the corner of his eye, he noticed two motionless fur-balls lying dead a little distance away, completely intact. A bolt of recognition hit him. When the next bloodstained critter leaped at his throat, he took an exaggerated swing sending its lifeless form flying far away from the action. As it flew, several fur-balls broke away from the group in pursuit. The dead fur-ball hit the dirt with his hungry companions only a few feet away. The body skidded to a halt but instead of tearing into their dead friend, the pursuing fur-balls peeled away and rejoined the group.

Sol's attention to the sideshow cost him. One fur-ball got to his leg and another to his back. He cried out in pain and K'nal came to his aid. The giant tore off and crushed one and then another of the offending creatures only to have two more tear into his own shoulders. The Frorian howled in pain. They were being overtaken.

Sol grabbed K'nal's head, forcing him to meet his eye. "Throw me!" he yelled. He could see the confusion in the giant's dark brown eyes. "Throw me!" he repeated. Fortunately there was no argument. K'nal grabbed Sol by his chest plate and with a quick pivot launched him into the air. Sol hit the ground in a forward roll and stumbled to his feet. He looked back to see that, as expected, about half the creatures had broken off the group and were now on his heels.

Sol ran as fast as he could, circling back toward K'nal to get within shouting distance. "Curl up in a ball! Stop moving! Be still!" he shouted to his partner. K'nal dropped to his knees and curled his body, covering his head with his hands.

The crowd cheered as the creatures swarmed over the Frorian, hiding him completely from view. They knew what was coming, they had seen this before. K'nal would thrash and scream, trying to free himself.

Lysik cheered with the rest of the crowd. He silently chastised himself yet again for never before attending the bouts. It was as if he had found a home in the Coliseum, this beautiful place where bloodshed was celebrated and depravity cheered. It was a church of carnage, complete with worshippers. He watched the spectators almost as much as he watched the fighters. Their faces radiated in a dazzling array of emotions: fear, rage, glee, sorrow, and lust. He had been in the stands all day, reveling in the spectacle and waiting for the current bout. He could hardly believe the day was almost over.

He could also hardly believe that the fighter before him, the one fleeing from the herd of oversized dust bunnies, could possibly be his prey. True, the two had survived longer than the fighters before them, but as far as he could see it was the Frorian that held the bulk of the talent. That Shadon had shown such angst over such a man was laughable. In fact, Lysik laughed out loud at the thought, comfortable in the fact that no one would pay him any mind.

But with the laughter came a touch of disappointment. He had heard tale after tale of the fighting prowess of Sol and he couldn't help but be intrigued by the possibility of testing his daggers against the slave. He needed no grand forum such as the Coliseum, just a private fight and the knowledge that he was better. The idea of besting the best pleased him. Of course, based on what he was seeing today, the slave might not even be worthy of his time.

He shrugged any disappointment aside with a smile and kicked back, ready to watch the fighters be ripped to shreds.

Sol watched as the fur-balls engulfed K'nal, praying that his hunch had been right. As he neared he could see that despite being covered in the vicious creatures, K'nal did as he was told and stayed still. Even on the run, Sol marveled at the trust it took for K'nal to drop his weapons and hit the dirt. Sol ran past the pile of fur and just as he had hoped, the crowd cheered again as the rest of the fur-balls abandoned the stationary Frorian to join their companions in chasing Sol.

Already weary from battling off the creatures, he knew he wouldn't be able to keep up his sprint for long. He hazarded a look over his shoulder, estimating that their efforts until now had cut the fur-balls' numbers roughly in half. Unfortunately, that still left nearly a hundred of the hungry beasts hot on his heels. He could feel the creatures slowly closing on him and his lungs were burning. He scanned the floor as he ran, searching for some means to rid himself of his entourage.

With his eyes off his path, he didn't see the discarded head of K'nal's giant war hammer. The trip sent him lurching and stumbling forward. Rather than attempt to right himself, he dropped his weapons and hit the ground, quickly curling into a ball. The creatures were on him in an instant. He fought a scream as sharp little claws and teeth cut into his skin and the smell of dried blood overwhelmed his senses. Somehow he managed to stay still and just as with K'nal, the fur-balls soon lost interest. He peeked out under his arm after a few moments to see the herd again working the stadium walls, looking for an escape route.

If Sol was happy to have found a brief reprieve, the crowd was anything but. Boos and jeers rained down on the cowering fighters. Despite their predicament, Sol knew they couldn't risk the crowd's displeasure for long. He slowly raised his head and saw that K'nal had done the same. The intensity of the booing was steadily increasing. The fur-ball herd was still working its way along the wall when the trash started to fly. From all areas of the stands, spectators shared their displeasure by chucking refuse at the fighters. Although both Sol and K'nal were close to the center of the floor, and therefore unreachable by even the best tosses, the trash did catch the attention of the fur-balls.

One by one, the creatures peeled away from the herd to pursue falling litter. Slowly the swarm decentralized, spreading out to give chase.

Sol saw their opportunity and signaled to K'nal. The giant understood and both fighters gradually rose to their feet in unison. The crowd cheered but still the trash rained down. The mob had found entertainment in distracting the fur-balls, in becoming part of the spectacle. Still unnoticed by the creatures, the fighters slowly collected their weapons. With a nod from K'nal and a deep breath, Sol waved his makeshift batons above his head.

Predictably, his action caught the attention of a few but not all of the fur-balls. The majority of the creatures were still spread out chasing trash. Even as they closed, the group that chose to engage Sol lost several members to pursue a rolling head of cabbage. The ones that made it were quickly disposed of. Their flying bodies and Sol's motion caught the attention of a few more fur-balls and the cycle repeated. He looked over to see the same pattern transpiring for K'nal. The creatures were as vicious as ever but now their numbers were manageable. They had done it.

A new cheer roared up from the crowd. Not only would their heroes live but this time they, the crowd, had helped. The mob knew that they were part of the victory and after the last fur-ball fell, the two fighters made it known that they knew it too. They bowed to their audience, thanking them for their hides, tattered though they may be.

Lysik applauded with the rest of them, sincerely entertained by the thrilling bout. Like his fellow spectators, he was glad to see the fighters leave the arena alive, though his joy was motivated purely by the assurance that today's victory had granted him his opportunity to have a hand in their eventual demise.

And the crowd! The wonderful, fickle, stupid mob, ready to turn on their favorite pair at the drop of a hat. For the first time since receiving his assignment from Shadon back at Fort City, the assassin felt truly at ease with his mission. Today had proved how very simple it would be to turn the crowd against the would-be hero. A fighter's past deeds mattered little; it was all about his performance that day. With such a short collective memory, Lysik was sure he could turn the public against the slave. And with that certainty came an equally important realization: the gladiator need not die to fall. All that mattered was that he loses the favor of the mob. After that, Lysik could deal with him as he saw fit.

That prospect opened up a delightful new realm of possibilities. Not only would he complete Shadon's mission but he would do so in his own way. It would be a good show, he would see to that. In the end the crowd would turn, the partner would die, and the gladiator would fall. Then Lysik would finish it on his terms. If the slave was fit to fight, he would finish it with his daggers. If not, then he could take his time. Either way, he would look into the slave's eyes and watch his arrogance drain from him in the same steady stream as his own life. The hero that never was would know in his final breaths that despite his feats on the Coliseum floor, he was nothing more than any other slave of the Empire.

He was nothing.

Sol struggled along the corridor, trying to ignore his body's protests and to keep up with the young guard. His arms ached from swinging the makeshift batons, his legs burned from sprinting, and it felt as if most of his skin had been scraped off. Even with his numerous complaints he had still managed to come out of the bout in better shape than K'nal. The two fighters had hardly been given a moment before the guards split them up to go to their respective cells. A moment had been enough to see that the giant was in a bad way. Large patches of fur had been completely torn out and what remained was stained in blood. Deep cuts covered his face, including one gash over his left eye which had swollen shut, and as the giant limped away Sol could see he was missing an ear.

Hobbling after the guard, Sol considered the bout. Those damn furballs were a menace. He wondered where they came from. Wherever it was, he silently promised himself never to go there. He imagined a landscape completely devoid of life, roamed by vast herds of the vicious creatures. Pity to the poor hunters whose job it was to capture the fur-balls and bring them to the Coliseum.

Whoever those men were, Sol now suspected that they hadn't acted on Lysik's orders. As close to death as they had been, the whole situation felt too chaotic to be part of some devious scheme. Any man calculating enough to torture a victim for days on end would have a plan that was spelled out to the letter. No, the fur-balls were probably just another attraction dreamt up by the promoters. Whatever the case, they had been lucky to get out alive.

Now he just needed to concentrate on staying that way. He didn't think any of his wounds were too bad if he could get them clean and maybe administer a few stitches. Supposing the fur-balls didn't carry any nasty diseases, and that he could ward off infection, he would likely be okay in a couple days. Mainly he just needed to rest, a prospect that seemed unlikely as they passed the entrance to the tunnel down to the lower levels and his cell.

"Are you lost?" he asked the blond-haired guard leading the way. The pimpled youth couldn't have been more than sixteen.

"I don't think so," the guard replied, sounding less than certain.

Sol sighed. "If you're taking me to my cell, you missed the tunnel."

The guard ignored him and kept walking.

"Then where are we going?" He was in a foul mood. The pain radiating from his hip didn't help the matter.

"Just following Slink's orders," the guard clarified, as if that explained everything.

"Well there's your first problem," barked Sol. "You're new here, right?"

He nodded.

"You'll learn soon enough that nobody listens to that creep."

"So I've been told. The other guards are awful to him. They're always putting him down or pulling pranks on him." The guard shrugged. "I don't think he's all that bad."

Sol laughed. "You'll get there. Believe me. I mean, have you seen the way he treats the women? He's a pig."

The youth eyed him. "You've known him a long time?"

"Too long," Sol confirmed.

"Could've fooled me." He stopped and motioned to a door. "We're here."

Sol had been too busy bad-mouthing Slink to pay any attention to where they were going. He was surprised to see they now stood outside the door to the women's barracks. "Why are we here?"

"I asked Slink that very thing. He said he was doing a favor for a friend." The youth eyed Sol. "I can only assume he meant you."

Confused, Sol opened the door.

"I'll wait here." The guard moved to the side as Sol entered the barracks.

The room was dark, save for a half-circle of flickering candlelight cast upon on the far wall. In the low glow Sol could see the silhouettes of the women who called the barracks their home. They sat and stood in a semicircle at the periphery of the light, blocking its contents from his view. The scene was still, there being neither movement nor sound. None turned as Sol made his way slowly down the rows of bunks toward the silent congregation.

He had spent a good portion of his life here, although he hadn't set foot in this room again since the morning of his first bout. It held many memories. He had been born here. Later, he took his first steps here and lost his first tooth. But in spite of its history, this wasn't a happy homecoming. Though he knew not what awaited him in that ring of light, a dark sense of foreboding settled over him. He thought about turning back, content in not learning the meaning of the scene. He didn't want to know. But still he continued. Something drew him to the light, like a moth to the flame.

And then he was there, in the light. Faces turned to greet him; some he knew, and some he didn't. It hardly mattered; he didn't see any of them. His eyes saw only the lone face bathed in candlelight at the center of the circle. The face of an old cook, resting at the head of the bed. Oci's face.

The circle parted respectfully to grant him entrance. He didn't notice. He drifted to the side of the bed and knelt, taking her hand. Her hand was warm, though she didn't return his gentle squeeze. The scene returned to stillness. Sol's concentration lay solely with the gentle undulation of the sheets. With each rise and fall he compelled the next breath to come. He willed all that he was, all that he had ever been, into her next breath, then the next, and then the next. They might have stayed that way for minutes or years; there was no time.

Finally, Oci stirred and struggled to speak. Someone handed Sol a cup of water. He lifted her head ever so gently and trickled the liquid past her cracked lips. The water helped and she settled. Opening her eyes, she smiled at Sol.

"You're here," she whispered groggily.

"Of course," he assured her.

"I asked Slink. He's a good boy."

A knot rose in Sol's throat. "Yeah, he is."

Her smile faded to a worried frown. "Are you hurt?"

"No," he lied, "just dirty."

She smiled again. "No surprise. I've never known a boy more prone to dirt. I remember when you were young…" she trailed off, closing her eyes. Sol returned to meditating on the sheet. In a short while she stirred again. "Sol," she said, this time fully awake and aware. He squeezed her hand to assure her of his presence. "Sol, it's time for me to go."

"Don't say that," he protested.

"It's okay, dear. I'm ready."

Even though he didn't want to, he believed her. "You're not in any pain?"

"There's no more pain," she assured him.

He nodded. "Where will you go?"

She smiled. "I'm not sure. Some place big and open, where you can see the sky for miles. And pine trees," she added, "I've always loved the smell of pine trees."

Sol half-chuckled, half-sobbed. "I'm really going to miss you." He held her frail hand to his face. "I don't know what I'll do without you."

"You'll live," she said simply, "and you won't let this place get to you."

He nodded, though this time he didn't believe her. He gingerly kissed the back of her hand. "I love you," he said.

There was no answer. She had drifted off again, eyes closed and mouth slightly agape. Sol returned to his silent vigil, surrounded yet alone. The composition of the semicircle changed as its members came and went, attending to their duties. Sol didn't notice. She stirred several more times during the night, mumbling random words and inaudible phrases, but nothing coherent. Shortly after midnight the sheets fell still, rising and falling no more. Oci was gone.

Sol stayed where he was, her hand in his. After a time the crowd started to break up, drifting off in twos and threes. Still Sol remained. He didn't hear the respectful condolences. The faces of the circle were lost to him. He was numb. He felt nothing. One thought stuck in his mind: he wouldn't let them take her. They wouldn't dispose of her like the average corpse. Not Oci.

But come they did. He felt them walk up behind him, still kneeling on the floor.

"It's time," said a voice.

Sol looked over his shoulder to see the guard that had lead him here. With his new uniform and shock-blond hair he looked so young, so naive. Turning back to Oci, Sol shook his head. "No," was all he said.

The young guard laid a hand on his shoulder. "We have to," he persisted.

Sol shrugged off the hand, unmoving.

From over his other shoulder came a more familiar voice. "She was always good ta' me."

Sol turned and regarded Slink. The guard's tear-rimmed eyes were on Oci and the pain on his face was clear. "She was good to everyone," Sol agreed.

Slink looked him in the eye. "I'll take care of 'er. I promise."

Sol believed him and nodded. "I want to go with you."

It was Slink's turn to shake his head. "Can't risk it. You're not even supposta be 'ere."

Sol wanted to argue but held back. Instead he nodded again and stood. He bent over Oci, kissing her forehead in a final farewell before turning to leave with the young guard following silently behind. This time as he walked back down the aisle he saw the women. The old cook had touched every life here. In each face he could see the pain he felt, though his own face remained blank and hard as stone. When he reached the door the young guard followed. Several of the women moved to help Slink with the body.

Sol didn't look back.

11.

They walked back to Sol's cell in silence, a fact he was grateful for. Every noise, every scuff of their feet on the hard stone floor, felt like an intrusion on the solemn quiet. The living rock of the Coliseum walls seemed to mourn the passing of one of its best. Sol slowed slightly to let the guard leading him pull ahead, craving some privacy.

Oci's gone. As he walked the thought ran through his mind again and again. With it tumbled a mix of numbness and emotion the likes of which Sol had never known. He hurt so badly, yet he felt nothing. He cried, but no teardrops fell. There was anger there, too. Anger that such a woman, such a strong and good woman, had been forced to succumb to this place. Anger that she would be replaced by another slave as casually as a clockmaker might change out a failed cog. Like all slaves, himself included, she was expendable.

There was fear there, too. Fear for the path that Oci was now on. Over the years he had spoils who represented nearly every religion, creed, faith, and conviction come through his cell. Some were devout, many suddenly more so due to their sudden awareness of their own mortality. Most of the women shared little bits and pieces of their beliefs and a few dumped them upon him as if their very soul depended on it. He always tried to listen politely, no matter how inane or trite the preaching. As far as he could tell their beliefs all had a few things in common. Of chief concern was that if you were good in life, good things awaited you in death.

In the long, lonely nights he spent in his cell Sol had contemplated the afterlife, wondering if not only his whole life but his whole existence was to be spent in the Coliseum. He had heard a number of theories on the subject. One said that a person's spirit returned to the place they most loved to do the things they most loved for all eternity. While that sounded nice in passing, the thought of spending eternity in even his favorite places in the Coliseum struck him as far from paradise, not to mention that even the most enjoyable activities would become torture after the first few hundred years. He was a bigger fan of the belief that the spirit was able to come and go anywhere it pleased, commingling with other spirits in this world and in the next. What "the next" constituted was up for debate. If you were good in life the next world was anything from clouds and harps to vast green pastures or white sandy beaches. If you were bad the options slimmed considerably and almost all of them involved fire.

He hoped for his sake and for the sake of those he loved that there was more than this world. He wanted to believe, tried to believe. After all, if he had ever met a good soul, he was sure it was Oci. She deserved paradise. He hoped beyond hope that she was there now, in whatever her perfect next world might be. What kept the fear at the surface was the doubt. As much as he wanted to believe, to have faith, as some called it, something kept him from it. A part of him, the part that couldn't be reasoned into the unreasonable, refused. He wanted there to be more but he couldn't make himself believe that there actually was.

After what seemed like an eternity they reached his cell and the young guard opened the door to let him in. He stumbled into the shadows without a word, eyes on his feet, feeling more than hearing the door shut behind him. A different movement from the far corner of his cell put him on alert. *How appropriate*, he thought. Lysik must have been waiting for him. He guessed he would find out soon enough what the next world contained.

The figure moved out of the shadows, long, curly auburn hair letting him in on his error.

"By the Gods!" Korra exclaimed as Sol also stepped into the light. He still wore his armor, gore desecrating its usual shine. It was his face, however, that elicited her exclamation. Dried blood matted the hair to his head, contrasting with his pale, sunken features and his bloodshot eyes rimmed with dark circles. She moved to him, sure by his drooping posture that he was close to collapse.

"No!" He backed away, hands extended to maintain separation. "Guard!" he yelled. He didn't want to share his cell. He needed to be alone. The guard was too far gone to hear his call, though. She was there for the night.

"I'm sorry I left things like I did," Korra said, misunderstanding the hurt evident on her face. "I didn't want to hear what you were saying. Please, let me –"

"Stop," he interrupted. "Please stop," he pleaded with an expression of such profound sorrow that it silenced her immediately. "I need some time."

Korra nodded, confused and hurt but seeing the obvious need in her companion. She moved away silently. Sitting with her back to the wall at the head of the bed, she pulled her knees up to her chin, wrapping her arms around her legs to try and make herself as inconspicuous as possible.

Sol nodded, grateful for the effort, and slumped to the ground with his back against the opposite wall in much the same position. A heavy silence engulfed the cell.

Sol stared blankly ahead, not seeing Korra or his cell. An entirely different scene played out before his eyes, a scene from a long time ago.

The small, furry form lay motionless in Sol's hands.

"Whitey?" he whispered. The albino rat's soft, white fur was cool to the touch; the body was limp. Large tears rolled down Sol's face. "Whitey, are you ok?" he asked, though in his heart he already knew the answer. The question, as they sometimes are, was just a diversion, a way to avoid the reality of the situation for a few moments more.

The tunnels under the Coliseum were filled with rats. They were a constant problem, always gnawing their way into food stores and spreading fleas. Guards and slaves alike were forever battling against the pests: plugging rat-holes, rigging traps, and setting poison. The measures kept the population in check but just barely.

Sol had been acutely aware of the vermin his whole life. Countless were the times that Oci had put him to work chasing them out of the pantry. He could hear them at night, their little claws tapping on the hard rock floor as they scurried around the barracks. New arrivals at the Coliseum learned quickly not to leave their blankets draped onto the ground, lest they awake during the night to a rat running across their belly. As a rule the slaves hated them, but while Sol couldn't deny their more loathsome attributes, there was something about the little critters that he found fascinating. He watched them when he could, when they weren't aware of his presence, as they sniffed and scurried about. They seemed so curious, always probing into corners and crevasses with their long noses. He loved how sleek and shiny their fur coats were. Like boys are wont to do, he wanted to have one of his own.

Through one of those wonderful twists of childhood luck, his wish was granted one day in a kitchen pantry. After wrestling aside a sack of rice taller than himself, Sol was amazed to find a tiny baby rat huddled in the corner. Unlike every other rat he had ever seen, instead of brown or black this little fellow was white as snow with bright pink eyes. It was also quite young. Sol approached the rat carefully and was happy to find it docile enough to touch and even pick up. He presented it to Oci as Whitey, his new pet. Oci was less than thrilled about the boy's selected companion but she also saw how much it meant to him. It wasn't long before Whitey was a regular guest in the kitchen and barracks.

The living arrangements were simple. Because of the inevitable conflict between a pet rat and living in the women's barracks, Whitey stayed out of sight most of the time. For the most part the rat lived in Sol's shirt, going wherever the boy went as his constant companion. When the barracks or a hallway was relatively empty he would take Whitey out to play. He taught the rat to come to his name and sit back on his haunches for a treat. Despite being born a wild rat, Whitey never bit and he was very clean and tidy, as even wild rats are. In short, he was the perfect pet for a lonely boy.

And now, after two happy years, Whitey wouldn't wake up. Sol had noticed the rat was sleeping a lot more in the last few months and eating less. He had no idea how long rats tended to live and he had found Whitey's age difficult to guess since he was already white. It was something a child wasn't supposed to think about, a pet's mortality, even in a place like the Coliseum where the grim specter of death was always present.

It was still early morning and although many of the slaves were already up and attending to their duties, the barracks were relatively quiet. Sol sat up in his bed, the same one he had been born in, cradling his lifeless pet.

"He was a good friend," Oci said.

Sol startled. He hadn't heard her approach. "The best," he agreed. He struggled against the tears with the pride of a boy but soon lost out to emotion.

Oci joined him on the bed, hugging him to her ample bosom. "It's okay to cry, but not too much. Shouldn't shed too many tears for an animal that lucky."

Sol looked up at her, puzzled. "What do you mean?"

"Whitey had a good life, probably the best one a rat ever had. He always had food and nobody ever tried to trap or poison him. And in the end he passed peacefully in his sleep next to someone he loved and who loved him." She smiled sadly. "We should all be so lucky."

Sol ran his hand lovingly over the rat's soft white fur. "I wish he could stay around forever."

"Now don't say that. Whitey had it good but I don't think any creature would want to stay in this place forever. I certainly don't. Do you?"

He thought about it and then shook his head, more because he knew that's what Oci wanted than because of any certainty on his part. "But we are here forever." It was as much a question as a statement.

There was a long pause. A tear rolled down the cook's plump cheek. "Maybe, maybe not. You never can tell." She wiped the tear away and stood. "Now why don't you say goodbye to your friend and let me take care of him."

Sol stroked the rat's fur a final time. "Goodbye, friend." He felt like there was more to say but those were the only words he had. He handed the rat to Oci who smiled before turning and making her way out of the barracks.

Sol stayed in bed, wondering where rats went when they died.

Sol rubbed his eyes, back in the present. He wasn't sure how long he had sat there but he knew it was long enough; there were things to be done. He tried to stand, feeling pain course through his weary body for the first time since entering the women's barracks. He staggered, leaning heavily on the wall. Almost immediately there was a welcome shoulder to lean on as Korra moved to help him.

"Thanks," he said after she deposited him on the bed.

"Sol, I'm sorry," she started. She had obviously been waiting for an opportunity to speak.

He stopped her with a gentle finger held to her lips. It was an intimate gesture that clearly took her by surprise but she didn't flinch or pull back. He let the finger fall away. "The woman who raised me, my mother in every respect but blood, passed away this night," he explained calmly.

"Oci?" she asked, her own sorrow evident. "Oci's dead?"

Sol was sure he had never mentioned Oci to her, but somehow he wasn't surprised. That the old cook had made an impression on a Spoil, only here a few weeks, filled him with warmth. That's who Oci was. That's how she would live on in the lives of every man or woman to ever come through this place. He nodded. "How did you know her?" he asked, genuinely interested.

"She brought us food. I don't think she was supposed to, but she told us that since she practically raised the guard keeping watch she wasn't too worried. She seemed very kind," she answered with a sad smile. "I'm sorry."

"I am too," Sol admitted, "but I'm glad you were able to meet her. She would have liked you."

They sat quiet for a long moment, each in their own thoughts. Sol looked her over for the first time since he'd entered his cell. She looked different; most notable was the lack of sequins or lace. Instead she sat comfortably in thick wool pants and a top of the same fashion as the fighters wore. Her face looked better, too. No new bruises marred her features and her cheeks, though sunken, seemed less hollow. "You look better," he said, unable to hide the wonder behind the statement. He had seen dozens of women decline before his eyes. Never had he seen one reverse the trend.

"Slink," she answered with an odd smile. "He's been taking care of me. I haven't visited another fighter for almost a week. I don't know why."

Sol shook his head. "I've known that guy for a long time. Now it turns out I don't know him at all." He stood. "I think it's time that changed." Moving to the door he called for the guard, louder than before. When no one answered he called again and then a third time. Finally a blond-haired head poked around the corner. "I need to see Slink!" Sol called to him. The head nodded and then ducked back behind the wall.

While they waited he returned to the bed. He addressed Korra after taking a deep breath, his tone low and serious. "When we spoke before, you said that you had contacts outside of the Coliseum. If you could get word to them, you're confident that these contacts could and would not only hide us but move us, and that they could smuggle us out of the city?"

She grabbed his hands, her face lighting up. "Yes," she almost yelled, "I know it!"

He pulled his hands away from hers. "Don't get too excited. We're a long way from out, but if you're as well connected outside these walls as you claim –"

"Which I am," she interrupted, no less excited.

"Well, there's no one, with the possible exception of Grall, that knows inside these walls better than me. If it's possible to escape, which I'm not sure it is, we've probably got a better shot than anyone."

"And, if you're not sure if escape is possible," she chimed in, smiling, "then you're not sure it's *not* possible."

He returned the smile. It was true. Except for a brief moment in his youth, Sol hadn't spent much time contemplating escape. It had always seemed like an exercise in futility, a waste of time. He had known that even if he made it out of the Coliseum he would be alone and exposed in a world he knew nothing about. Like a fish in a fishbowl, what good does it do to jump out?

He sighed. "Okay, so is it possible?"

Footsteps in the hall interrupted their conversation. Slink tinkered with the lock before letting himself into the cell. Sol stood and the two men, the fighter and the guard, regarded each other eye to eye. For once there were no quick insults, no banter. It was quiet for a long moment before Sol spoke. "Did you take care of her?"

"Yeah, as best I could." Slink's voice cracked, his eyes downcast.

"She thought a lot of you," Sol said. It was something he had never thought he would admit to the guard.

Slink smirked, shaking his head. "She thought a lot of everyone."

Sol nodded. "That young guard, the one with the blond hair."

"Bryant," Slink offered.

"Well, Bryant told me you're the reason I was able to say goodbye." His tone was flat, unreadable.

"I thought you'd wanna –" Slink began, stammering slightly.

Sol interrupted. "And now Korra tells me you've been taking care of her, keeping her from other fighters."

"Well she was 'bout used up an' –"

Sol interrupted again. "Why?"

Slink ran a nervous hand through his greasy hair, glancing at Korra. "No reason, I jus' –"

"Why?" he pushed. He suspected he knew why but he needed to hear it directly from the guard.

"You're my friend," Slink mumbled, shrugging his shoulders. "And with Oci gone, you're 'bout the only one I got," he added softly.

The cell was quiet while Sol contemplated the man before him. Nothing had changed. Slink stood slouching, his ratlike face and disheveled uniform looking as it always did. He was the same insufferable guard he had always known, yet he had just called him friend. The guard had gone out of his way, and not without risk, to give him a chance to say goodbye to a woman they both loved, a woman that had been right about him. She had been right and because of that he had shown the guard mock kindness, more for entertainment than out of any kind of benevolence. "I'm afraid that I haven't been nearly as good a friend to you as you have to me. I'm sorry," Sol said, extending his hand.

Slink glanced at Korra again, obviously embarrassed by the scene. "Don't mention it," he said, shaking Sol's hand for the first time. Regaining a bit of his composure, he gave Sol a wink. "I'll leave you two alone to, uh, reacquaint yourselves."

To the surprise of both the guard and the Spoil, Sol stopped him. "Stay. We have some matters to discuss that I think you should hear," he said, aiming a meaningful look at Korra.

Korra's eyes went wide. "No, he shouldn't."

"We're going to need help," Sol argued. "I've already spoken to Grall –"

Korra's jaw dropped. "You what?" she interrupted.

"And he wouldn't hear a word of it," Sol finished.

"A word a' what?" Slink asked, confused as ever.

Korra brushed the question aside. "I'm sorry, Sol, but you can't tell him," she said with an air of finality.

Sol gave a derisive chuckle. "Can't?" he asked with raised brow. "I hate to burst your bubble, *Lady* Korra, but I need to make one thing very clear: in here, I'm in charge. We will do what I say, when I say it, or we won't do anything at all. Understand? Slink will hear what we have to say. With his leave, of course," he added quickly. Slink nodded with a grin, still uncertain as to what he was being included but enjoying the prospects none the less.

Korra's eyes widened with surprise. She fumed and sputtered angrily for a moment. Sol braced for a tongue-lashing but she regained control, calming enough to regard him with a molten glare. "Okay," she said through clenched teeth, "while we're in here, you're in charge."

Sol noted her careful wording. He could tell she wasn't used to taking orders and he knew that once they were outside, she would demand control. That suited him just fine. At that point he would be out of his element and he definitely was no stranger to taking orders. It made more sense to have a single person calling the shots at one time, anyway. Whatever action they decided to take it would require precise coordination. Even then, there was still a pretty good chance they would fail. If they didn't work together, they didn't stand a chance.

Sol rubbed his temples. "Very well, then. We've got a lot to cover." He motioned for Slink to join Korra sitting on the bed. The guard obliged, though he got a bit closer to Korra than she seemed to prefer. Sol continued after she scooted away, addressing the guard in all seriousness, "What I'm about to tell you I do so as a friend. You may want to include yourself in it, you may not. Whatever your choice, I must ask you, as a friend, not to tell another soul."

Slink nodded warily, clearly unsure about what he had gotten himself into.

Though he wouldn't admit it, Sol was anything but sure of the situation himself. He was willing to believe that he was only now noticing a side of Slink that had been there all along, hidden where Sol had been unwilling to look. And there was little doubt that having a guard on their side, even one as low on the totem pole as Slink, could prove invaluable. Still, if he was misjudging their newly solidified friendship even slightly, telling the guard could prove their downfall. He glanced at Korra, whose expression conveyed her obvious disagreement, and took a deep breath. "We want to escape," he said simply.

The effect was immediate. "Well it's about damn time!" Slink burst.

Korra gawked at the guard. "You've been waiting for this?" she asked with obvious disbelief.

"For far too damn long," Slink confirmed. "I hate this rotten pace." He turned back to Sol with a smile. "When are we leaving?"

Sol couldn't help but return the smile. Despite his initial uncertainty, he was hardly surprised at the guard's reaction. Slink had as much of a reason to hate this place as anyone, if not more. "We don't have time to go over the details so I'll summarize." He told Slink of their previous discussions, Korra's contacts outside of the Coliseum, and their limited timeframe, even going so far as to include Vance's warning about the Empire's assassin, something Korra hadn't yet heard about. As he spoke he watched the guard carefully for any clue that might reveal any misgivings he might have. Enthusiasm was all he found in Slink's reactions, with only one exception.

"We should leave the Frorian," Slink said after Sol finished.

Korra gave a sarcastic chuckle. "Well it's a good thing you don't have any say in the matter."

Sol shot her a look.

"Listen, don't get me wrong. I appreciate everything you've done for me," she addressed the guard. "You've probably saved my life. But this is bigger than any of us. K'nal's going."

Sol shook his head. "I'm sorry, I hate to say it but I agree with Slink. K'nal stays."

Korra sprang to her feet. "What?"

"I don't like it any more than you do," he said. It was the truth. K'nal had proven to be a noble companion and capable fighter, and Sol had nothing but respect for the white giant, but there were other matters to consider. "Let's break this down. What needs to happen for us to get out of here?" He continued before anyone could answer. "We need an avenue out. We need weapons to give us a chance should we need to fight. We need to be together as a group, with weapons, on a path out, so that we can meet up with one of your contacts who can sneak us out of the city. Sound reasonable?"

"Yeah, but –" Korra tried to argue but Sol cut her off.

"Bringing K'nal makes everything more difficult," He continued. "Here we three sit, easy as can be, but figuring out how to arrange for K'nal to join our little party will be some trick. Plus, he's too big. He's too big to fit into a crate to smuggle out. He's too big to hide once we're outside. He's too damn big!" Sol shook his head. "I'm sorry, Korra, I really am."

Instead of yelling at him as Sol had expected, Korra returned calmly to her seat. "I'm sorry, too." Sol nodded, considering the matter settled, ready to continue. "Because if K'nal stays, so do I," she added.

Slink scoffed. "Well that's a fine how do ya do. Maybe we don't need you ta' go, either. Ya ever think a' that?"

"We do need her," Sol corrected, fully aware of the predicament Korra was putting them in. "Without her contacts, we won't stand a chance."

Korra nodded to acknowledge Sol's grasp of the situation. He thought about threatening to call the whole thing off but dismissed the possibility just as quickly. Their feet were firmly set on this path and they would walk it until its end. "Very well, K'nal goes," he conceded, immediately feeling better despite the fact that he had no idea how they would pull it off. He took a seat on the floor, taking a moment to look each of his companions in the eye. He smiled. "So, how do we do it?"

The rest of the night was spent pouring over every idea, big or small, that could possibly lead to their freedom. The time passed quickly while in argument and slowly while in contemplative silence. During several of the latter, Korra drifted off into fitful slumber only to startle awake with a cry after a few moments, much to Slink's amusement. Sol was exhausted but knew that sleep was impossible with his mind racing like it was. After so much time spent denying even the thought of freedom, the chance for the real thing, however slight, was like a feast for his consciousness. His mind had been starving for this night and each idea or possibility that crossed it only added to the hunger.

The others were hungry too; he could see it in their eyes and hear it in their voices. Like any living thing, the primary and overwhelming desire was simply that of self-preservation. To escape afforded their only real chance of survival. But within the trio even this desire varied, not in fearsome intensity but in expectation.

For Korra, Sol figured, even with her risky position within the People's Resistance, she had always expected to live and die free. She had people outside of the Coliseum and big plans she fully intended to complete once they escaped. Slink, on the other hand, Sol doubted that he had ever expected to leave the Coliseum again. He also doubted that he had many friends, if any, to welcome him back. Still, he was of the outside world and he probably had old haunts and favorite diversions to look forward to.

Sol had no plans or expectations. The places he wanted to go and the things he wanted to see were straight out of bedtime stories. The outside was nothing but a collection of tales told by guards and spoils; diversions and nothing more. Only now was he willing to admit to himself that the chance to escape, to survive to see the outside, was solid and real. The newly formed thoughts of freedom were tangible; he could hold them in his mind. Beyond that he was chasing daydreams.

The three conspirators discussed and argued through the night with the morning arriving all too quickly. It was agreed that Slink should update K'nal concerning their plans, a task the guard wasn't exactly thrilled about, and also after some debate that it was best for Slink to take Korra back to the spoils' barracks as usual. The guard had been bending far too many rules for what he was now a part of. They all agreed it would be best, with the exception of continuing to exempt Korra from her responsibilities as a Spoil, for him to keep a low profile by playing by the rules.

They had made some progress, agreeing on a few important issues and even hatching a crude plan. It was a good start for a short night but as he watched Korra leave, Sol knew the single tear rolling down her cheek was one of frustration. He felt it too, although he tried to stay positive. As far as he knew there had never been a successful escape from the Coliseum, but if anyone had a chance he was convinced it was their little group. They had the brains, they had the brawn, and they certainly had the desire.

The dark cloud that hung over the whole affair was what they didn't have: time. Lysik was coming; for all he knew the assassin was already here.

12.

Children ran through the streets toward the Coliseum, anxious to catch a glimpse of the odd spectacle. They pushed their way through the crowd that had gathered around the small enclosure, fascinated by what they saw. A group of men, not much bigger than some of the children, sat and stood in the center of a large cage, warily eyeing the group. They were dressed only in loincloths and had long black hair and tan skin, which was covered in exotic-looking tattoos.

"Straight from the forests of Calampsha!" a large man with a bushy mustache informed the crowd. "Little buggers begged me to bring them to civilization. Said that their tree gods demanded that their fiercest warriors fight in the Coliseum."

"They don't look fierce," a child near the front commented. He was right. The huddled group of diminutive men looked anything but fierce.

"Why, that's because these are gentlemen warriors," the big man explained. "Gentle as a lamb outside of a fight. Here," he said, handing the child a small melon, "why don't you give 'em a snack."

The child looked to his mother who nodded her assent, then held out the melon through the bars of the cage. One of the pygmies rose to his feet and approached the boy. As was the custom of his people, he bent low into an exaggerated bow before taking the melon and returning to the center of the cage to divide it amongst his group. The crowd clapped, enchanted by the little warrior gentleman.

From across the street the assassin watched with a smile on his face. Just as he had hoped, the people were taken by the tiny savages. Things were progressing perfectly.

Another welcome sight approached from down the street: an old man with a long, gray beard and a huge black woman in a large, floppy hat. Waving and nodding to passersby as they approached, the well-known bards scrutinized the pygmy enclosure curiously.

"What's all that about?" the old bard asked after greeting the assassin, nodding toward the crowd.

"Fuel for the fire," Lysik answered cryptically, "and none of your concern."

The old man stroked his whiskers. "Fair enough."

"Where is your young friend?" Lysik asked. "Does he consider himself above answering my summons?"

"Not at all, not at all," the old man responded quickly, obviously looking to placate the dangerous man. "I told him to concentrate on your orders and leave the conversation to the grownups."

Lysik nodded, not convinced in the least. It was far more likely that the old bard had been wise enough not to bring his brash young colleague into a situation where the boy's tongue would get him into serious trouble. The old man's foresight was admirable. "And how are my orders progressing?"

The large woman nodded excitedly, her wide-brimmed hat flopping. "Just wonderful!" she chimed, clearly hoping to please the assassin. "Our fellow bards have concocted some wonderfully creative stories and have been relaying them to the public for almost a week. Things are going wonderfully."

"Wonderful," Lysik sneered, eyeing the overly exuberant woman with disgust. He turned back to the old man who picked up the thread of conversation.

"The stories should work." The old man ticked off the storylines on his bony fingers, "They say the slave's grown impatient with how easy the bouts are and that he's demanded a challenge *worthy of his greatness*. Information's been leaked about his practice of poisoning the tips of his blades and his preference for young male spoils. There's even one rumor going around about the unnatural relationship he has with his Frorian fighting partner." The old man's expression made it look as if he'd just eaten something particularly unpleasant.

Lysik smiled, delighted by the bards' creativity. "And our new hero?"

"Already taken care of," the old bard assured him. "Hand picked him myself. He's skilled enough to be admired but not so skilled that this problem will crop up again. And he's veteran enough that all the new attention the bards are paying to him won't seem too strange. I've even taken the liberty of having a shiny new set of armor made, just so he looks the part."

Lysik nodded, truly impressed. Their visit with the tortured young bard had been more effective than he had expected. Of course, that word had gotten out concerning what eventually became of the young man surely only helped the matter. "Very good," he said, "carry on." Satisfied, he crossed the street toward the pygmy enclosure. With a wave he caught the attention of the large, mustached man who immediately stepped out of the crowd to meet him.

"Was there any problem getting them?"

The handler shook his head. "No problem. All the hunters had to do was drug their water hole. Easy as pie." He chuckled. "Good thing, too. Little buggers are wicked deadly with a blow gun or a spear."

"They will be given bows," Lysik instructed.

The big man frowned. "No good. Little buggers ain't never seen a bow and arrow in their life. Won't have a clue how to use the damn things."

Lysik smiled. "That's the idea."

The handler eyed the assassin. "Well, should I give 'em the bows now so they have some time to practice?"

"They will be given the bows immediately before the bout. There will be no practice or instruction. Do you understand?" He rested a hand on the handle of his always prominently displayed dagger for emphasis.

The handler nodded, understanding but certainly not liking the situation. Of course, he wasn't about to question this particular client. "Yes, Sir," was all he said.

"Good." Lysik turned and walked toward the Coliseum entrance, where a guard stood ready to let the assassin in and holding his trusty suitcase of vials. "Now," he said to himself with a wicked grin, "I have some preparations to make."

Something was wrong.

Sol cast a sideways glance at the stone-faced fellow leading him through the Coliseum tunnels who was one of four heavily-armed soldiers, not Coliseum guards, escorting him to his usual pre-fight holding cell. Not once had he ever walked this path with anyone but Grall. In fact, this was the first time he had ever seen more than a pair of soldiers in the Coliseum at one time, and certainly never below ground. On rare occasions city soldiers would assist with the transfer of particularly notorious prisoners into the Coliseum but that chore always ended at the entrance to the tunnels. As far as he knew, his current escort was a Coliseum first.

The timing was off, too. He hadn't been summoned for a bout this early in the day for years. Veteran fighters always fought late in the day, it was the natural progression of seniority. Saving the best bouts until the afternoon built tension and kept the 'fans in their seats. Normally he wouldn't be making this walk for several hours yet.

So, more accurately, everything was wrong.

"Not your usual duty assignment, eh boys?" Sol tried to fish for a little more information. The butt of a spear shoved into his back was all the response he received. He wasn't surprised. They hadn't answered any of his questions when they showed up at his cell. Conversation was limited to the largest of the four barking an order to fall in and shut up. Not that he really needed any hints to guess what the sudden irregularities meant. There was really only one explanation: today was the day. Lysik had taken control and there was little he could do but play his role. He was trapped.

They reached the holding cell and the soldiers shoved him inside. As usual, K'nal was already there. The giant met his eye with a raised brow, acknowledging the peculiarity of the situation. "We are here early, brother," he said as they shook hands.

Sol nodded, taking his seat across from the Frorian. "Indeed."

"I take it you also missed your usual escort."

Sol continued to nod. "Four city soldiers and not a Coliseum guard to be seen."

"For me as well," K'nal confirmed. "Peculiar."

Sol didn't answer. When he finally spoke his voice was as heavy as his spirits. "Slink told you of my situation, of who pursues me?"

K'nal nodded gravely.

"Then you no doubt understand that as my partner you are bound to the same fate."

K'nal nodded again.

Sol sighed. "I fear our time has come."

"Perhaps." K'nal shrugged.

"Which means that our hope of escape has been for nothing."

K'nal shook his head. "No, brother, hope is never for nothing."

Sol tried to clear the knot from his throat. "K'nal, I'm really sorry that –"

The Frorian stopped him with a raised hand. "Today is not for apologies and I do not want yours."

Sol hung his head. On the one hand, he was grateful not to have to share his feelings. On the other, he was sorry not to be able to take what was likely his last opportunity to speak his mind. He kept quiet, though. He had dragged K'nal into this mess, so the least he could do would be to honor his partner's wishes and drop it.

Silence settled over the cell and neither fighter stirred. It was an oppressive quiet, one that seemed to smother noise in order to perpetuate itself; thick and difficult to break, like wading through syrup. Eventually, Sol raised his head. "Back during the Dybuk fight, when my legs were pinned and you were about to raise your ax, I saw you say something to the monster. What did you say?"

"To the Dybuk?"

"Yeah."

K'nal muttered a guttural string of growls and grunts that Sol recognized as the Frorian's native tongue.

"What does it mean?"

K'nal took a long moment to ponder before speaking. "I think you might call it a tribute," he frowned, shaking his head, "or perhaps an apology. It is difficult to explain."

"Please try."

K'nal's brow creased in contemplation. "There are some battles without victors, only survivors. Battles that should have never been fought. To those that fall it is the custom of my people to offer a prayer that they might know that their lives were not taken without regret. I offered the prayer to the Dybuk as a fellow monster so far from home."

The knot returned to Sol's throat. "Do you miss your home?"

"No," K'nal corrected, "I miss my people. We are what you call nomads. We follow the game that sustains us. All of the tundra is my home and I do miss it. But more, I miss my people. It is they that I fight for." The Frorian paused. "Who do you fight for?"

The question was simple but it hit Sol, cutting through the fog of doubt that had been clouding his mind and triggering a memory he had long since forgotten. He heard Grall's voice echo through time to answer the question. "You're going to go out there and do what you have to do, not because you're fighting for you but because you're fighting for me and for Oci and for everyone else in here. This is your home. You're fighting for your home."

Faces flashed through Sol's mind: Grall's, Oci's, Slink's. He thought of Korra and of the Spoils that had preceded her. He remembered the faces of the women in the barracks lit by dim candlelight after Oci's passing. He recalled the face of a young man as his impaled body slid down the shaft of a spear.

"I fight for all of us," he answered. "Everyone here in the Coliseum, these are my people."

"And what of this killer sent by the Empire? Who does such a man fight for?"

Sol's eyes darkened. "A man like that fights for no one."

K'nal nodded. "Then we may well prevail," he said with conviction.

Sol raised a brow and the Frorian continued, "We must win. We have so much more to lose."

Sol couldn't help but smile. K'nal's logic on the matter was painfully simple, like that of a child's, yet it contained within it a power and strength that couldn't be denied.

"We will win the day," he said. "We will fight for our people and fight for each other and because of that, we will win. And perhaps that will buy us the time we need."

K'nal nodded, satisfied. "Come, brother, I need to meditate upon the coming battle. I am sure you need to do the same."

Sol nodded and once again the cell grew quiet; a fragile quiet, easy to break.

Sol wasn't naive. He knew the assassin's plot would likely spell their doom. He knew that even if it didn't, there would be a next time, and a next, until they were finished. It was as it had always been.

But he also knew, as K'nal had reminded him, that he had a say. He was the one on the floor, his floor, and he would not submit just because the Empire had deemed it so. This was his home, these were his people, and he would fight to the death for them both.

Sol knelt in the dusty dark facing a familiar large wooden door. Behind him stood K'nal, fingering the edge of his large double-headed battle ax. Both fighters had been equipped with their favorite weapons, which was a pleasant surprise to be sure. A long broadsword rested in its sheath, strapped diagonally across Sol's back with a matching short sword on his hip. Being properly armed furthered the confidence of the warriors, bestowing a feeling that whatever awaited them on the other side of the massive wooden door, they had a chance. Both fighters tensed as the chains whined and *clinked* and the door began to rise. A moment later they ran out into the suns and heat of the Coliseum floor.

They were met by a large quantity of shrubs and small trees filling the Coliseum floor. The potted plants weren't more than chest height on Sol and not dense enough to block the spectators' view from the stands but they still limited visibility for the fighters on the floor. It was an odd scene to be sure but it wasn't the faux forest that was most unnerving; they had dealt with props such as these before. It was the unusual murmur emanating from the stands that troubled the fighters. The sound was low and angry and the scattered applause that accompanied it only seemed to highlight its hostility. Eventually, the overpowered applause faded away all together.

They stopped at the edge of the fake forest. Through the foliage Sol could just see the closing of a door along the side wall of the Coliseum. What or who it had been opened for remained out of sight.

Sol craned his neck but couldn't see over the vegetation. "Can you see what they are?" he asked K'nal, hoping the Frorian's height might give him an advantage.

K'nal shook his head. "Not well. But there many and they are small and fast."

An image of a fur-ball-like creature flashed through Sol's mind but he quickly dismissed it. A repeat performance wouldn't hold the crowd's attention. Whatever they faced it would be something new.

"Is there a strategy to their movements?"

The Frorian shrugged. "If there is, I cannot see it. Did you notice that the plants have been anchored?"

Sol nodded. Every pot and crate that held a plant had been anchored to the Coliseum floor with thick cords of wire. There would be no eliminating the obstacles by simply knocking the plants over.

"In we go, then." Sol motioned K'nal forward and the fighters waded into the shrubbery. Even given the gravity of the situation, Sol enjoyed the sensation of entering a forest, fake or not. It wasn't his first prop forest but the others had been composed entirely of painted wooden cut-outs of trees, so this forest was the most authentic he had ever been in. He hadn't spent much time around real plants and he loved how they smelled and the way their leaves trembled in the slight breeze. The novelty of the experience strengthened his conviction that they had to succeed today. There were simply far too many things in life left to experience.

Out of the corner of his eye he saw a diminutive figure dart from one tree to another to their left. He blinked in amazement, unsure of his own eyes. He turned to get a better look and another darted across the path in front of them.

"They're tiny people," he told K'nal, shocked at what he'd seen.

"I did not know humans came even smaller," K'nal pondered.

"Neither did I," he admitted.

Another pygmy darted across a clearing to their right. They stood no taller than Sol's hip and were practically naked, their only clothing consisting of a small loincloth. What they lacked in draping they made up for in body paint. Every one of them was decorated with a dazzling array of colors and designs. Each one carried appropriately small bows and quivers full of appropriately small arrows.

"They're trying to surround us," Sol announced. Though the vegetation wasn't dense the pygmies were taking full advantage of it, timing their movements and using their diminutive size to their full advantage.

"They have surrounded us," K'nal corrected, moving close to Sol.

The sound of small feet scurrying across the sand behind them confirmed the giant's claim. The pygmies were all around them. As he backed toward K'nal, Sol wondered why they hadn't already attacked. Something didn't feel right. The pygmies had the advantage of position, numbers, and terrain. What were they waiting for?

"We need to get out of these trees," Sol announced. They tried one direction, then another. Every turn they made was greeted by the scamper of little feet, always in the periphery and just out of reach.

"What now?" the Frorian asked.

Sol looked around, trying to see their situation from a new angle. The little devils darting around them had every advantage, all because of a bunch of damned potted plants. *The plants!*

"If we can't get out of the forest, we'll bring it down around us. Use your ax and I'll cover you."

K'nal did as he was told and put the giant war ax to work cutting a clearing in the faux forest. The sudden aggressive action seemed to be just what the pygmies were waiting for. From every direction, miniature archers emerged from the foliage, sending a swarm of arrows flying at the two fighters. Sol hit the dirt with K'nal right beside him. Much to his surprise, not even one arrow came close; several did not even leave their respective archer's bows successfully.

The crowd groaned.

Rather than relief, their opponent's apparent incompetence left Sol with a feeling of dread. He looked up to see two more pygmies fire arrows well off-target, noting the expressions of fear on their small faces.

Sol tried to push his anxiety aside as both gladiators jumped to their feet, intending to use the poorly aimed volleys to their advantage. K'nal charged toward a group of three archers who were fumbling with their bows with Sol right on his heels. One archer managed to nock an arrow and fire wildly at the oncoming pair but neither fighter even needed to duck to dodge the misfired projectile.

In that moment, Sol's whole world came to a crawl. Everything slowed, everything fell silent. They charged in slow motion toward the fumbling pygmies and all he could see was the fear etched on their faces. His stomach sunk. It was all wrong, he realized. Something clicked.

"STOP!" Sol cried. It was too late. His world had returned to normal speed and that speed was too fast. K'nal swung his ax in a deadly arc aimed to fell the group of three with a single stroke. The little men were defenseless.

Were it anyone else, the three would have died, but for the first time in his considerable experience on the Coliseum floor, Sol used his speed and agility to save his opponents life; three lives, in fact. With the handle of his long broadsword in one hand and the blade flat against the other, he dove to intercept the powerful swing. K'nal's ax caught the flat of his blade and shattered it, driving the head of the ax into Sol's breastplate and hurling the fighter into the pygmies, knocking the whole party into a tangled heap.

"Brother!" K'nal waded into the pile and picked Sol up by his breastplate. The metal's shiny surface was badly dented from the deflected blow, but still whole and un-pierced. The three pygmies, also whole and un-pierced, scurried away.

Sol gasped for breath, wishing the Frorian would handle him a little more gently.

"Are you insane?" K'nal questioned, obviously convinced he already knew the answer.

Sol slapped at the tree trunk of an arm holding him off the ground. "Put me down!" K'nal dropped him and Sol fell to his hands and knees, coughing and gasping for breath.

"Why did you do that?" K'nal asked, his back to Sol. The Frorian stood poised with his ax positioned defensively against the onslaught he expected at any moment.

Still on his hands and knees, Sol looked around. They were still surrounded by small painted figures, who mostly still held their bows at the ready, but their positioning was purely defensive and their expressions of confusion and fear assured Sol that he had done the right thing. He struggled to his feet, undoing the straps that held his chest and back plate on, allowing them to fall to the floor.

"I will not yield," K'nal growled over his shoulder.

Sol moved to the white giant, laying a hand on his arm. "Look at them, brother. I don't want to say any more prayers for battles that shouldn't have been fought. These people aren't our enemy."

K'nal looked around at the faces of the small humans around him. He lowered his ax. "Very well, brother. But what now?"

"Now what, indeed?" Sol mumbled as he looked to the stands.

The crowd seemed as uncertain as the fighters. A general grumble issued from the stands but for the most part the mood was curious. Spectators craned their necks, anxious to see how the unusual standoff would end. Sol suspected that it was only the novelty of the situation that held their attention and kept frustration in the lack of action at bay. If the mob loved one thing it was something new.

Sol nudged the Frorian. "They want novelty? We'll give 'em novelty. Follow my lead." He stepped to the center of the pygmy ring, holding his weapons out from his sides; his shattered broadsword in one hand and his short sword in the other. A nervous hush fell over the crowd as everyone concentrated on the odd spectacle. Sol turned in a slow circle, searching the faces of the small painted figures and stopping when he found what he guessed to be the leader of the band, an older looking pygmy flanked by several particularly stern-faced fellows.

A step toward the elder pygmy confirmed his suspicion as the flanking figures took an aggressive step forward with their bows raised threateningly. Sol stopped, never taking his eyes from the leader's, and gave a slight bow. The elder pygmy seemed to understand and issued a command in a string of quick syllables, his entourage obediently falling behind him. Sol continued his approach with slow and measured steps, his expression blank. He knew that even with their limited skill with the bows they had been given, any misunderstanding at this range would end with him resembling a pin-cushion. A half a dozen paces from the leader he stopped.

He held the weapons out in front of him with slow, deliberate movements. With his eyes still locked with the leader's he shook his head, his face twisting in an exaggerated frown. In one overly dramatic motion, he dropped the weapons, letting them clatter to the ground.

The elder tribesmen regarded the large man for a long moment. He gave a single nod and then glanced at K'nal, still standing where Sol had left him.

Sol gave the Frorian a nod. The white giant approached and reluctantly copied Sol's routine, dropping his ax on the growing pile of weapons. The pygmy leader nodded again and issued a series of commands to his people. One by one, the pygmies left the ring and joined their leader, pausing only to drop their bow and quiver on the pile.

The sight pained Sol. He supposed he should be glad that his plan was working but every bow that fell on the pile only helped seal the pygmies' fate. Had he not intervened, they would have died at his and his partner's hands, but refusing to fight would assure them their doom. Sol grieved for them, witnessing the dignity the little people displayed and the loyalty they showed to their leader.

An abrupt end to the silence brought him back to the moment. Grumbles of understanding rippled across the stands as the mob collectively recognized that, novelty or not, their morning's entertainment was in jeopardy.

Though it was rare, it wasn't unheard of for a fighter or even a group of fighters to refuse to fight. The situation always resolved itself quickly enough when the fighters or creatures still willing to battle put a quick end to those who weren't. If worst came to worst, the fighters scheduled for the following bout could always be sent out to put an end to any objections. Through some twist of fate, today's unusual match had been scheduled as the last one before the lunch break, a time normally reserved for executions, so there were no other fighters waiting in the wings ready to resolve the situation. The grumble in the stands began to escalate into a roar.

K'nal nudged Sol, nervously eyeing the stands. "Again, brother, what now?"

Sol's mind raced. If there were no spare fighters available to take care of them then the task of cutting them down would likely fall to the guards.

As if on cue, the doors to the Coliseum floor rattled open to admit a large cadre of guards, the four grim-faced city soldiers leading their slow, steady advance. The crowd's pitch increased, welcoming the sight.

The crowd!

Sol grabbed K'nal's arm. "Boost me up onto your shoulders."

The Frorian eyed him suspiciously. "What are you going to do?"

"I'm not sure. Just hurry!"

Without another word, K'nal picked him up by the waist and tossed him up so that he was standing precariously on the giant's broad shoulders.

"People!" Sol shouted. "Listen to me! Everyone!" he yelled but to no avail. The crowd was too loud.

K'nal, catching on to Sol's plan, provided the solution. Without warning, the Frorian cut loose with an ear-splitting roar that sent Sol teetering on his perch and the pygmies backpedaling. Even the guards and soldiers halted their slow march. The effect was immediate, with nearly every spectator holding his or her tongue in order to see what had prompted such a mighty bellow.

Sol froze; the spotlight was firmly on him now. He had spent a good part of his life in front of these stands. He was used to having thousands of eyes follow his every move, but never in his wildest dreams had he thought of actually speaking to the mob. After a moment of tense silence K'nal gave a quick shrug of his shoulders, the motion nearly throwing Sol to the ground but managing to persuade the nervous fighter to find his voice.

"People!" he bellowed. "I am Sol, Son of the Coliseum! You know me! You have watched me grow up, watched me fight, watched me kill!" The crowd cheered at that. Sol continued quickly, trying to build momentum.

"You have shared this place with me. This is my home! You are my family!" The sentiment elicited more cheering, louder even than before. Sol glanced nervously at the guards, who had resumed their advance.

"Brothers and sisters, I tire of killing!" The crowd's tone changed, shifting to more of a grumble. He was losing them. He couldn't make this about him. It had to be about them.

"Like you, I am tired of being controlled, tired of living my life under the heel of their boot!" Instead of pointing at the approaching guards he directed the crowd's attention high in the stands, toward the luxury boxes. The grumbling continued but its tone shifted. It grew angrier, more urgent.

"I am tired of being a pawn!" The clamor in the stands increased further still. The advancing guards stopped again, eyeing the angry thousands with trepidation.

Sol continued, trusting the clamor of the crowd to carry his words. "I will be tired no more! It ends today!" he cried, his fist elevated dramatically into the air. "Fight! Fight with me! Fight for your freedom!"

The crowd erupted, the groans and grumbles mixing with fanatic cheers to form a single overwhelming growl, as if a great beast had suddenly awoken from a long slumber. Scuffles broke out in the stands and trash rained down onto the floor. Up in the luxury boxes, hired bodyguards barricaded the doors lest the rabble outside take out their frustration on the gentry within.

Sol hopped off K'nal's shoulders.

"Interesting course of action," the Frorian said.

Sol shrugged and turned to the guards and soldiers that had closed on their little group. The pygmies were now huddled around Sol and K'nal.

"Kill them!" the leader of the soldiers ordered, indicating the whole group.

Before the others could even draw their swords, a veteran Coliseum guard brought them to a halt. "Belay that order!" he said, eyeing the angry crowd. "We cut them down here and we all die. Take them inside and we'll deal with them later."

The soldier, none too pleased with interference from a mere guard, started to argue but then appeared to think better of it as the chaos of the stands began to pour onto the floor, with spectators climbing down the walls and heading their way. "Fine. You take the pygmies and we'll handle these two," he agreed. The soldiers corralled the two fighters at spear-point and led them away before the guards could issue any argument.

K'nal caught Sol's eye as they were herded off the floor. He shared the white giant's unease. True, they had defeated the assassin's plans and managed to make it off the floor alive, but this wasn't a normal victory. They had spoken out against the Empire with its most ruthless killer waiting for them in the wings.

There was no doubt that repercussions would come swiftly.

13.

The Coliseum was in chaos.

What had started as a few isolated scuffles above ground had now spread into a full-fledged riot. True to the nature of the Coliseum, the spectators-turned-fighters assaulted one another with utter abandon. Those who weren't fighting were either part of the mad scramble toward the exits or being trampled by it. The few city soldiers whose normal duty included little more than ushering people to their seats were nowhere to be seen, having fled early in the turmoil. In several places the violence in the stands had poured out onto the Coliseum floor. Guards emerged from the tunnels meaning to help, but without a plan or direction they merely added to the mayhem.

Things weren't much better below ground. Guards and slaves raced every which way, no one with a clear idea of where they should be. One of the main corridors was completely blocked by a raging battle between guards and a group of criminals scheduled to be executed later in the day. To top everything off, somehow in the pandemonium a jungle cat had gotten loose from its cage and was now tearing through the tunnels, followed closely by a pack of handlers with nets.

Sol and K'nal were prodded by the grim-faced soldiers through the turmoil. The constant pokes from the spears at their backs left little doubt of their fate should they decide to try and use the chaos to their advantage.

"Where to?" Sol heard one of the soldiers shout over the noise. The answer was lost in the clamor but it became clear soon enough as they made their way back to their usual holding cell.

A sudden panic seized Sol as the cell door opened. He knew their actions had derailed the assassin's well-laid plans. There was little chance any more attempts would be made before the public. This time Lysik would come for them, for him. He couldn't just sit in this cell and await his fate.

He turned on the soldiers, knocking spearheads aside with a roar. He was on the nearest one quick as a flash, landing a punch across his jaw with one hand and reaching for the soldier's sheathed short sword with the other. He had no plan and no real hope for escape; he fought only to stay out of that cell. The short sword flashed out of the scabbard, spelling certain doom for the dazed soldier. Sol raised the weapon to strike and then hesitated. Even in the grip of panic the implications of what he was about to do bore into him. Not once, in all his years in the Coliseum, had he raised a hand against anyone off the Coliseum floor. Even during his time in the Pit, where men regularly fought and killed for their survival, he had managed to avoid conflict. Now he stood, sword raised, ready to kill.

Two things saved the guard: Sol's hesitation and K'nal's massive arms. During Sol's brief moment of indecision the giant reached out, lifted Sol clean off the ground and carried him into the cell, the sword clanking harmlessly aside. Not willing to question their good fortune, the soldiers slammed the door shut after them.

Sol struggled against the Frorian's hold, furious at the interference. K'nal let go once the door closed behind them, sending Sol toppling to the floor. He was up in an instant, pressing aggressively at the giant.

"You had no right to interfere!" he insisted, swinging a fist at the Frorian for emphasis.

The small cell allowed little room to dodge but K'nal showed no sign of concern. "The guards were nearly on you. You would have died," he stated calmly.

Sol groaned. "I would have died fighting. At least I could have gone down my way."

"Was that really your way?"

The question hit too close to his feelings during the earlier moment of hesitation. He silently cursed the giant's perceptiveness. "Dead is dead. Because of you I won't even have a say in how I go. I'm trapped."

K'nal nodded. "Now you know."

"Know what?"

"How it feels for the rest of us to be in this place."

The truth of K'nal's words hit Sol full force. Physical detention was nothing new. What drove him to panic was the loss of control. His fate had never been entirely his own but within the confines of the Coliseum he had always retained some modicum of power over his day-to-day life. That control had been stolen away and it frightened Sol like no foe or beast ever had. He recognized that fear. It was the same fear he saw in the eyes of every Spoil he had ever invited into his cell.

Sol's shoulders slumped. "I'm sorry," he said.

K'nal nodded and moved to his usual bench. Sol joined him, the two fighters back in their customary spots sitting across from one another, knees touching in the little cell.

"So what now?"

K'nal leaned over and laid a hand on Sol's leg. "Now, brother, we wait."

Lysik was furious.

If he had been allowed to handle the situation his own way from the start, without all this nonsense for the benefit of the public, the slave would be dead and the problem would be on its way to being forgotten. But Shadon didn't want to solve a problem; he wanted to take down a hero. In an ironic twist, by validating the slave's status as a folk hero, the Empire had granted him far more power than otherwise would have been possible.

In all of the assassin's careful planning, all the time and effort he had invested to assure that today went as it should, he had never even considered the possibility that the fighter wouldn't fight. It was ludicrous. All the effort he had put in! Bards had been working overtime for days spreading word of the *true* nature of Sol, the supposed hero of the Coliseum. Then there was the slave's replacement. The hero-to-be had been scheduled to appear after the mid-day executions. With his unknown-to-him poison-tipped blades, he had been assured a valiant victory. Now he wouldn't even see the Coliseum floor.

Much to his chagrin, that was exactly where Lysik now found himself. As chance would have it, one of the first scuffles broke out in the section he had been sitting in. As the violence spread, he was left with the choice of battling his way up to an exit or dropping down the wall onto the Coliseum floor. His choice of the latter had started a flood of people picking the floor over the stands.

Now he waded through the same chaos he had hoped to avoid. Dagger in hand, he cut a skilled path through the unarmed rabble, making his way toward a door he had seen several guards emerge from. Most of the mob gave him a wide berth after witnessing the fates of the first few that didn't. Perhaps it was this show of respect that marked him or perhaps it was Lysik's fine attire, so obviously out of place in the underprivileged of the lower stands. Regardless, a pair stepped into Lysik's path, clearly singling him out for trouble. The huge men were undoubtedly brothers, most likely twins, one differing from the other only by a well-aged scar cutting diagonally across his bearded face. The easy way they carried themselves in the chaos told of countless bar room brawls, but had they known the danger they now chose they might not have treaded so lightly.

"Where do you think your goin', pretty boy?" the scarred brute asked mockingly as they circled in on their prey.

The other laughed at his brother's clever joke. "Yeah, pretty boy, where you goin'?"

"Charming," Lysik mumbled to himself. In an instant the dagger left his hand and was planted deeply into the latter's eye. The big man stopped mid-laugh and dropped to the ground, dead. His brother followed him down with a mournful howl, cradling his fallen sibling.

"Coward!" the brute blurted at Lysik. "You didn't give him a chance!"

Lysik smiled at the naivety of the accusation. He unsheathed a second dagger concealed in his high top boot. "True," he agreed, "but what chance did the fool really have?"

Outraged, the growling brute charged in full force. The swift assassin deftly sidestepped the charge, ducking below the outstretched arms of his assailant, while at the same time drawing the razor sharp dagger across the man's unprotected abdomen. It was over in the blink of an eye. Lysik stood as the brute stumbled past, clutching his belly in a vain attempt to keep his bowels on the inside of his skin.

Lysik moved to the first fallen brother, retrieving his other dagger before wiping both blades clean on the man's shirt. "Sorry I can't stay and play but I'm in a bit of a hurry." No answer came from his other attacker, now on his knees staring blankly at the pile of his entrails lying on the sand. Lysik continued once again toward the door, this time completely unopposed.

He ducked inside the tunnel entrance. "You're with me," he informed the first guard he came across. Together they weaved their way through the increasingly empty tunnels, most of the chaos having already erupted out onto the Coliseum floor. They reached the room in which Lysik had stored his trusty bag of bottles. "Go get the slave Sol and bring him here," he instructed the guard.

"And the Frorian?"

"Damn the Frorian!" Lysik growled. The guard turned to scurry away but Lysik stopped him. "On second thought, bring Sol to me, then kill the Frorian."

The guard nodded and departed, leaving Lysik to prep. He had assumed he would have all the time in the world to deal with the fighter and he so hated working under pressure. For a moment he considered just killing the fighter outright. He didn't need any information. There was no substantive reward to be gained from drawing it out.

But no. He did need something from the fighter, the slave that had caused so much trouble and foiled his well laid plans. He needed more than just the slave's death.

He needed the wretch to want to die.

Sol and K'nal crouched as best they could in the cramped holding cell, their attention trained on the cell door. They both agreed that the assassin would act quickly in the wake of his failure and that their best chance lay in never actually meeting the man. They would try to use the mayhem of the moment to fight their way out and after that, who knew? All they could do was focus on the next step and the next task involved overwhelming however many armed soldiers and guards that came to call.

Rattling keys warned the two fighters of their escort's approach. The scuff of feet on the stone floor hinted at guard's shoes rather than the rhythmic stomp of a soldier's boots. And by some stroke of luck it sounded as if there was only one. Sol caught K'nal's eye and the Frorian nodded, signaling his readiness. The key clicked into the lock, the door swung inward, and both fighters pounced. K'nal reached for the guard but to the giant's surprise Sol threw a shoulder into him, sending both fighters tumbling against the wall.

"Well hello to you, too," Grall chuckled, looking down at them from the open doorway.

Sol looked up at the old guard and smiled sheepishly. Had he and K'nal been in opposite positions instead of chuckling, Grall would have likely already had his neck snapped by powerful furry arms.

The smile quickly faded, though, as Sol recalled what errand Grall must be on.

Grall noticed the change. "Relax," he said, "I'm here of my own accord."

K'nal sat up, rubbing his side. "Then perhaps given the circumstances you should have announced yourself."

"And miss that little show?" Grall chuckled. "Not likely."

"So why are you here?" Sol stood and brushed himself off.

"The assassin's here in the Coliseum. What do you plan to do about it?"

Sol gestured to K'nal. "We were planning to take out the guard and head up top."

Grall scoffed. "Then what? There's only one exit and you know it. Even if you made it into the streets you'd be surrounded. This place is on lockdown. All the fighters and slaves are locked in their rooms and most of the guards are up top helping with the riot. The tunnels are practically deserted." The old guard grinned mischievously. "I say you stick to the plan."

"What plan?" K'nal asked, still sitting on the ground.

"The escape plan Slink's been bragging about for the last week."

"What?" Sol barked. "That snitch ratted us out!"

Grall held up a hand. "Calm down. He did no such thing."

"But you said–"

Grall interrupted. "Slink's never been very good at keeping a secret. I could see that he was stewing about something and sure enough he started dropping hints after a few days. 'Can't wait to get a decent meal' and 'I'm not gonna miss seeing your ugly mug' and the like. The other guards stopped paying attention to Slink years ago but after our talk I put two and two together and figured it out. I told Slink that you wanted me to have the basics of the plan to cover your backs." The guard shrugged.

"And he spilled." Sol frowned. "Remind me to smack that guy the next time I see him. So you think we have a chance?"

Grall shrugged again. "It's hard to say. I figure you'll either end up out and free, or dead. I've heard of this Lysik fella. I think I'd take either of those options rather than meet up with him." The guard clapped. "So why are you two still here? You've got a plan, the door's open, get going!"

"We are not armed," K'nal pointed out.

"Like I said, the tunnels are deserted," Grall reiterated. "There's no one to fight."

Sol shook his head. "It's no good. We need Korra. Without her it's hopeless once we're outside."

"Don't you worry about her," Grall assured. "You go and I'll bring her to you."

Sol's eyes widened. "Then you're coming with us!"

Grall put a hand on Sol's shoulder. "No, son, I'm not."

"You're still following procedure."

The old guard chuckled. "I'm not sure letting fighters out of their cell during a lockdown with the intent to escape counts as following procedure."

"He has a point," K'nal agreed.

Sol could only nod. "So he does. Are you sure I can't change your mind?"

"I am."

Sol nodded sadly. "Well then, I guess we had better be on our way."

K'nal stood and Grall lead the way down the hall. He had been right; the place was emptier than Sol had ever seen it. When they reached the main corridor he brought the group to a stop. "This is where we part ways," he told the fighters.

K'nal complained, "I would still feel better if I had a weapon."

Sol ignored him. "It won't take long before someone notices we're missing," he told Grall. "Hurry and get Korra and we'll meet you downstairs."

"Yes, Sir," the guard teased, already on his way.

Sol wanted to tell Grall to be careful. He wanted to thank him and tell him how much his help meant. He wanted to convince him to come with them. Instead he just watched the guard move down the corridor and eventually round a corner.

He turned to K'nal. "Follow me and stick to the shadows."

Whether the tunnels seemed empty or not, Sol knew that somewhere in this Coliseum the assassin was hunting for them. He could feel malevolent eyes peering from the shadows, searching them out, and he knew that if they didn't move fast, those eyes would find them.

"They're gone."

Sitting next to a bed already rigged with restraints, Lysik looked up from arranging his bottles on a nearby table. "What?" he asked. The statement was so ludicrous he assumed he must have misheard the guard.

"I–I'm sorry," the guard stammered. "I found the soldiers that lead them off the floor and then I went to the holding cell they said they took the fighters to, but they weren't there," the guard spoke very quickly. "I thought maybe I went to the wrong cell so I searched the other holding cells and they weren't in any of them. So then I went to find the soldiers again and–"

Lysik stopped him with a raised hand. "Were the cells intact?"

"What?"

"Were any of the damn doors broken down?" he shouted.

"No, Sir."

Lysik closed his eyes and rubbed his temples.

"I'm sorry, Sir, but what does that mean?" the guard asked after a moment.

"It means," Lysik explained impatiently, "that somebody let them out."

"But, Sir, that's impossible."

Lysik stood and drew his dagger. "Yet that seems to be exactly what has happened." He motioned to the bed. "Now I suggest you go find them before I invite you to take their place."

Eyes wide, the guard started to stammer another apology.

"NOW!" Lysik roared.

The guard scampered out the door, calling for his compatriots to aid him in his search.

Lysik started out on the guard's heels but then turned back. Rifling through his collection he picked out two small bottles: a red one and a green one. He tucked one into his right pocket and the other into his left, then took off after the guard.

The tunnels were all but empty as Lysik tried to catch up with the search for the missing fighters. Attempting to follow the sound of racing feet, he turned down one hall only to find it dead-ended into a storage area. Retracing his steps proved a failure when he ended up at an unfamiliar stairwell. He cursed his luck. It was only his second time in the labyrinth that was the Coliseum's underbelly, a place it took guards months to learn their way around. Even though he was loath to do so, he was just about to start calling for help when a guard rounded a corner, heading for the stairwell.

Lysik pointed at the ratty looking fellow. "You there! Take me to see your Captain."

The guard looked over his shoulder, obviously unsure if he was the one being addressed. "What?" he asked, after he confirmed there was nobody behind him.

"Your Captain, you cretin," Lysik explained. "I need to see him now."

The guard chuckled. "An' jus' who the 'ell do you think you are to be ordering me about?"

The assassin resisted the urge to kill the man where he stood and begrudgingly explained. "My name is Lysik. I'm a representative of the Empire."

Understanding flashed upon the guard's face and he swallowed hard. "Of course, Sir, follow me, Sir."

Relieved to be on the hunt again, he fell in behind the guard. "Do you know if they've been found?"

"Who's that, Sir?"

"By the Spirits, man! Two fighters have escaped, didn't you know?" He held off further chastising, having noticed an odd expression settle on the guard's face. Hurt? Anger? It was hard to say.

"Which two?" the guard asked in a quiet voice.

"The fighter Sol and the Frorian," Lysik replied, watching the guard closely. His attentiveness allowed him to just avoid colliding with the guard when he suddenly stopped dead in his tracks, the color drained from his face. Lysik grabbed the man by his collar and shoved him against the wall, the tip of his dagger pressed against the underside of his chin.

"What do you know?" the assassin hissed.

"Nothin'!"

"I don't believe you." Blood trickled down the guard's neck from the tip of the dagger, the sharp blade keeping the guard pinned against the wall while Lysik reached into his pocket and produced a small red vial. "Open your mouth," he commanded.

The guard clamped his mouth shut, eyeing the bottle and pressing his lips tightly together.

Lysik twisted the dagger just slightly, eliciting a grunt of pain. "Open your mouth or I'll cut off your lips and save you the trouble."

The guard's eyes darted around frantically, sweat beading on his brow. Another twist of the dagger coaxed him to open his jaws, his eyes clenched tightly shut. With one deft move the assassin popped the cork off the vial and poured its contents into the guard's awaiting mouth. Lysik stepped back, sheathing his blade.

The guard immediately broke for the empty passageway.

"That poison won't let you get far!" Lysik called after him.

The guard stopped and slowly turned back. "Poison?"

Lysik held up the red vial. "One of the nastier concoctions I've ever come across. It's a delightful combination of very deadly and also very slow acting. And as I'm sure you're already noticing, those who take it invariably wish it wasn't the latter." The guard, who was indeed already doubled over and holding his stomach, didn't respond. "There's only one antidote and it's almost impossible to find," Lysik chimed, letting the potion work for a long moment to provide proper motivation before adding casually, "and I happen to have a bottle of it right here." He held up the small green vial from his other pocket.

The guard stumbled back toward him, still hunched over, desperately reaching for the green vial. "Please," he moaned.

"Ah, ah, ah," Lysik chided playfully, "perhaps if you play your part well enough we can work something out, but first you need to tell me what you know. Let's start with your name."

The guard slumped against the wall. "Veritalious," he answered, fighting back tears.

Lysik chuckled. "Veri–what?"

"Slink," he moaned. "They call me Slink."

"Appropriate. Do you know who let the fighters out of their cell?"

Slink shook his head, still hunched over and holding his stomach.

"Do you know where they are?"

More head shaking.

Lysik sighed in frustration. "Well, then do you know where they'll go?"

This time Slink nodded.

"Good," Lysik said, truly pleased with how the situation was evolving, "and where is that?"

"Please, gimme the bottle and I'll tell ya whatever ya want," Slink begged.

The assassin shook his head. He spoke slowly, enunciating each word like one would for a particularly dimwitted child. "This is the last time you will be reminded. You will do whatever I say and maybe, if you perform well enough, I'll give you the bottle. If I have to tell you again I will pour the antidote out onto the ground." He paused letting the threat sink in before continuing, resuming normal speech again, "Now, where are they going?"

"They're tryin' ta' escape," Slink half-spoke, half-moaned. "They're plannin' ta' hide in empty crates and smuggle themselves out. They'll go ta' the big storage room."

Lysik nodded, satisfied with the plan. "And you know this because you were supposed to go with them," he guessed, curious about the guard's involvement.

Slink nodded, his eyes downcast.

Lysik laughed. "The hapless guard gets conned into helping a pair of slaves escape, only to be broken-hearted when he's betrayed and left behind. How pathetic."

Slink moaned and slumped forward further.

"You will lead me to them," Lysik commanded.

Slink staggered to his feet and lurched his way down the empty passages toward the largest of the Coliseum's storage rooms, with the assassin following close behind. As they traversed the tunnels Lysik collected any stray guards they came across so that they had added six to their hunting party by the time they reached the door to the storage room. They stopped outside of the storeroom door and Slink reached for the doorknob.

"Not so fast," Lysik said, stopping him. "We have no way of knowing if they're armed."

"What if they are?" scoffed one of the guards. "There are eight of us."

Lysik flashed an angry look at the guard. "If you contradict me again, there will only be seven." The truth of it was that he didn't intend on underestimating the formidable pair again. Of course, that didn't mean he was about to share his concerns with a group of lowly guards. He turned to Slink who had dropped to his knees and was currently hunched over in a ball. "You're sure they're in here?"

The miserable figure nodded, looking up and extending his hand.

"Not yet," Lysik said. "You have one more task to perform." He pushed his way past the huddled guard and opened the door a crack, just enough to peek in. The storeroom was large and square with no side rooms or cubbies and only the single entrance. Empty wooden boxes were piled up to the ceiling, filling most of the room. He saw no movement and heard no sounds. As he had hoped, the fugitives had probably already stowed themselves away. With how crowded the room was with wooden crates, it hardly mattered.

He kicked Slink to get his attention. "Bring me lanterns, full ones." He motioned to the oil lamps hanging from crude brackets on the wall.

Slink slowly complied, moaning and groaning the whole time. The other guards watched the scene with puzzled expressions but wisely kept any questions to themselves. Slink returned with two recently filled lanterns, the light from their dusty glass globes bringing harsh contrast to his contorted features. When he tried to hand the lanterns to the assassin, Lysik made no move to take them.

"Those are for you," Lysik explained. He opened the door for the guard. "Toss them in. Burn the crates and your friends to the ground."

Slink stared at the open doorway, lamps in hand, an expression of horror etched on his pale face.

"You can't do that! There are supplies in there!" the same guard that had spoken up earlier protested.

The dagger was out of its sheath and leaving Lysik's hand before his companions could even start to nod their assent, its blade finding its mark in the hollow of the unfortunate guard's throat. He fell to his hands and knees, reaching up and pulling out the dagger. Blood spilled onto the stone floor and sprayed onto the other guards' legs. The guard quickly collapsed, gurgling and spitting blood with his last breaths.

The other guards, temporarily paralyzed by the gruesome scene, went for their weapons.

"Don't be foolish," Lysik warned, another dagger already in hand and cocked back to throw. "I gave him fair warning. Now I give you the same."

The guards eyed the dagger and exchanged doubtful looks. One by one they sheathed their weapons. The assassin sheathed the dagger and turned his focus back to Slink who stood exactly as he had before the interruption, beads of sweat running down his face.

"They betrayed you," the assassin reminded. "They were going to leave without you. You don't owe them anything. And besides," Lysik held up the antidote, smiling as the guard's eyes shifted between the open door and the little green bottle, "you don't have a choice."

Slink blinked several times and then slowly nodded.

"Be ready. They may try for this door," Lysik warned the guards.

Slink heaved the first of the lanterns through the doorway into the dimly-lit storeroom, tossing the second in toward the other side of the room before slamming the door shut behind him. He held out his hand again, his other holding his stomach. He moaned pitifully.

Lysik laughed and tossed him the bottle. "Here, you've earned it."

Slink caught it and immediately pulled out the stopper, tipping his head back and inverting the bottle over his open mouth. Nothing came out. He shook the bottle but still not a drop trickled out. The bottle was empty.

Lysik laughed loudly, the sound echoing off the stone walls.

"You said…" Slink stammered, his eyes wide with shock.

"*You said! You said!*" the assassin mocked, a wide smile on his face. "You consorted with slaves. You planned to desert your post and help them escape. You really think I would let you walk away from that? You are a fool."

Slink staggered backward against the wall, holding his stomach. Without another word he turned and staggered slowly down the hall, the sound of Lysik's laughter following him into the dark.

The assassin watched him go, still laughing. The serum he had given Slink would wear off soon enough. Even the dimwitted guard would probably figure out the supposed "poison" only induced severe stomach cramps and not death. He wasn't worried about the rat at the moment, he wasn't going anywhere. Later he would track him down and finish him off in the manner best befitting a traitor.

For now he was far more concerned about what was going on behind the storeroom door. He cracked the door open slightly, the bright flicker and steady roar of the growing flames spilling out into the hall. The dry, aged wood of the crates popped and cracked as the fire consumed them.

But that wasn't the sound the assassin was listening for. Lysik closed his eyes and listened for the sound of victory. He listened for the slaves' screams.

K'nal crinkled his nose and craned his face toward the ceiling. "Do you smell smoke?"

"I can't smell anything over this stench," Sol said in a nasally voice, pinching his nose shut.

The Frorian tested the air again and then nodded. "I definitely smell smoke. Something is burning."

"It's not just a torch or a lantern?" Sol asked, not sharing his companion's concern.

K'nal shook his head. "It is wood smoke and it is getting stronger."

Sol shrugged. "We've got bigger things to worry about. Help me move this crate," he said, pointing to a large wooden box.

K'nal took one more sniff of the air, his sensitive nose warning him again that the smoke smell was increasing, then did as he was asked.

Still the assassin waited.

Fire roared through the cavernous store room, transforming it into a raging furnace that consumed the stacks of dry wooden crates with terrifying speed and intensity. Only minutes had passed and already the flames were starting to die down. And still Lysik hadn't heard what he was waiting for. No man or beast died quietly when taken by fire, a fact he knew from experience. The Frorian had quieted the Coliseum crowd with a single bellow earlier, leaving little doubt that his cries of agony would be heard even over the roar of the flames. Something was wrong.

Lysik crouched down low to get out of the smoke and ordered two of the guards into the storeroom to investigate. The men hesitated, eyeing the clouds of black smoke billowing out the door. Lysik said nothing but simply reached for his dagger. The guards got the idea and plunged into the room, covering their faces as best as they could with their sleeves. Long moments passed. Just as the assassin was about to send in another pair, the first two guards stumbled out, hacking and choking as they collapsed on the floor of the passageway.

"S'no good," one of them managed to choke out. "Room's been completely torched."

The second guard nodded, continuing the report as the first fell into a violent fit of coughing. "True enough. Anything in there's either burned or choked to death."

The assassin nodded and the group of guards made to disband away from the smoke, thinking their mission complete.

Lysik had a different idea. "Spread out," he ordered. "Search the tunnels, every cell and passageway. Tear the place apart."

"But Slink said they were in that storeroom," a confused guard chimed.

Lysik reached for his dagger but settled for the cringes the unsheathed weapon inspired, not being sure which of the group had questioned his order. "The rat obviously lied," he explained. "Search everywhere. Bring me that guard, bring me those slaves, and do your fucking job!" he shouted. The guards dispersed, nearly trampling each other in their efforts to distance themselves from the volatile assassin.

Lysik stayed put, fuming. He wasn't concerned that his prey might escape. Where could they go? They were trapped somewhere in the Coliseum's bowels. No, what troubled him was the continued insolence this whole situation seemed determined to heap upon him.

He would not be embarrassed by these slaves again. "They will pay," he promised to himself, "they will pay dearly."

"The smoke seems to be dissipating. That is good." K'nal announced as they added another crate to the stack.

"Wonderful," Sol panted, not really caring one way or the other. He stepped back to survey the makeshift barrier they had constructed. The pile of crates and debris significantly narrowed the wide walkway that ran along the underground Trash River. Situated between the huge room's single ramped entrance and the massive metal grate that spanned the river's exit tunnel, Sol figured the barricade would provide a little cover if the situation called for a fight.

Just as importantly, it had given them something to occupy themselves with while waiting for Grall and Korra. Unfortunately, they were out of things to pile up. "I think that's about as good as it's gonna get," he told K'nal.

The two fighters hunkered down behind the barrier to wait. It had been a long time since Sol had been down to the Trash River. Over the years he had found that many of the things that frightened him as a child held little fear for him as an adult; the Trash River was an exception. Its putrid black water swirled and frothed before pouring into the rock on the far side of the metal grate, resulting in a constant and horrid sucking sound that echoed around the cavernous room. Sol eyed the rickety metal trellis that spanned the walkway over the water and anchored to the rock wall on the far side of the river. Many a time he had been tethered to that same trellis, always seemingly ready to collapse, and sent into the Trash River to cut out some rotten debris caught up on the grate. Dangling inches from the sucking black hole, gagging from the smell, crying from fright, he had never suspected that the Trash River might one day end up being his only hope of freedom.

Crouched next to a giant Frorian, an assassin of the Empire hot on his heels, and getting ready to jump into the black hole that had been the terror of his youth. It seemed there were a good many things he hadn't anticipated.

14.

"Where are we going?" Korra asked the old guard again.

Grall had taken her from her cell without fanfare or explanation. Since she had been expecting Slink to fetch her for a visit with Sol, she had assumed the old guard was just taking his place. Korra was familiar enough with the tunnels by now, however, to know they weren't headed toward Sol's cell.

"Downstairs," Grall answered.

"Slink hasn't been giving me to other fighters, only Sol," Korra risked, afraid that her regular duties as a Spoil had resumed.

"Yes, I'm well aware of your little arrangement," Grall replied, his expression blank.

The two walked in silence for a short while, Korra eyeing the old guard nervously. She knew that Sol had faith in Grall but as far as she was concerned he was still a guard and not to be trusted.

"Are we going to see Sol?" she asked, probing for more information.

Grall halted, regarding her with a frown. "I have worked for his whole life keep any nonsensical thoughts of escape out of that boy's head. And then you came along." The statement hung in the air accusingly.

"And what right did you have to steal hope from a child?" Korra bristled.

Grall shook his head. "You don't know what it's like living your whole life in this place. Hope like that, impossible hope, it can drive a man to madness."

"You're a hypocrite," Korra accused.

"What?"

"You're telling me that you've lasted as long as you have without any hope of something better on the outside?" she scoffed. "You're either a hypocrite or a liar."

Grall gaped at the petite female slave who had just called him, Captain of the Guard, a liar. She visibly tensed, expecting to be slapped.

Instead, Grall laughed. "I can see why he likes you. You're right. Partially, anyway. I wasn't wrong to keep Sol's hopes grounded in the Coliseum," he insisted, "you just haven't been here long enough. You can't understand." He continued quickly, cutting her protest short, "But I do have hope." He resumed walking. "I have a son."

Korra fell into step beside him. "On the outside?"

He nodded. "Same age as Sol. In two years I'll retire and go find him. That's why I'm staying behind."

Her eyes widened. "Staying behind? Is that where you're taking me? Are we escaping?"

Grall nodded again. "It's now or never. I wish there was another way but there's no time. The gears are turning and it's either the Trash River or the assassin now." The old guard didn't sound overly hopeful.

"It'll work," Korra assured him. "That river has to come up somewhere right?"

Grall answered with a doubtful look.

"It'll work," she said again, undeterred. "How long has it been? Since you've seen your son?"

"Almost sixteen years." He glanced at Korra, noting her troubled expression. "What?"

"But what about Sol?"

"He doesn't know," Grall admitted.

"You never told him?"

The old guard shook his head. "Part of keeping him grounded."

"Well, all right, but that's not what I meant. You have no idea how your son feels about you or whether he even wants to see you. He might not even be alive."

Grall halted suddenly, his hand cocked back to slap her. He stopped, breathing hard, struggling to calm himself. "You have no right," he growled.

"But Sol," she continued relentlessly, "he trusts you. He looks up to you. You're like a father to him."

"I am not his father!" Grall yelled. "And he is not my son."

Korra said nothing, the quiet of the tunnels amplified after Grall's outburst. He resumed his march, faster this time, and she fell into step behind him.

She couldn't know the pain her words caused the old guard. His whole life in the Coliseum had been structured, propped up and strengthened with the anticipation of one day being happily reunited with his son. Everything he did was shaped by this hope. He battled constantly to keep out the very doubts that Korra had so easily deduced. He had to. His decision had been made long ago; to push aside worry and distraction and commit himself to one day finding his boy. It was what kept him going.

But what about Sol? Her protest echoed in his head. He had tried to maintain a sense of distance with the slave, some objectivity, like a good guard should. There were always ways to rationalize the liberties that were allowed. Having never been outside of the Coliseum, Sol's situation was different. He had to have someone there for him or else he would go mad. Sol needed him.

Of course, Grall knew as he marched through the tunnels, as he had known for the past twenty-two years, that there was much more to it than that. How could he forsake one of his boys for the other? Were the ties of blood stronger than the last two decades? Even now, as he put all his future hopes at risk in a crazy attempt to help Sol escape, he battled with these questions.

So distracted was he that he didn't hear the quiet footsteps approaching them from an adjoining passageway and very nearly collided with the guard that had intersected their path.

"Sorry, Sir," the guard stammered.

Grall dismissed the apology with a gesture, far more concerned with the guard's current path. There was only one room down this particular corridor: the one that housed the Trash River. The entrance to the room was about a hundred feet around the next bend.

"Where are you headed?"

The guard shrugged, "Just continuing the search." He cast a confused look over Grall's shoulder. "What's with the Spoil? I thought we were on lockdown."

Grall glanced back over his shoulder at Korra, who was trying her best to look inconspicuous, before turning to level a stern gaze at the guard. "I've already searched the room below. It's empty, continue your search elsewhere," he ordered. He grabbed Korra by the arm and started to brush by the guard.

"You didn't answer his question." a voice pointed out from the intersecting corridor. A second figure stepped into the lamplight from the shadows behind the guard. "What is that slave doing out of her cell?"

The assassin needed no introduction; both Grall and Korra knew who the finely dressed figure searching the bowels of the Coliseum must be. Korra's knees weakened, only Grall's tight grip keeping her upright.

"She was servicing a fighter when the lockdown was announced," Grall explained smoothly. "I was just taking her back to her cell."

"Aren't the fighters housed several levels above us?" the assassin asked suspiciously.

"I was taking a shortcut," Grall answered, eyeing the guard, who would no doubt know this to be a lie. The poor fellow only stared at the ground, looking like he wanted nothing to do with the conversation.

"I see," Lysik rested a hand on the hilt of his dagger, "and you don't think your time would be better spent searching for the escaped fighters like all guards were commanded to do?"

"Of course, Sir. Let me drop this one off and I'll get right back to it." Grall started to pull Korra back up the path they had just come. They would have to wait for the assassin to move on before continuing down to the Trash River. He could only hope that Lysik would continue his search in a higher level.

"Stop," Lysik commanded.

The pair halted and Grall turned around, noting that the assassin was not looking at him but at Korra.

"Turn around," Lysik commanded, addressing the Spoil. Korra slowly complied with her head bowed and her long hair masking her features. The assassin reached a hand to her face, lifting her chin. She flinched out of his grasp. Next he grabbed her hair, roughly jerking her head back and exposing her face to the lamplight.

"I have seen this face before," he announced, smiling.

Korra's eyes widened.

"You, my dear, have just made my day." He patted her on the cheek. "Delivering you to Shadon might just make up for the rest of this mess."

"You," he said, pointing at the guard still standing at the entrance to the intersecting corridors, "take this slave up to my room up top."

"I can take her," Grall offered, recognizing that the situation was quickly slipping from his grasp.

"No, you will accompany me down to the lower level."

"But I just said it's already been searched," Grall objected.

"And I don't believe you," the assassin sneered. "You'll have to prove it to me."

The guard glanced nervously between Grall and Lysik, now standing eye-to-eye. Korra stood frozen next to Grall with her eyes wide. Nobody moved. Suddenly Korra cried out, diving for a knife tucked into Grall's wide belt.

The old guard's reaction was automatic. With practiced ease born of thwarting dozens of similar attempts over his long career, Grall turned her up the corridor, pinned her against the wall, and twisted the knife safely from her grip.

"Please," she begged, sobbing. "I can't let him take me."

Lysik chuckled. "So predictable." He nodded to Grall, "Pretty quick for an old man. I may have underestimated you." He took several stepped down the passageway.

Grall didn't hear him. His attention was focused on the weapon he had wrestled from Korra. He stared at the small carving knife, its wooden handle polished smooth from so many hours of use. Sol's most precious possession; he had taken it away as punishment for hoping. He rubbed a callous thumb over its carefully sharpened blade and knew that the time for a decision had come. There was no way around it. The Spoil was to be led away, and then he and the assassin would go down to that room and they would find Sol. A choice had to be made.

He released his hold on Korra and she turned to face him, her tear streaked expression hard and bitter. "For your son?" she asked.

"For my boy," he answered with a sad smile.

He stepped aside and the guard moved to take Korra back up the passageway, obviously relieved to be out of the company of the assassin who was, at the moment, squinting down the dimly-lit corridor, his hooked nose giving him every appearance of a hawk closing in on his prey. The guard shoved Korra, sending her stumbling up the ramped tunnel. She glared back over her shoulder at Grall.

It was the glare that let her see what the guard didn't: the hilt of Grall's short sword smashing down on the back of his head. The guard toppled forward, unconscious. Grall spun on his heels, his blade slicing wildly in front of him and just barely deflecting the dagger thrown at his back. The dagger clattered away behind them.

"You're a fool," Lysik sneered, his second dagger already in hand.

Grall readied himself but the assassin hung back. "I'm curious what you intend to do now," Lysik mocked. "Fight your way out and live happily ever after with your little family of slaves?"

Grall didn't answer. Neither did he take his eyes of the assassin as he reached behind him, holding Sol's carving knife out to Korra, who had just finished wrestling the sword out from underneath the unconscious guard. "Give this to Sol," he said. "Tell him I'm sorry for ever taking it."

She took the blade, positioning herself behind the old guard.

Grall scowled at the assassin. "You're down a blade," he pointed out. "Let us pass and you can blame it on the guard. There's no one here to know the difference."

Lysik scoffed. "Where's the fun in that?" He casually flipped the dagger into the air, easily catching the spinning handle on its descent. "I'm in no hurry."

"We are," Korra mumbled just loud enough for Grall to hear. She was right; it was only a matter of time until another guard decided to search this particular stretch of tunnels. The last thing they needed was company.

Grall took a deep breath and moved in.

The assassin met him halfway, taking a wide swipe at Grall's belly. The old guard parried the attack and went onto the offensive, but Lysik effortlessly dodged several wide swings of his sword. The two separated and Lysik fell back a step. Grall pushed in. Again they met, again no hits were scored, and again Lysik fell back a step.

Grall had spent most of his life in these tunnels. He was better armed and with the downward slope of the corridor he had the higher ground. Despite these advantages, the old guard knew he was in trouble. Years of working with some of the best fighters in the Empire had bestowed him with the uncanny ability to accurately judge the merit of a combatant. Lysik's parries came too easily, deflecting his attacks with little exertion or effort. He on the other hand was already breathing hard, sweat beading on his brow. Even though he was slowly gaining ground he knew he would not get the better of the assassin. He was being toyed with.

Grall glanced back at Korra. Catching her eye, he inclined his head slightly down the tunnel. She nodded just as subtlety and crouched onto the balls of her feet.

The exchange didn't go unnoticed. The assassin rushed in dagger first, just as Grall had expected. Catching his wrist, the old guard turned him up the passageway and pinned him against the wall, just as he had done to Korra moments earlier.

"Now!" he yelled.

Korra sprang, rushing to squeeze past the tangled pair.

Unfortunately for them both, Lysik was far stronger than Korra. With a well-aimed elbow across the face he broke the old guard's nose and the blow sent Grall staggering back into Korra. No longer pinned, the assassin dropped into a spinning crouch, his blade lashing out wickedly into Korra's thigh as she stumbled past, sending her sprawling onto the tunnel floor. Adjusting the grip on his dagger, Lysik pounced with his dagger raised high, poised to finish the Spoil in a single thrust.

Luckily for Korra, it wasn't Grall's first broken nose.

The old guard grabbed Lysik's raised arm, ignoring the blood streaming down his face, and put all of his considerable bulk behind the effort of swinging the assassin through the air back up the corridor. Lysik somersaulted neatly onto his feet and spun around, a big smile on his face and his second dagger in hand, his roll having ended right beside his discarded weapon.

Grall wiped a sleeve across his face, grimacing more at the sight of the assassin once again fully armed than the pain of the broken nose. Making matters worse, the unconscious guard was no longer unconscious. Grall caught only a glimpse of the man's back as he scurried up the passageway, calling out for his fellow guards with every step.

They were officially out of time.

Sol stopped pacing, unsure of what he was seeing.

The two gladiators had spent most of the last half hour crouched in silence behind their makeshift barricade, their proximity to the constant sucking sound of the Trash River's outflow making conversation difficult. Eventually the inaction had started to grate on Sol and he had settled into walking back and forth between the barricade and the river's edge. Now he abandoned the pacing to sprint to the aid of the armed figure that had half-crawled, half-hopped into the cavernous room.

"K'nal!" he called out. The Frorian was already on his feet after having noticed Sol's sudden action.

They both reached her about the same time and Korra collapsed into K'nal's arms. Sol immediately moved to her leg, using his hand to put pressure on the wound. The cut was deep and bleeding badly. He quickly tore off both of his sleeves and began to bandage the wound.

"Where's Grall?" he asked as he worked.

"Back up the tunnel," Korra groaned, her face contorted with pain. "He's with the assassin."

Sol finished the makeshift bandage and the flow of blood stemmed. The dressing would help but the wound would need stitches to heal properly and there would be no walking on it for some time.

"Take her. Take your chances with the river." Sol told K'nal. "I have to go back for Grall." He had already explained where in the river the grate didn't reach the ground. At this point the Frorian knew as much about their escape path as he did.

He expected Korra to object, to want to leave the guard behind. Instead she handed him the guard's short sword. "We stand a better chance against that river together. Go get Grall, we'll wait for you."

K'nal nodded his agreement and Sol took the sword, turning and sprinting up the corridor. Almost immediately the noise of the sucking water was replaced with the sound of battle. He rounded the bend in the tunnel to find Grall and the assassin trading attacks and parries at a furious pace. The old guard was hardly recognizable. A gash on each cheek had been added to his broken nose and his shirt was bloodstained from a long diagonal gash across his chest. Despite his wounds, or perhaps because of them, the old guard fought fiercely, pushing the action at every opportunity.

The assassin remained untouched.

Glancing up between parries, Lysik smiled at Sol's approach. "I was afraid you weren't going to make it!" he called out jovially over the ring of steel.

Grall glanced back over his shoulder, his eyes meeting Sol's and his determined expression turning to one of shock. "No!" he cried out. "Go! Get out of –"

His protests came to an abrupt end, his eyes widening, his jaw going slack.

Sol skidded to a halt, the breath stolen from his lungs.

Lysik smiled over Grall's shoulder, his daggers buried deeply into the old guard's ribs. Slowly, ever so slowly, he lowered Grall off his blades onto the dusty floor. "I waited for you," he explained to Sol, casually wiping the blades on Grall's pant leg. "I was starting to think you were going to hide down there all day. But you never disappoint, do you?"

Sol didn't answer, didn't move. Somewhere deep within a voice compelled him to rush forward and defend Grall's final moments. He could see the old guard shake as he labored for breaths that wouldn't come. The voice cried for action, for revenge, but Sol couldn't move. All he could do was stare at the dying figure at the assassin's feet.

"Come now," Lysik chided. "Are you all out of grand speeches? A eulogy to remember your friends, perhaps?" He poked Grall with the toe of his boot and chuckled. "Or are you waiting for me to kill off the rest of them? Two down, three to go."

Coming up through his haze Sol grasped only a portion of the assassin's taunt. "Two?"

"Two guards," Lysik said. "After I'm finish with you I'll find the other two slaves' hiding place and take care of them. Slowly," he added with a wink.

Sol's stomach clenched at what he was hearing. Was Slink dead, too? Had they failed so miserably that they would all perish without even attempting freedom?

Even as this question clawed at him there was something else. Something the assassin had said tickled at the back of Sol's mind. It took a long moment before he figured it out. Twice the assassin had mentioned hiding and he certainly seemed in no great hurry to get down below. That could only mean that he considered his prey trapped.

Lysik didn't know about the Trash River.

That meant Sol could run. He could turn and flee right now, leaving this terrible scene behind. Lysik probably wouldn't even give chase; the assassin though he had nowhere to go. He could grab K'nal and Korra and jump in the river. Lysik wouldn't realize his mistake until they were gone.

But again that voice inside him cried out.

Killing was something that was part of Sol's life, part of his very existence in the Coliseum. Dozens, if not hundreds, of men had fallen to his blades. He was a killer because he had to be. He had no choice. Not once, in all those kills, had he genuinely wanted to destroy the enemy that had been provided for him.

He wanted to kill now.

"You." Sol's eyes blazed with hatred as he addressed his first true enemy.

Lysik's smile widened.

"You," Sol repeated, taking a slow deliberate step toward the assassin, "have invaded my home."

Lysik laughed, holding his ground. "Your home? You have no home, slave!"

"You have hurt my family," Sol continued, barely hearing the sustained taunts.

"What family? That fat old guard?" Lysik again toed the now motionless body, this time with force.

Sol winced on the inside but his expression betrayed only hate. "You are a sick and evil person." Sol halted his approach mere paces from the waiting assassin. "And now, you will die."

"So be it," Lysik said simply before charging. The assassin lunged in and put his daggers to work, thrusting one high and one low.

Sol spun under the high dagger, turning the low dagger to the side before using the momentum of his spin to slice in low on the assassin's hip.

Lysik was ready, blocking the attack with one dagger only to thrust in high at Sol's throat with the other.

The maneuver was quick but Sol was quicker. He dodged nimbly to the side of the assassin's dagger and swung his sword high, scoring a hit on Lysik's forearm.

Both fighters fell back.

"Not bad," Lysik said, no longer smiling. "For a slave."

Lysik charged in again, this time feinting low before arcing his blades high. Sol stepped in close, expecting the maneuver and locking up both daggers with the pommel of his sword and thrusting a well-aimed knee into Lysik's groin. The assassin hunched over only to have Sol plant a roundhouse across his face, sending him sprawling to the floor.

At the same moment as Lysik fell, four armed guards rounded the bend of the tunnel from above. Seeing the assassin on his hands and knees the guards charged in, giving Sol, whose focus had been locked on Lysik, no time to react. They quickly overwhelmed him, one blade knocking his sword clattering to the ground while another thrust into his shoulder. He cried out, his rage blinding him to the pain, but they were already upon him, pummeling his head and body with the hilts of their swords. Sol fought back as best he could but the blows were coming too fast. Stars danced before his eyes and he could feel the sweet dark of unconsciousness closing in around him.

"Enough!"

The guards obeyed the assassin's command, falling back to leave Sol in a crumpled bloody heap on the floor. They retreated up the tunnel a few paces behind Lysik, who was once again on his feet, but had blood running down his face from a wicked gash below his right eye. "On your feet," he hissed.

Sol shook his head, trying to clear the cobwebs from behind his eyes. He wanted to get up, knew he had to get up, but his feet and his brain seemed to have stopped talking. The fact that there were two fuzzy Lysiks scowling down at him didn't help anything. Eventually, he managed to get his legs under him, standing and shaking his head once again.

"Pick it up," Lysik ordered, pointing to the sword.

Sol did as he was told, retrieving his weapon and then falling immediately on the defensive, the assassin having granted him no time to recover. Lysik rushed in and the two met again, the action much the same as before except that now it was Sol taking the majority of the punishment. Try as he might, his wounded shoulder just wouldn't respond as it should, to say nothing of the stars still dancing on the periphery of his vision. This time when Lysik came in low he barely managed to block the initial attack, the clumsy parry stealing none of the assassin's momentum and allowing Lysik a brief opening at Sol's torso. Sol cringed as Lysik's dagger raked across his ribs.

The hit left Sol reeling, not as much from the pain as from the realization that came with it. However brief the opening, his side had been completely exposed. Had the assassin wanted to he could have finished the fight with a single thrust. Just as he had done with Grall, now the assassin was toying with him.

The opportunity for reflection was brief. Lysik lunged in again, putting Sol on the defensive. The pain from the gash across his ribs had cleared his head a little and he managed to parry a series of attacks before the assassin gained the advantage, clubbing the hilt of a dagger into Sol's temple. The guards standing behind Lysik cheered as Sol hit the ground.

Again the stars danced on the edge of Sol's vision, mocking the futility of his efforts. He clenched his eyes shut, opening them again to find that he had fallen mere paces away from the motionless old guard. Grall didn't appear peaceful in death; the assassin's handiwork was all too visible. The sight of his mentor lying dead on the floor sobered Sol considerably. He knew there were four armed guards ready to pounce should the assassin fall but at this point that hardly concerned him. All that mattered was that Lysik never again see daylight.

He picked himself off the tunnel floor and turned to face Lysik, spitting a mouthful of blood on the floor. "Let's finish this."

This time it was Sol's turn to go onto the offensive. With a growl he lunged at the assassin, using the momentum of the Lysik's parry to carry him into a spin, his sword angling ominously at his opponent's neck. The speedy assassin managed to block this, too, but the force of the attack necessitated both blades to halt the short sword, leaving Lysik momentarily defenseless. That was all Sol needed to step in and land a wicked uppercut to Lysik's gut. Sol grunted in satisfaction as he felt the snap of a breaking short rib.

Lysik lashed out wildly with the sudden pain, forcing Sol into a momentary retreat. Immediately he stepped back in, using the assassin's uncoordinated defense to his advantage. With a quick flourish he forced the swinging daggers high, changing his course and thrusting in low to score a hit on Lysik's thigh. The assassin fell back, eyes wide with surprise at the sudden swing in the fight's momentum.

This time when Lysik attacked it was clear there would be no more toying. The speed of his attacks doubled and the blows were aimed to kill. Sol adjusted his own tactics as best he could but shs shoulder, which continued to weaken, made the pace of action difficult to maintain. Step after step he fell back, unable to mount any offensive in the face of the rapid assault. He knew that if he was to have any chance he would have to act soon; he simply couldn't keep this up. But even as he was pushed back, he recognized that it was the fury of the assassin's attacks that might be his salvation. Lysik had traded speed for variability. Every series of attacks was the same, repeated in rapid succession. That meant that every opening in the assassin's defenses, too brief to take advantage of independently, could be anticipated. If he was quick enough, he might be able to strike.

Lysik's constant assault left him little choice. Sol bided his time, waiting for the series of attacks to repeat. When it did he took his chance, extending himself in a necessarily awkward thrust at the assassin's midsection. The blade hit but the window had been too brief and the assassin too fast. The sword cut into Lysik's side, scoring a grizzly but not fatal wound.

Had Lysik continued his attack, judging the hit for what it was and not overreacting, Sol would have been finished. Instead the assassin batted the blade away, knocking the sword from Sol's weakened grip and losing one of his own blades in the process. Recognizing the opportunity, Sol grabbed the wrist of the hand holding the remaining dagger and forced it against the tunnel wall with all his might. The two grappled for position, Sol slamming the assassin's dagger hand against the wall over and over. Finally the dagger flew free, Sol kicking it away down the tunnel and through the entrance of the Trash River room.

Keeping his grip on Lysik's wrist, Sol threw his hips toward the assassin and spun, hurling Lysik over his shoulder. The assassin hit the ground with a loud *thwack*, his head bouncing sickly off the stone floor. Sol was on him in an instant; his hands found the assassin's throat, intent on squeezing the life from him. Despite being stunned from the fall, Lysik still managed to put up a fight, punching at the gash across Sol's ribs and gouging at the wound on his shoulder.

It mattered not at all. Sol held and squeezed, his eyes locked on the assassin's. He knew the guards, charging in to aid the assassin, were almost upon him. All he could hope was that he would stay conscious long enough to finish the job. A cry arose as they closed in, their swords raised.

But it wasn't their swords that caught Sol's attention. It was the cry. There was something very familiar about it.

Then they were on him, not with their blades or even their fists as he had expected, but crashing and tumbling bodily on top of him in an angry heap. The impact knocked Lysik's throat from his grip.

"No!" Sol screamed, punching and kicking with the last of his strength to get his hands back on the assassin. A pair of hands tried to pull him away from the pile and he swatted them away.

"Well there's a fine how do ya do," complained a familiar voice.

"Slink!" Sol exclaimed, extracting himself from the pile and rising clumsily to his feet with the guards help.

"Who'd ya expect?" Slink asked, pulling him along toward the Trash River room.

Sol silently chastised himself for believing the assassin. It must have been Slink's cry that he had heard. The guard had come to his aid, barreling into his comrades from behind.

"We gotta hurry!" Slink rushed him into the room. On the river's edge Korra leaned on K'nal, motioning for them to hustle.

Sol stole a glance over his shoulder and saw the assassin had extracted himself from the pile and was in pursuit with a couple of the guards in tow. They were only a dozen paces behind and closing. It was going to be close.

The race was decided by inches. Sol felt a hand grasp at his shirt from behind just as he and Slink barreled into their friends, knocking them into the river's churning black water. The cold of the water threatened to steal the air from his lungs as they swirled in a tangled mess deeper into the darkness. Whether the chase was over or not, he couldn't tell. All he could do now, all any of them could do, was swim for their lives.

Swim for their lives and for their freedom.

15.

Three guards strained against the rope but still it would not budge.

"Pull, you lazy rats!" Lysik barked, growing more impatient by the second. The first guard he'd thrown in after the slaves never so much as resurfaced after entering the black water. He had been in the act of tossing in a second when another guard suggested a rope. So tethered, the second guard had submerged just as quickly as the first and now, after several long minutes, seemed to be stuck in his underwater tomb.

"Enough, leave him!" Lysik ordered.

The trio ignored him, still heaving on the line, presumably not willing to abandon another comrade to the underground river. A pair of guards standing off to the side, not having enough length on the rope to join the pulling, eyed each other nervously.

The assassin drew both of his daggers. "Drop that rope or you're going in after him."

Several angry glances later the guards reluctantly complied. They released their grip in unison and the line zipped away, disappearing into the churning river.

"Let's go," one announced to the others. The trio moved to join the pair as they moved toward the room's exit. A howl of pain stopped all five; a dagger was buried in the foot of the guard that had spoken.

"We're not done here," Lysik growled, his second blade at the ready.

The injured guard leaned down and pulled the dagger from his foot with a muffled yelp. "Yes, Sir," he said through gritted teeth, "we are." With that he chucked the blade, sending it spinning through the air in a high, lazy arc over Lysik's head directly into the Trash River.

Lysik gaped at the spot where his prized dagger had disappeared beneath the flowing water, furious to the point of speechlessness. He pivoted, his other dagger raised, ready to avenge its mate. Just before the blade left his hand, somehow Lysik reconsidered his actions despite his rage. Standing before him were five veteran guards, grim-faced and armed to the teeth. Individually, they wouldn't pose a problem, but if they rushed him as a group, especially down a blade, he could be in serious trouble.

"We'd rather die fighting you than go in that river." The injured guard seemed to have read Lysik's thoughts.

The assassin lowered his blade. "The slaves that went into that river are dead. You saw them drown with your own eyes."

All the guards nodded, clearly believing with all their hearts that no one could survive the black water.

"Go," Lysik dismissed the group and then turned to contemplate the water.

"They're dead." he told the empty room, the guards having already made their hasty retreat.

He believed it, almost.

Minutes passed and still he stared at the river. The constant sound of the sucking black water echoed off the room's cavernous stone walls. He shivered, his injuries hurting all the worse for the cold. The ribs would take weeks to heal properly and the gash in his thigh was deep enough that he might walk with a limp the rest of his days. More than these, he begrudged the scar he would carry after stitching up the gash under his eye, a constant visual reminder of his failure in handling the slave.

Finally, he shrugged and turned to leave, dejected but willing to accept that his mission was over. He had killed the bard and the slave; that was the gist of what had been expected of him.

"I did my job," he said to himself, not believing for a minute that Shadon would agree.

Lysik sighed. He would have to go back to Fort City. Making his report to the General and managing to keep his hide might prove to be the most difficult part of this whole mess.

Sol was dead; he was sure of it.

His entire existence was cold and dark; darkness so black as if to have never known light. There was no up or down, no sense of time. All he could do was tumble blindly through the void he now found himself in.

Many times he had wondered, back when he was alive, if there really was an afterlife, some final destination determined by one's deeds, where he would end up. He had always tried to be good, to mind Oci and Grall and treat his spoils with respect. If there was an afterlife, he had hoped that maybe he would earn his way into a good one.

But he had also killed. Regardless of the reason or the circumstances he had been forced into, he had killed so many. According to his sources, scared, half-naked women with their own end in sight, killing was a sure way to end up in a far less pleasant hereafter.

Tumbling through the cold darkness, Sol figured the bad of his life must have outweighed the good. This certainly wasn't heaven so it must be hell. The Spoils had been wrong, though. There was no fire.

Or was there? He could feel his lungs burning, though he certainly saw no flames and smelled no smoke. Something deep within him told him to swim up through the void, whatever direction up was. He tried to comply but he was tumbling so quickly that up wouldn't stay up and any effort to reach it was wasted. The fire in his lungs was close to bursting and he had a fleeting thought of how odd it was to feel as if you were going to die when you were already dead.

Suddenly, instead of tumbling through the void the void was tumbling and rushing by him; he had hit something. So numb was every part of him that he couldn't tell what it was and frankly he didn't care. He clung to the thing, a tree limb perhaps, as it lifted him from the void.

Sol hit the ground hard, coughing and spitting up fetid water. His lungs still burned and it was no less dark, neither was it any warmer. In fact, it seemed even more frigid, but alive he must be. How else could he feel so awful and so happy at the same time?

Hands found him in the dark, slapping his back. The coughing eventually lessened only to be replaced by vomiting as his body tried to purge itself of the tainted water of the Trash River.

"Sorry," he mumbled to the hands after the convulsions stopped.

"Don't worry, I did the same thing." It was Korra. She pulled him away from the mess and began to remove his wet clothes.

Sol tried to reason through what was happening but his mind seemed to have slowed to a crawl. All he could comprehend was how cold he was. He didn't protest when after having been stripped, Korra had him lay down on a pile of something that felt like crispy dry leaves. Neither could he muster any surprise when she, also naked, laid down with him, wrapping her body around his.

How long they laid like that, naked and cold, Sol couldn't tell. Eventually, their combined body warmth thawed his mind enough that he was able to form a few coherent thoughts.

"Where are we?" he asked through chattering teeth.

Korra was shaking almost as bad as he was. "In a cave," she said.

"Where's K'nal?" He rubbed his hands over her back, hoping the friction would warm them both.

"He's off looking for Slink."

"Looking?" The cave was completely devoid of light. He couldn't imagine *looking* for anything.

He felt Korra nod her head against his bare chest. "He can see, somehow. He said something about winter in his homeland and seeing heat."

They fell silent, shivering against one another, their ears straining for some sign of K'nal. Finally, they heard the sloshing footfalls of the giant's approach. K'nal dropped a limp form before collapsing beside them, sopping wet and shaking to the point of convulsions.

"I do not think that he is alive," they were able to make out through his tremors.

Sol crawled over to where he heard the body drop, groping its frigid form and trying to feel for some sign of life. His hands moved to the neck and felt no pulse; neither did they feel breath at his mouth.

"He's dead," he announced. Neither of his companions reacted.

A great pain welled up inside Sol. It was his fault they were in this mess and that everyone he cared about was dead or dying. He and his remaining friends would perish in this dark hole. He would never taste freedom. He recoiled into himself, the sorrow and self-pity threatened to overwhelm him more than the cold ever could.

He cradled Slink's head in his hands. The guard had risked and given so much to take this chance at escape. He thought of how Oci had stood up for him, how badly he had been treated by his fellow guards, even by Sol himself. The realization washed over him that he would never be able to repay Slink for his friendship. It was too late.

He heard a low moan in the darkness nearby and knew that K'nal was in real trouble. They were all in real trouble and if he didn't do something soon, they would all die. Slink had done something. Slink, Korra, K'nal; they had all saved him. Even Oci, so long ago, had saved him. The time had come for him to return the favor. He owed it to Slink not to give up.

Knowing what he had to do, he ran his hands over the body, not finding what he was looking for.

"Was anyone able to hold onto a blade?" he asked the darkness.

He heard Korra shuffling around but K'nal didn't even answer.

"Yes," she answered finally. "I have your knife."

Not really caring whose knife it was, Sol crawled over and took the blade from her. He immediately recognized the smooth, wooden handle and short blade of his carving knife. He couldn't imagine how Korra had come to possess it but at the moment there were more pressing issues. Putting his questions aside, he focused on the task at hand.

"Pile up this crispy stuff," he told Korra. As she worked he groped around the dark, working farther and farther from his companions. More than once he put his hand into something he hoped he would never learn the origin of. In the end he found what he was looking for.

"Korra!" he called out. He had tried to keep track of his route as he crawled around but with no success.

"Sol?" she replied.

"Guide me back! Keep talking!"

She did, mostly by complaining how terribly cold she was and how worried she was about K'nal. He made his way back to their group, his own hands barely able to grasp his knife in their numbness.

"Where's the pile?"

Korra guided his hands to the crispy pile and he went to work trying to get a spark by striking his carving knife against the piece of loose stone he had found. He knew not all stone sparked against metal, especially when it was damp like everything in this cave was, but he had to try. Time after time he struck the stone and time after time nothing happened. His hands ached with effort and lack of dexterity, several times dropping the stone into the pile. After what seemed like an eternity, a few small sparks flew from the blade onto the pile. Those first sparks didn't light and neither did the second or third. Korra caught onto the game and began gently blowing on the sparks as they landed and soon enough the crispy pile started to burn and burn fast.

"We need more fuel!" Sol cried, searching the cave in what seemed like blindingly bright light.

Before he could move the small pile had burned itself out. Korra groaned.

"Get another pile," Sol ordered. "I'll be right back."

In the brief light he had seen a heap of refuse in the far corner. The Trash River must occasionally flood and leave deposits when it receded. He could only hope some of it was dry enough to burn. Again he set out on hands and knees into the dark and again he called for Korra to bring him back, returning to the pile with some bits of relatively dry wood and other unidentifiable prospects for holding a flame.

"We've got to hurry," Korra pleaded.

Sol didn't need prodding. He hadn't heard a peep out of K'nal for far longer than he liked. He set to work on the pile. This time luck was with them; sparks flashed through the dark on the first strike, igniting the pile. Korra worked hard to pull in more of the crispy groundcover while Sol held the old bits of wood in the fast-burning flame, pleaded with them to catch. For a long moment the wood seemed as if it would only snap and fizz. Finally, smoke started to pour forth and a flame came to life.

Sol added the other bits of litter he had found to the growing flame.

"More!" he barked. Korra was already using the light to scour the cave for combustible scraps. Soon they had the fire roaring so large that they had to roll the half-conscious Frorian back from the flames, which was no easy task in itself. Steam rose from K'nal as they both tried to squeeze water from his fur.

"Come on, big guy, wake up," Korra pleaded.

Slowly, the blessed heat of the fire worked its magic, bringing the white giant back to life.

"Slink," K'nal groaned.

Korra shook her head. "I'm sorry. You did the best you could but he was already gone. His body is over there."

"No, it's not." Sol stood over the figure lying motionless on its side.

"What are you talking about?"

Sol shook his head. "This isn't Slink." He rolled the body over with his foot. It was one of the guards that had chased them to the edge of the river.

"Did they get Slink?" Korra asked.

"I don't know. I thought he went in with us."

"He did," K'nal spoke up. "He knocked me in."

Sol and Korra exchanged worried glances. If Slink hadn't surfaced by now, there was little hope he was still alive.

"You keep the fire going," Sol said. "I'll go look."

Sol searched as much of the cave as the light from the fire would allow. The cavern was immense. At one point he stood on the downstream edge of the fire's light and chucked a loose stone into the darkness. Wherever it hit it was too far away for the sound to reach Sol over the gurgle and splash of the Trash River. As he searched he collected more scraps for the fire, although there were precious few to be had. In time he abandoned his search and returned to his friends.

"No luck?" Korra greeted him, spreading their wet clothes out on the rock around the fire to dry.

Sol shook his head. "But don't count him out just yet. I've already made that mistake once. He'll turn up." He wasn't sure why he felt so optimistic about Slink's chances but he just couldn't bring himself to dismiss the crafty guard.

Korra looked less than convinced but the Frorian nodded his approval. K'nal had used strips of the dead guard's shirt to re-bandage Korra's leg and he motioned Sol over to attend to his wounds. As he worked they discussed their next move, everyone agreeing that they should depart as soon as possible. The disagreement arose concerning what they should take on their journey.

The argument started with Sol pointing out that there was no way of knowing how long it would take to reach the surface and that they were completely without provisions. It would be foolish, he said, to leave a source of meat lying untouched. At first Korra didn't understand what it was that Sol was referring to. She caught on quick enough when he produced his carving knife and moved over to the dead guard.

"No!" she protested loudly. "You are not going to butcher that man like some animal!"

"Meat is meat," K'nal said with a shrug.

"Listen," Sol said, "you can go explore the cave for a little while. That way you don't have to see anything. K'nal and I will take care of it. We'll even cook it."

Korra just stared at him, her jaw slack.

No matter what they suggested or how delicately they approached the subject, Korra would not budge. In the end they agreed to leave the body, taking only the rest of its clothes. The extra layers would help the two humans stay warm. Plus, as Sol pointed out, when they found Slink he would need something dry.

What to do with the fire was a simpler problem. They didn't have the proper materials for a torch so all they could do was wrap up a hot coal in some damp debris and carry their remaining fuel with them, hoping they would find some more along the way. That only left the question of how they would find their way.

"You will have to rely on me," K'nal offered. He explained that in his home there was no sunlight for months out of the year, so his people had developed the ability to see slight variations in heat in order to hunt and survive in such dark times. K'nal assured them that he could guide them well enough without a torch, although he admitted that the consistent cold of the cave made seeing difficult even through his gifted eyes.

They humans dressed as dry and warm as the cave would allow, and the three companions set out, reluctantly leaving the dwindling fire behind to wander in total darkness. Sol carried the coal pouch and K'nal carried Korra, since her wounded leg made it impossible to keep up on her own. After the first misstep and near fall by K'nal, she moved to the Frorian's back, clinging on piggy-back style to allow K'nal free use of his arms. Sol wasn't quite so lucky. He tried to walk beside K'nal, one hand on the Frorian and one protecting the coal pouch, but after several nasty bumps and scrapes he fell into step behind the white giant, using K'nal's movements to guide his steps.

They traveled like this for hours. The water's path must have eased considerably, because the sound of flowing water fell away to an almost inaudible trickle. So complete was the silence of the cave that any noise they produced seemed an unwelcome invasion. As such, conversation was sparse and when they did speak it was in hushed tones. It was in this manner that Sol asked Korra how she came to be in possession of his carving knife.

"Grall gave it to me," she answered groggily. Between blood loss and near hypothermia, not to mention running for her life, Sol could understand her exhaustion. The rhythm of the march and the soft warm fur of K'nal's back had nearly lulled her to sleep.

"To you?" Sol asked.

"Yes, to give to you. He said he was sorry for taking it in the first place." She paused. "He told me something else, too, that he had a son."

Sol stopped briefly, his legs momentarily frozen in shock. "He never told me," he said after stumbling blindly to catch up to K'nal.

"He told me that, too," she said.

"How could he have never told me?" Sol couldn't understand. Grall had always been tight-lipped about his past, but to leave out something as important as family…what else didn't he know? "And why did he tell you?" he asked, not quite able to keep the hurt from his voice.

"I'm not sure," she admitted. "I think he knew that by the end of the day, one way or another, he was going to have to choose."

"Choose what?"

"Between helping you and seeing his son."

Sol had no answer to that. The trio marched in silence again for some time. It was K'nal that eventually spoke up.

"For a father to do what he did, he honored you."

"Yes, he did," Sol agreed.

"You need to honor him in return," K'nal continued.

'How?"

"Find his son. Tell him about his father," the Frorian spoke with certainty, like there could be no other course.

Korra disagreed. "They'll be tearing the city apart looking for us." Her tone was respectful but insistent. "There's no way we'll be able to look for Grall's son."

"We can decide that when the time comes," K'nal said, cutting off any further argument.

Likely, no argument would have come. Sol was too overwhelmed to decide. On the one hand, K'nal's suggestion had an inherent truth to it. He should find Grall's son; he owed his mentor that much at least. On the other hand, Korra's protest made perfect sense. At the moment it was just nice to know he was being included in whatever she had planned for the outside world.

Besides, perhaps it wasn't his place to find Grall's family. The old guard had obviously kept it from him for a reason. What else might he find if he looked? The thought made him realize how little he knew about any of his companions.

"Do you have any children?" he asked.

"Of course not," Korra answered.

"I was talking to K'nal."

"Sorry."

"I have many nieces and nephews," K'nal answered. "I miss them very much."

The three continued their long march in pleasant conversation. K'nal told them more about his homeland, about hunting on the tundra, and the ways of his people. The usually stoic Frorian sounded almost wistful when recounting the cruel conditions of the southern wastes. Korra chimed in occasionally, supplying a little background for Sol's benefit when she could. Sol kept quiet. K'nal's deep baritone was reassuring; his stories gave Sol hope that one day he would be able to look upon his own past, his memories so full of loved ones lost, and feel the same sense of nostalgia.

In time the stories trailed off and the three plodded on in the silence, each deep in their own thoughts. Sol tried to feel whether they were climbing, but if they were the slope was too gradual to tell. The river, which they had been walking beside all the while, had left its banks, forcing them to wade through ankle-deep water. The soft plod of feet had been replaced by rhythmic splashing as he and K'nal pushed through the cold water. With nothing to see, all he could do was slog on and try to block out the vision of Grall being slowly lowered off the assassin's daggers.

The sense of failure for not killing Lysik hurt Sol deeply. He had let Grall down. The irony of the situation mocked him. The one man he had wanted so badly to kill he hadn't been able to.

"It is getting warmer." K'nal's announcement drew him from his thoughts.

"We must be close to the surface!" Korra said, the relief in her voice palatable.

"I am not so sure. I do not smell outside air. I smell something…unpleasant"

Sol sniffed the air and he could hear Korra do the same, but neither of the humans could detect anything different, at least not at first. Further on he caught the first hint of a smell, so faint that he wasn't sure he trusted his nose. A short while later the stench was undeniable and, as K'nal had said, most unpleasant.

"Well that explains the heat," Korra said. "It's sulfur. We must be coming up on a hot spring."

Sol wasn't sure what sulfur was but he did appreciate the steadily rising temperatures as they continued toward the source of the smell. His feet were numb from the cold water and his lips had started to tremble again, despite his efforts to resist. The further they walked, the warmer the water became. After a while, a pleasant heat filled the entire cave.

He was almost forced to enjoy the warm water fully when he crashed into K'nal who had suddenly stopped his march.

"There is a light," K'nal said.

Sol peeked around the white giant.

"I see it," Korra said, having looked over K'nal's shoulder.

Sol saw it too. A greenish-blue glow splashed through the darkness a couple hundred yards in front of them. In the total dark of the surrounding cave, the glowing water seemed to hover in mid-air.

"What is it?" Korra asked.

"I do not know," K'nal answered, "but it is coming this way."

K'nal was right. While the radiant light wasn't exactly making a bee-line for them, it was meandering in their general direction.

"Can't you see what it is by its heat?" Sol asked.

"The whole chamber is hot because of the spring. I see like you see now."

Sol assumed that meant the Frorian had switched back to normal vision. "If it's unfriendly, we're not in any shape to defend ourselves," he pointed out.

"Trying to flee in the dark would be futile," K'nal responded.

"Let's just see what it is," Korra suggested.

The three waited in tense silence as the glowing waters came ever closer. As they did they could just make out a human-shaped silhouette in the light of the glowing water.

"Is it a Spirit?" Korra asked.

Just then the silhouette stumbled. Splashing loudly, it failed to gain its balance and toppled into the water.

"Clumsy Spirit," K'nal observed.

A familiar voice echoed off the stone walls. "Aw for the love a'," followed by a string of expletive-laced curses.

"Slink?" Korra asked, her disbelief obvious.

Sol was already splashing through the water toward the figure, his actions sending up their own spray of glowing green light.

"Who's 'ere?"

Sol bounded straight up to the former guard and wrapped him in a bear hug.

"It's 'bout time!" Slink wheezed through the crushing embrace.

Sol chuckled and released his hold. "Sorry. We were sightseeing. How did you get so far ahead of us?"

"Ahead? I thought I was behind! I 'ad one 'ell of a time getting outta that river. By the time I did, I couldn't find nobody. I figured I'd missed you so I scurried to catch up. I was 'alf-frozen by the time I found this 'ot spring. I been kickin' around 'ere, tryin' to figure out what ta' do."

"You thought that we would leave without you?" K'nal asked, he and Korra having joined them.

"Well, I wasn't sure," Slink answered with a sheepish look.

Sol laid a hand on his friend's shoulder, his voice serious and sincere. "We're in this together. You have my word: no one will be left behind."

"Not even you," Korra added.

All the humans laughed. Not understanding the joke, K'nal frowned disapprovingly at Korra's comment, drawing further laughter from his companions.

"How far have you explored?" Sol asked when the laughter died out.

"The warm water peters out a bit further on. I think the river goes back in its banks and there's dry land, but the cave gets cold again so I didn't go far. I'm soaked to the bone." It was true. Slink's features were rodent-like at the best of times. Right now, in the green glow of the water, he looked like some kind of otherworldly drowned rat. "Oh, and the glowing fades out when the water gets cold."

"It must have something to do with the hot spring," Korra said

Sol agreed. "The warm water's nice but we need to keep moving."

"Right. All I want to do is get out of this blasted cave and get me a nice big bowl a hot goulash, like my old ma used ta' make."

"Bowl of what?" Sol asked.

They set out, Slink's description of his favorite dish igniting a string of conversation about hot baths, big meals, and comfortable beds. The cave changed just as Slink had described, the river returning to its banks and its frigid temperatures. On the first spit of dry land they made as much of a fire as they could and gave Slink the dead guard's relatively dry clothes. The fire didn't last long enough to dry his own waterlogged garments so they left them behind and resuming their march with Slink taking his place behind Sol, grumbling good-naturedly about Korra's traveling accommodations.

The conversation lasted for some time, each of the four sharing things they were looking forward to on the outside. After several hours of hiking the talk trailed off and they walked in blind silence once again.

For the first time, Sol fully considered the uncertainties of his life outside of the Coliseum. Everything had happened so fast. In the short time they had to plan their escape, he had forced himself to concentrate on the task of getting them out. Since being pulled from the river and beginning their cave trek, his focus had been on the loss of Grall and finding Slink. Now he had nothing but time to consider his future.

Uncertainty was something new for Sol. For the last six years he awoke each day not knowing who or what he would fight, yet he could always count on the fact that there would be another fight and that he would either win or die. The question was only how long he would survive.

There might not be another fight. It was a prospect he had never considered. Why would he? It would have been a waste of time. Now it was a possibility as solid as the stone on which he walked.

And it scared him.

He knew it shouldn't. He scolded himself for not being overjoyed. Part of him was; the part that didn't want to kill anymore. The hope that he would never again have to watch the life drain from a stranger's eyes was deep and sincere. But there was another part, a smaller part, but still there nonetheless, which wondered what he could possibly do now. Fighting he knew. Fighting he was good at. He had spent most of the last six years fighting. He didn't know anything else.

As he trudged through the dark he realized how blindly he was approaching his future. His companions had all lived on the outside. They knew about things like taverns and money and when it was appropriate to approach a woman. Other than Oci, he hadn't been alone with a woman that hadn't been forced into his company in years.

Slink stumbled slightly behind him, pushing him into K'nal's back. They had all been losing their footing more often; the constant march was wearing them down. Still they trudged on.

Slink's presence reassured Sol. Unless the outside was even more different from Coliseum life than he thought, he at least wouldn't be any more socially awkward than the inept former guard.

"I need to rest," K'nal announced a few hours later. The four companions hunkered down where they stood and tried to huddle together for warmth, a situation that inevitably lead to Korra slapping Slink before repositioning herself next to Sol. The break was a brief one. The hard ground stole warmth and comfort, but it was their ever increasing hunger that spurred them on.

No one could agree on how long they had been in the cave but the argument centered on days, not hours. They were managing to stave off thirst by lapping up water from one of the many trickles that worked their way down the cave wall but between losing their last meal after expelling the Trash River's fetid water and their constant marching, whatever meager energy reserves belonged to a slave had been used up long ago. Hunger was a constant companion now, a fifth presence in the dark.

At first Sol had regretted leaving dead guard behind. They were hungry and as K'nal had said, 'meat was meat'. Plenty of time to consider Korra's stance on the subject had changed his mind. She obviously abhorred the idea and as the group's best representative of the norms of the outside world, Sol guessed that most outsiders would feel the same. For better or worse, they had left the Coliseum behind. Even if they had only traded one underground prison for another, Sol was determined to start acting like an outsider.

Twice more the cycle of march and break repeated, each time the rest coming a little sooner than the last and lasting a little longer. They all took unofficial turns to try and raise the group's spirits. Korra offered encouragement, K'nal recounted stories, and Slink told bad jokes. It was Sol, though, that kept the group looking forward. He felt that they were in this mess because of him and that it was his responsibility to get them out. He took turns carrying

Korra and when Slink's complaints started wearing on already frayed nerves, he even carried the man for a short time until the former guard's pride got the better of him. When they stopped to rest he attended to Korra's wounds, tearing off parts of his own shirt to re-bandage her leg. On and on they hiked through the never-ending dark and not once did he complain, not once did he let them give up.

But still the cave continued.

It had been hours since any of them had spoken and twice as long since their last rest when K'nal finally gave them some good news. "I smell fresh air," he said.

Again, none of the humans could tell any difference but they trusted the Frorian's nose enough by now not to question. They hurried along with as much as energy they could collectively muster and their efforts were rewarded by a noticeable steepening of the cave floor and the river cutting more deeply into its stone banks. The grade slowed their pace but the change in surroundings, evident even to the blind humans and so very welcome after the mundane consistency of the last who knew how long, raised their spirits.

Once again conversations arose about being on the outside. Status updates were requested so frequently from K'nal that eventually he simply stopped answering them. By that time it hardly mattered; they could all smell fresh air. And there was something else. A great rumbling noise could be heard from somewhere far ahead. As anxious as they were to press on, K'nal was forced to slow their progress further in order to pick his way over an increasingly precarious path. The cave floor continued to rise and the river cut ever deeper, leaving the troop's path on the edge of a sheer face. The going was tough for K'nal and nearly impossible for the blind humans. Still Sol pushed his companions, picking them up every time they stumbled. They were all tired and probably should have stopped for a rest long before but K'nal's next announcement swept away all thoughts of stopping.

"I see light."

"Sunlight?" Slink asked over the roar of tumbling water.

"No," K'nal answered. "It appears to be moonlight."

Korra cheered and they pressed on, moving just as fast as before, though it seemed so much slower. As the path continued to narrow they were forced to crawl, lest they risk slipping into what had grown into a sizeable canyon. The danger was secondary at this point. They could all see the moonlight now, flooding the giant cavern up ahead from which the great roar of water originated. Ignoring their bruised and bloody knees they crawled on, anxious to see the exit.

In time they did. Their path came to a sudden end at the tip of a precipice, the floor and walls of the cave having fallen away sending the river plunging into darkness. The little sliver of rock jutted out into a great void, illuminated by a circular hole in the massive cavern's domed roof. The ceiling was not high and the hole was only about twenty feet directly above their heads, but the smooth, arching walls, shiny from the waterfall's mist in the moonlight, left no doubt about the futility of trying to climb up to the opening. Below them it was impossible to tell how far down the waterfall went but the roar of water echoing around them was deafening.

They were trapped.

"We'll have to go back!" Sol shouted over the roar. "There must be another way!"

K'nal shook his head. "There were no other paths."

Korra and Slink slumped down together on the floor, exhaustion finally overtaking them.

"No," Sol pressed. "We have to move on."

"Yeah, an' where do we go, eh?" Slink asked.

Sol looked around, desperate for some sign of an overlooked path. The truth was that he was just as tired as everyone else and it was that very fact that spurred him on. He feared that if he stopped then he might not be able to start again, but even in the dim moonlight it was easy to see that there was nowhere to go. "We'll have to jump," he announced.

"What?" Slink barked. "Into the waterfall? You're nuts!"

Korra sat up and laid a hand on Sol's arm. "You're exhausted. Let's sit for a while and rest. It will be light soon and we'll be able to get a better look at things.

"Please," she added when Sol made no move to relax.

He relented, agreeing that seeing their situation in sunlight might prove to be beneficial. The four tired companions curled up there on the rock slab, huddling together as much to assure that they didn't roll off into the void than for warmth, and slept.

16.

By the time they awoke the suns were high overhead, framed by the hole in the cave's ceiling and illuminating the massive chasm. After days of total darkness their eyes adjusted slowly and it was a while before they were able to see their situation more clearly. Unfortunately, no matter how well lit, their predicament hadn't changed. The water-polished walls of the chasm were just as slick and unclimbable and the cave's depths just as unfathomable. Indeed, even with sunlight pouring in the waterfall's bottom was still out of sight, its waters tumbling into a dark mist several hundred feet below their precipice.

One thing the light did reveal was how perilous last night's path had been. Looking at the narrow wisp of rock, Sol wondered whether the humans would have even attempted it had they known what they were crawling over. Between the state of their only escape route and K'nal's continued assurances that there were no other paths they could have taken, there was very little they could do other than sit tight.

It was a good thing, too. The simple fact was that they hadn't the strength left for much else. It had been days of constant and difficult hiking since their last meal. The final push to get this far had sapped their remaining strength. Sol and K'nal tried shouting for help for a time, but even that was exhausting, not to mention futile. There was little chance that anyone on the surface could hear even the Frorian's bellows over the waterfall's echoed roar.

It wasn't long before the suns moved past the hole and the cave steadily sank back into darkness. The four companions huddled together again, supporting each other with physical contact instead of words. Very little had been said all day and Sol suspected it had less to do with the noise of the waterfall than with the hopelessness of their situation. Korra had been especially quiet, sharing a few sad smiles and little else. He couldn't blame her. They had come so far; it seemed impossible that they would fail with freedom in sight, but there just wasn't any hope left.

"Maybe you was right 'bout jumping, eh?" A voice over Sol's shoulder proved he wasn't the only one thinking along those lines.

He leaned against Slink and the former guard nudged him in recognition. Another body squeezed closer as well.

"I can't believe it's going to end like this," Korra said.

Sol turned to her, their faces inches apart. Even in the waning light he could see she had been crying. The three humans jostled together as K'nal's great white arms encircled the group.

"I would rather it end here, free with friends, than on the Coliseum floor," he said in his stoic way.

The humans traded smiles and nods. "I never thought I would die free," Sol admitted.

There was a long silence, each deep in their own thoughts. Sol considered K'nal's words. Here he sat in the arms of his friends, outside the Coliseum for the first time in his life. Yes, he would die, but he would die free. And he would die on his own terms.

"Let's get some sleep," he said. "Tomorrow we'll see just how far down that waterfall goes."

The others nodded, having drawn similar conclusions. They shifted their pile but stayed close, finding comfort in each other's presence. It took a while, but one by one they drifted off. Sol was the last to fall asleep and when he did his fitful slumber was punctuated by strange dreams full of faces he hadn't seen in years; friends he had lost, men he had killed. He awoke several times, disoriented, unsure of his surroundings, and puzzled by the circle of stars overhead. Once he awoke with the sensation that he was falling and he was sure that he had rolled off the precipice. It was only the rock on which he laid that convinced him he was still grounded. This continued throughout the night, drifting in and out of sleep until sometime in the early morning hours when he was awoken by something bumping against his face. At first, thinking it was just Slink who had the habit of being an active sleeper, he tried to ignore it. But the bumping persisted and eventually he was forced to open his eyes.

What he saw didn't make sense. It was a loop of thick rope. The line floated inches from his face, glowing silver in the pre-dawn moonlight and resembling something along the lines of a ghostly hangman's noose. He sat up a little and tentatively touched the thick cord. It seemed real enough. He pushed it and it swayed gracefully away before swinging back. The whole scene felt no more or less real than the earlier parade of faces or the dream of falling. As such, it seemed the most natural thing in the world for Sol to pull himself up to stand with one foot in the rope loop.

And then he started to rise. He looked up to the hole in the roof, not able to discern any difference in the night sky. He slowly ascended toward the circle of stars, his muscles aching as he tried to hold on to the cord. He looked down on his sleeping friends. They were still cuddled up and completely unaware of his departure. Part of him wanted to call out to them but a larger part was worried that his voice might somehow break the rope's spell. Besides, by now he was high enough that they probably couldn't have heard him over the waterfall's echo.

The final few feet were the hardest, the rope scraping him against the rock and very nearly toppling him down onto his sleeping companions. Bloody knuckles and all, somehow he managed to hold on. Before he knew it friendly hands were dragging him onto level ground.

He was on the surface.

"By the Spirits, man, you look awful."

Sol couldn't believe his ears. "Vance?"

"The one and only." With his tattered clothes and his stubbled face, he looked much the same as he had during their last meeting. But the defeat that had haunted his eyes had been replaced with resolve and as he smiled at Sol the effect was so profound that he could have been a different man entirely.

"But how–"

Vance interrupted him, thrusting a canteen into his hands. "Drink this first."

Sol did as he was told. It was some kind of soup, cold and spicy. It was the most delicious thing he had ever tasted. He only got a couple swallows down before Vance yanked the container away.

"More than that and you'll vomit," he explained. "Besides, I'm sure your friends are just as hungry and there isn't much to go around."

"How did you know we were here?" Sol asked.

"I didn't," he said with a smile, "but I'd rather not have to tell this story four times. Let's get everyone topside and go from there."

Sol put his questions aside and modified the rope loop as Vance backed the two horses that had pulled Sol up closer to the hole. Sol shouted down to his friends but not surprisingly they didn't stir. He tossed down a shower of pebbles, several of which stuck Slink with enough force to finally wake him. Sol watched as the former guard looked around, obviously confused as to what had hit him and to where Sol had gone. Slink peered down into the waterfall abyss and for a moment Sol worried that the former guard was thinking that he had jumped and would follow. It was about that time that Slink saw the rope. He grabbed the line and tugged.

Sol tugged back.

Suddenly animated, Slink shook Korra and K'nal awake. The three peered up at the hole and Sol could see their faces, though he doubted with the backlighting that they could see his. After some discussion, Slink helped Korra fit the loop around her waist and Vance urged the horses into a slow walk. Up she came, the loop around her body sparing her some of the scraping Sol had experienced. He helped her up over the edge and they embraced, tears running down her cheeks.

"We made it," he assured her.

She smiled and then spotted Vance. "Who is that?"

"A friend. Let's get the boys on the surface and then I'll make introductions."

Twice more they repeated the maneuver. Slink managed to bump his head on the cave ceiling and the rope strained ominously under the Frorian's bulk, but it wasn't long before they were all exchanging hugs, handshakes, and soup from the canteen.

"This is Vance," Sol introduced their rescuer. "He's the only person I know outside of the Coliseum."

"Wait a minute, Vance Rutinal?" Korra asked. "The bard?"

Sol chuckled. Vance's fame had always been part of their visits' playful banter but he had never been sure how well-known the bard actually was.

Vance bowed slightly. "Retired, I'm afraid. The Empire has about as much use for me now as I do for it."

Korra glanced nervously between Sol and Vance. "But you work for General Shadon. You've been a bard of the Empire for as long as I can remember."

"Korra—" Sol started but Vance interrupted.

"No, she's right. Even an artist can claim only so much impartiality. I have lived for many years on the Empire's patronage. Even more than that, I have prospered through the toil and suffering of a man I now regard as a friend." Vance turned to Sol. "Most of what I have," he paused, "or had, I acquired by recounting your bouts to the Empire. I've used you for my own gain as surely as the men who forced you to fight in the first place. For that, I owe you my deepest apologies." The former bard extended his hand to the former gladiator.

Sol smiled and shook his hand at the wrist. "I'm in a forgiving mood."

"Is that why you have waited for us for so long?" K'nal asked.

"In part," Vance admitted, "although to be honest I was planning on departing in the morning. You four cut it pretty close."

"Yeah, we're good at that," Slink said with a chuckle.

Vance continued, "When I was a young man and unknown, I started out with nothing. All I had was the love of a good story. Now I'm an old man and I once again have nothing. But I still love a good story and I have a nose for finding one." He looked over the group. "You may be out of the Coliseum but I'll wager your stories are just getting started. I've been following the stories of othere my whole life. I think it's time I joined one. Besides, for better or worse, the Empire and I have some unfinished business."

"Wha's that supposed ta' mean?" asked Slink.

"Lysik killed his son," Sol explained.

"I'm sorry," Korra said, resting her hand on Vance arm.

"Thank you. But it would be more accurate to say that the Empire killed my son. Lysik was just a tool." A shadow passed over his eyes. "They will pay for what they have done. I swear on my life." The shadow lifted. "But I'm afraid you have me at a disadvantage."

"This is Korra," Sol made the introductions. "This is K'nal and you know Slink."

Vance shook hands with each of them and gave Slink a friendly pat on the back. "I heard that there was a guard in your group and I had a feeling it was you."

"The makeup of our group can't be common knowledge," Korra prompted.

"Come now, my dear lady, you don't think I got to where I am without connections do you?"

"Zat how you knew where we was?" Slink asked.

"Actually, that was just a guess." He motioned to the dark around them. "You can't tell at the moment but we're standing in what used to be a village, the village where I grew up in fact. When I was a young man we had to abandon our homes and move elsewhere. You see, the water, which we drew from the very hole from which you just emerged, had become tainted and was making people ill."

"How long ago was that?" Sol asked.

"About sixteen years."

"The Cave-In."

Vance nodded. "It wasn't until years later that I learned an underground river found under the Coliseum after a cave-in was being used as a trash dump. I always suspected that was the cause of village's problems. When I heard you four had perished in the same underground Trash River, I figured that if I was going to find you it would be here."

"Perished?" K'nal asked.

"That's right. Officially, you are all dead, drowned while trying to escape. Word is they lost two guards that were sent in after you. Which reminds me," he turned to Sol, "I have a gift for you." He motioned for them to follow, leading them to a wagon a short distance away. "My man in the Coliseum came across something in the chaos. With what it cost me I could have had new ones made for all five of us but I couldn't resist." He dug into the wagon, finding what he was looking for and handing it to Sol.

Carefully polished metal shone in the moonlight. "My helmet." He had never expected to see it again. It was his only physical tie to the Coliseum floor, part of the only home he had ever known. More importantly it was a gift from Grall; something from his mentor that he could take with him. "Thank you."

Korra was far more interested in the news of their demise. "This is wonderful! If they think we're dead, they won't be looking for us!"

"Given the events of the last six days, I'm doubt they would be looking for you, anyway."

"Six days!" Slink barked.

"What events?" K'nal asked.

"That performance from you and Sol. Your refusal to fight really set off a spark."

"The riot in the stands?" Sol asked.

"The riot was just the start. When it couldn't be stopped the anarchy spilled into the streets. At first, the bulk of the fury was aimed at the gentry, but as momentum increased the mob turned their attention to the palace."

"And since so few soldiers are kept in the Capital..." Korra chimed.

"There was little they could do to stop it," Vance finished. "The palace fell after the third night."

"And the Emperor?" Korra asked.

"Still hanging from the palace gates the last time I saw."

"Hasn't the army has made it to the city by now?"

Vance shook his head. "The events of the Coliseum were but a drop in the bucket and the ripples didn't stop at Astrolia's borders. Tension has been mounting throughout the Empire for far too long. Without a unifying event, dissent has been random and without focus. The fall of the Capital marked a break in the dam. I've heard of rioting as far away as Catalino. Everyone knew the army was stretched thin." He shrugged.

"But surely they will regain control."

"Probably," Vance conceded. "I suspect the Empire's forces will regroup around Shadon and Fort City soon enough. For now, however, the Empire is in chaos and I suggest we take advantage of it."

"Where we gonna go, eh?" Slink asked.

"And what are we going to do?" Vance asked.

Korra started to speak but K'nal stopped her with a hand on her shoulder. The white giant gestured toward Sol who had stepped away during their discussion. The silhouette of the former gladiator could be seen against dawn's first light, holding his trademark helmet to his chest and gazing at the eastern horizon. Korra limped to his side and wrapped an arm around his waist. The other humans stood to his other side, Slink laying a hand on Sol's shoulder. K'nal took position behind them, his massive presence sheltering the group. No one spoke. Around them, birds began their morning calls as the world awoke from its slumber.

There Sol stood, his past clutched to his chest and every friend he had in the world by his side. He couldn't know what paths lay before him or where they would lead. But he did know this: for the first time in his life he would choose his way.

He was free.

Sol smiled, hugged his friends closer, and watched his very first sunrise.

THE END

Acknowledgements

My sincerest thanks to everyone who helped this book come to be. Thank you to my beta readers, Lloyd Gaylord, Drew and Cathy Gaylord, and Jen and Matt Osterhoudt, who's input on early drafts was invaluable. A big thanks to my editor Robert Dowsett, who helped make this story everything it could be. Thank you to Luciano Chiaramonte, who pushed me to get this published. Thank you to my wonderful publishers, Murandy Damodred and Justine Dowsett for giving me this chance. And my biggest thanks to my wife, Hilary, for her unwavering support. You're my everything.

About the Author

Adam Gaylord lives with his beautiful wife, daughter, and less beautiful dog in Loveland, CO. When not at work as a biologist he's usually hiking, drinking craft beer, drawing comics, writing short stories, or some combination thereof. He's had stories published in Penumbra eMag, Dark Futures Magazine, Silver Blade Magazine, and Plasma Frequency Magazine, among others. Check out his stuff at http://adamsapple2day.blogspot.com or look him up on Goodreads.

To learn more about our authors and our current projects visit:
www.mirrorworldpublishing.com, follow @MirrorWorldPub or like
us at www.facebook.com/mirrorworldpublishing

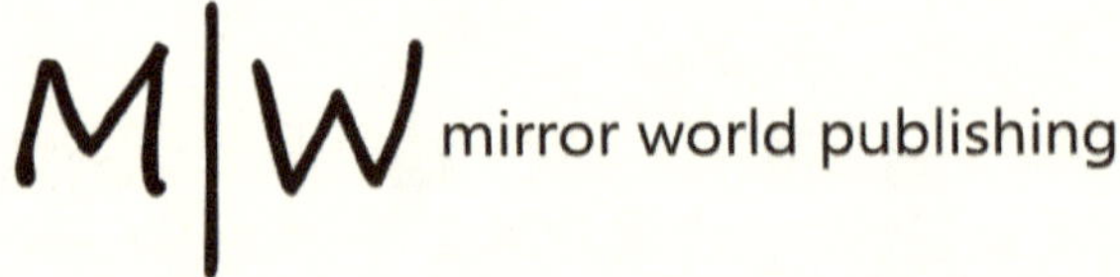

*We appreciate every like, tweet, facebook post and review and
we love to hear from you. Please consider leaving us a review
online or sending your thoughts and comments to
info@mirrorworldpublishing.com*

Thank you.

ADAM GAYLORD